GW00864459

Brian Allen Levine was born in 1966 and read law at Downing College, Cambridge. He lives in West London and the South of France with his wife, three children and two dogs.

This is his first novel.

To our friends
Ollie and Jo
from
Eve and Bob,
Brian's parents.

© Copyright 2006 Brian Levine.

All rights reserved. No part of this publication may be reproduced, stored in a retrieval system, or transmitted, in any form or by any means, electronic, mechanical, photocopying, recording, or otherwise, without the written prior permission of the author.

Note for Librarians: A cataloguing record for this book is available from Library and Archives Canada at www.collectionscanada.ca/amicus/index-e.html

ISBN 1-4251-0620-X

Printed on paper with minimum 30% recycled fibre.

Trafford's print shop runs on "green energy" from solar, wind and other environmentally-friendly power sources.

Offices in Canada, USA, Ireland and UK

Book sales for North America and international:
Trafford Publishing, 6E–2333 Government St.,
Victoria, BC V8T 4P4 CANADA
phone 250 383 6864 (toll-free 1 888 232 4444)
fax 250 383 6804; email to orders@trafford.com

Book sales in Europe:
Trafford Publishing (UK) Limited, 9 Park End Street, 2nd Floor
Oxford, UK OX1 1HH UNITED KINGDOM
phone +44 (0)1865 722 113 (local rate 0845 230 9601)
facsimile +44 (0)1865 722 868; info.uk@trafford.com

Order online at:
trafford.com/06-2378

10 9 8 7 6 5 4 3 2

Julius

Brian Allen Levine

To Jane, Ollie, Georgie and Mia

'Between the acting of a dreadful thing and the first motion, all the interim is like a phantasma, or a hideous dream.'

William Shakespeare, *Julius Caesar*

'The (movie) business is a cruel and shallow money trench, a long plastic hallway where thieves and pimps run free and good men die like dogs. There's also a negative side.'

Hunter S. Thompson

1

I looked out over the sea of heads in front of me, all waiting breathlessly for me to die.   Up to the Gods, down to the pit, in the stalls and in the private boxes, seven hundred souls held their breath and directed their gaze to the lone figure on stage, dressed in a toga and covered in blood.   The spotlight tracked my face, my furrowed brow and agonized gasps. The audience held their breath as a trap-door opened up beneath me and down I went with the force of gravity, landing with a large thump onto a pile of mattresses on the floor.

Above me the trap-door shut quickly and a light clicked on. I lay in the dust, gazing up, trying to catch my breath. Dying took it out of me. It was the forty-fifth time I'd died, the forty-fifth time I'd had a laurel wreath knocked off my head. I could have strained to listen to the end of the play, but I just wanted to get it over with, take the curtain, a little applause and cut to the nearest pub.

That night I should have been at home. I should not have taken an underground train, I should not have purchased a newspaper and I should not have gone to work. Jews weren't meant to work on the Sabbath but my orthodox parents had died from Spanish flu when I was eight, leaving me to my less-Orthodox uncle Leo Katzen, a tailor. He'd read me Dickens and Shakespeare rather than the bible and he told me that I had a secret weapon.

'*Abe*', he used to say, '*you may be a Jew, but you sure don't look like one.*'

My mother had been a very beautiful white blonde Polack who moved to Germany where she met my father who'd already decided to move to England. I was born in East London with a shock of fair hair, one blonde head in a world of brunettes. I didn't much go for ringlets or a yarmulke or the discipline of Sabbath. I didn't need any of those things because I'd already decided what it was I wanted to be when I grew up.

I'd told uncle Leo and he was all for it, right up until the moment the bus ran him over in 1930. I was a young man of twenty, fresh out of a tailoring apprenticeship and ready for a new challenge. I was tall, some would say ruggedly handsome, fair-haired and strong. I didn't want to cut cloth. I wanted to be an actor and by late 1938 on a rainy night just off Shaftesbury Avenue that is exactly what I was.

The run had been a good one, but like all good things, the run was coming to an end, after forty-five performances. I was playing Julius Caesar in the play of the same name and this was the last night's performance. The pay was fine but no-one I acted with had any work to follow, including me. I'd have to go on the dole and queue for cheap bread and soup because acting didn't pay enough to tide you over the quiet times.

The rain had stopped now and the streets gleamed. The lights glowed brightly and the moisture had made the air virtually breathable. I looked out of a second floor window to see a throng of people streaming out from the foyer which was staffed by efficient young women from the outer suburbs, places with solid dependable names like Harrow and Whetstone and Barnet. It had been full tonight but they'd come for the play and not for me. Six weeks ago I'd been the stand in, only gravitating to lead when Michael Winterbottom caught bronchitis.

They'd given me a standing ovation that night and when they'd stopped clapping I headed to my dressing room for the last time, along a corridor lined with posters for *The Importance of Being Earnest*, *Othello* and *Sweeney Todd*. I used to collect the posters for all my plays and I took the one for *Julius Caesar* to add to my collection from my dressing-room wall, rolling it up and shoving it in a cardboard tube to stop it getting damaged.

I was never without my books, and that night on my dressing-room table, neat and tidy, framed by a large mirror surrounded by bright bulbs, sat my two leather-bound volumes, one a collected Shakespeare and the other *Turandot* by Schiller. I sat down and stared at my bloodied face in the dressing room mirror, the bright bulbs making me blink. The clock behind me told me it was ten-thirty. There was still time for a drink, if I was quick. I remember thinking I didn't need to bother with the make-up this time, that it could wait 'til I got home.

Outside the theatre, the rain had stopped long enough for the pollution to return, the fog of bus-fumes whisked by the taxi-cabs into a plume that covered the main routes in and out of London, and sank the small lanes into a smoky pall. In the small lane at the side of the theatre an old man with yellow teeth and a crinkly smile opened the stage door for me and doffed his cap. I don't think he noticed I was covered in stage-blood, or at least, that my face and hands were. His name was Harry, not that it matters. I had my duffel bag over my shoulder, the long cardboard tube poking out of the top, and my books under my arm.

'Goodnight Mister Goldstein, sir', he said, 'and may I say so sir you was great tonight, sir. It's a real shame'.

'Onwards and upwards!', I think I replied.

As I headed down the narrow street I passed a young couple giggling in a doorway. I looked at their happy, slightly tipsy faces and remembered that it had been a long time since I'd had female company. Amanda, wasn't it? Or maybe it had been Chloe...it was so long ago that I couldn't remember.

I passed a Chinaman under a streetlight and he nearly jumped when he saw me and my bloodied face. I must have looked like the Yorkshire ripper on the prowl. He muttered something quickly and sped off in the opposite direction. I turned down another dimly-lit alleyway that formed the cut-through to my favourite drinking hole, *The Prince Regent*. Ten-forty. Time for two pints, or even three.

The alley was gloomy and quiet and all I could hear was my footsteps on the cobble-stones. Had it been Chloe? Or maybe, maybe it had been Gloria?

Suddenly I heard something peculiar. I stopped and listened. It sounded like a scuffle coming from about twenty yards in front of me in a doorway.

'*Nein, nein, bitte*...please...stop!', pleaded a man insistently.

I slowly took off my duffel bag and put down my books on the cobblestones. I could hear muffled punches. I approached carefully, from an angle, away from the street-light, so they couldn't see me until I could see them. I edged closer and there in the doorway were the outlines of two men standing over a third, raining down punches on him.

Grunts of pain, fists against ribs. I walked steadily towards the doorway, my heart pounding and I looked down at my own hands, still covered in stage-blood. They weren't trembling. I'd just faced seven hundred people on stage. There'd be no problem facing just two.

4

Five yards now, closer, and closer still, the aggressors came into view. Two young thugs in black shirts with strange insignia – they were Moseley's lot – rained punches and kicks on a figure lying prone in the doorway, shielding his face with his hands. I could see the victim was a well-dressed man, not young, maybe in his late fifties, and he wore a camel-haired coat.

'You want *Geld*? Money? I can give you money. Here, take!', he whispered hoarsely as his hand went to his jacket pocket. He got another punch for that.

'I'm not after yer money, yer Jewish scum!'

'But I am not a Jew!'

The word *Jew* had a funny effect on me. It made me lose my temper. I gripped the blackshirt's collar and pulled him off the old man in the doorway. Both blackshirts, young ill-shapen hulks in their early twenties, dim faces topped with dirty hair, turned to look at me and my bloodied face, coming out of nowhere. I didn't swing at them, I just stood there and roared like a madman, a deep powerful actor's roar just like a caged animal. The blackshirts took one look at me, then each other and ran away down the alleyway, their footsteps clattering off and round a corner.

I knelt down to the man in the doorway and tried to help him up. He was breathing heavily and he looked like he was in pain. His eyes were shut, and he kept repeating '*I am not...I am not*' until he finally slowed and then fell silent. The man, realizing that the blows had ceased, opened his eyes.

'*Mein Gott!* What have they done to you?', he asked me, seeing my stage-bloodied face.

I saw his face clearly for the first time in the glimmer of the street-lamp a few yards away. It was craggy but aquiline, a large bony nose, bright blue eyes and high cheekbones, distinguished somehow despite the bloody lip and bruising. His accent wasn't harsh, more an educated mid-European drawl.

'Not what it looks like', I replied.

He wiped his lip and looked down at the blood on his hand, then at the blood on mine. He looked up and I realized he was staring at me like he knew me. He smiled and his eyes twinkled.

'You are the actor!', he laughed. 'You are...you are, *ein moment!*'

He hoisted himself to his feet creakily and I reached out to help him. He pulled himself up proudly to his full height, which wasn't much. He held his hand out formally to me.

'Hans Bosendorf!'

'Abe Goldstein.'

We shook hands and he winced.

'Can you walk?' How bad is it?', I asked.

Hans wiped the blood from his mouth.

'Nothing, young man, that a beer will not remedy'.

I liked him already.

The *Prince Regent* was full of men and women topping up their Friday night before last orders. The zinc-topped bar was awash with ale, the two barmen sweaty and pumping the taps like factory workers. We sat at a small table to the side. The other punters threw puzzled looks at the blood on our faces, in my case out of a bottle, in Hans Bosendorf's, the real thing. I rested my books on the table, the *Turandot* and the Shakespeare and took a long drink from the beer he bought me.

'It's good to be recognised', I said, licking my lips, tasting the beer. 'You're one of the few.'

'Just like you', he replied, clinking glasses with me and taking a long thirsty drink.

'My father was German', I said quickly.

6

'Really? *Konnen Sie Deutsch?*'

'Yes I speak German. I grew up with German everywhere. I suppose you'd call it Yiddish.'

'Ah yes, *Yiddish.*' Hans took a sip from his beer and leaned towards me. 'You know what I do, Abe Goldstein?'

'You have an expensive coat', I replied.

He also had smart shoes, a nice tie and a shirt that would have been well-ironed and white had it not been for the scuffle. Some kind of theatre-loving businessman perhaps, still with a grandish air about him even though he was disheveled and bloody. His coat was camel-hair and looked extremely expensive.

'I am in the movie business, Mr Goldstein, the suspension of disbelief for ninety minutes or longer, which is the trend these days. I have a great number of expensive coats.'

More beers arrived and Hans handed over a ten shilling note when the beers were only a few pennies. He pressed the money into the waitress's hand and squeezed her arm. I don't think he wanted any change. I watched him slide a business card into her hand.

'What are you doing in England?', I asked.

'Looking for what I could not find in Germany.'

'Real English ale?'

'*Nein. Ich suche* – I am looking for - a romantic lead who is strong and handsome, who speaks German and is available from the twelfth.'

'You must have hundreds like that in the Fatherland', I replied.

'Thousands. But he must have a sense of humour.'

'I see your problem.'

'Ha ha! *Sehr gut!* You Jews have a good sense of humour, do you not?'

'I suppose we have to. Especially where *you're* from.'

'I would wager you do not get the usual problems, though, do you? After all, I've never seen a Jew look less like a Jew in my life.'

He was right. Neither had I.

'But the name', continued Hans, 'is most unfortunate. *Abe Goldstein* would not work in Germany right now.'

'As of tonight, Abe Goldstein isn't working anywhere right now', I replied.

Hans leaned closer still, conspiratorially.

'Have you heard of Nathan Birnbaum?'

I shook my head.

'That is because he calls himself George Burns now, in Hollywood.'

'Hollywood', I murmured, loving the sound of the word.

'Ehrlich Weiss?'

'Sounds like my dentist.'

'Not quite. Ehrlich Weiss became Harry Houdini, Goldfish became Goldwyn and Cohen Pictures became Columbia Pictures. The forgettable Laszlo Loewenstein, or the unmistakeable Peter Lorre? These are all Jews who changed their names. It is what we in the business call marketing.'

Hans looked pleased with his pitch. 'And then of course there is the master', he added.

'The master?'

'Humphrey Bogart.'

'Bogart? What's his real name?'

'That *is* his real name. But he is also a Jew'.

I held out my thick leather-bound Shakespeare.

'What's in a name?', I asked.

'My dear Abe. Shakespeare didn't work in the movie business.'

He settled his gaze on my copy of Shakespeare's Plays and the *Turandot* by Schiller.

'Schiller', he announced emphatically. 'Julius Schiller.'

'Julius Schiller? Who's he?'

'He's you. Or he could be you, if you let me help you.'

'Julius Schiller?'

I took a long swig from my glass of beer.

'Last orders, gentlemen please!', announced the barman.

Hans pulled out a large wad of pound notes and signaled over to him. The barman's eyes lit up instantly.

'Two more of your most excellent London ale barman. And tell the others the last round is on me.'

The barman grinned broadly.

'Right you are sir!'

He got to work, fielding a crowd of punters scrambling for their last drink, each toasting us as they came away from the bar with their glass.

I murmured the name over and over, trying the sound and the feel of it. It sounded good.

Julius Schiller. Goldstein wouldn't work in Germany right now.

All I needed, Hans said, was to wear a nice suit and then he'd take me to the German embassy, just off Belgrave Square. He would say I was a displaced German wanting repatriation and that I'd lost my passport. Hans would vouch for me, say he had a job for me in Berlin. We'd get the passport that day and could be on the flight the next. He made it sound so simple, like he did this sort of thing every day.

9

'Maybe not every day', he admitted, 'but then you haven't heard what I'm willing to offer you to make it worth your while.'

I looked at the line of three beers apiece that Hans had laid on for us. The barman had locked the doors and we were now officially a private party, not subject to licensing regulations. We could drink until the money ran out, which might be a very long time.

'You mean, a salary?', I asked, maybe a little too keenly.

'Yes, of course a salary. Normally I screen-test, but I've seen you act, I've spoken to you, plus you saved my bloody life back there. I think I know what I'm dealing with.'

'What sort of salary?'

I'd gotten a pound a performance, eight pounds a week in the West End, which was good money, relatively. I was sort of hoping that Hans could match that.

'Let me see. I anticipate three months, maybe ninety days filming. What about a round four thousand Marks?'

'What?' I spluttered into my beer. I'd have been happy with four hundred.

'Alright alright. I'll make it five.'

'Five *thousand*?', I blurted out, trying to work out how much that was in English pounds.

***

I didn't get back to Maida Vale before five in the morning and I was lucky Hans had given me the money for a taxi because I was so drunk by the end that I could barely see. The black cab drew up outside my basement flat in a large white stucco house on Clifton Gardens and I poured myself out onto the pavement. I think I told the driver to keep the change, a three shilling fare and he got a pound. I was rich now. The one thing I remember was the look of contempt on his face as he left me lying on the ground next to a large oak tree with my books and my duffel bag, still with the cardboard tube sticking out of the top.

When I woke up, a few hours later, it was raining again and my head hurt. Then I remembered what Hans said and I started grinning. Five thousand Marks! I had stage-blood all over me but I had a whole weekend to rest before he picked me up at eight o'clock on Monday morning and took me to Belgrave Square. This would be my last weekend as Abe Goldstein. I better give him a good send off, I thought, as I picked myself up and headed inside my flat and towards the bathroom.

It was fate that I'd met Hans Bosendorf, and I wanted to go to synagogue and thank God personally. It was Saturday morning and I hadn't been for so long that I don't think anyone knew who I was. I'd come for Yom Kippur, the day of atonement, but I think that'd been last year not this and at that time I did have a lot of things to repent. However, today wasn't a day to repent. It might have been a normal Saturday for the rest of them but for me it was a day to rejoice.

When I turned up Castellain Road I positively beamed at the rabbi standing outside to welcome his worshippers. He was looking at a film star in the making. I'd put on my best clothes and shaved but he still looked at me like I shouldn't have been there, the tall blonde man with an Aryan face waltzing up to the front gate of his synagogue. I was even wearing a *yarmulke*.

I never understood why they separated the men from the women. You couldn't do that in the theatre. You'd have the women up in the circle looking down at the men in the stalls and vice-versa and no-one would watch the play.

'The fascists and anti-Semites hound us through ignorance', the rabbi intoned. 'It is merely ignorance. We should try and be tolerant of them and of all beliefs, as we hope all beliefs will be tolerant of us.'

Some hope, I thought, the image of the two thugs in the alleyway with their black shirts and dim faces flooding back to me. Hans was German but they beat him up because they thought he was a Jew. No-one had ever beaten me up for being a Jew.

'Sorry, God', I murmured to myself. I looked English or German or maybe even Scandinavian but I didn't look Jewish. The only thing that gave me away was my name and the thing dangling between my legs. I was doing something about the former and the latter would just have to live with it.

Five thousand Marks. It was hell of a lot of money, more than I'd made in the last five years. God would understand.

I spent the afternoon in the British library trying to gen up as much as I could about Germany. I wasn't as well-versed in world affairs as I perhaps should have been, and by the sound of it Hans would have me on a plane or a boat there soon enough, so it was time to learn.

From what I could gather from the newspapers – the German as well as the English ones – Hitler had helped put Germany's economy straight. He had introduced discipline and set up a variety of exciting youth programs. No mention of Jews anywhere, other than an advertisement by an obscure government department to assist in their repatriation to other countries.

I went back to 1933, concentrating on the *Volkische Beobachter* and the *Frankfurter Allgemeine*. It looked like the fascists had been doing what they'd done in England. Marching, burning books and smashing windows, even beating people up.

I'd thought of calling Isabel, asking her if she wanted to go out that night, my final fling as Abe, but I'd been to the bookshops along the Charing Cross Road and managed somehow to pick up a copy of *Mein Kampf* in the original German, by Adolf Hitler. I started to read it after tea and by the time I'd finished it at one in the morning I didn't feel like calling anyone, or going to sleep for that matter.

Monday morning came all too quickly, as I managed to sleep most of Sunday. Hans was early and I could see the black cab waiting through the bars on my front window. I checked myself quickly in the mirror and locked the door, skipping up the metal steps to street-level.

'*Guten morgen!*', he said to me, a big grin on his face. 'No second thoughts?'

I thought about telling him I'd read *Mein Kampf*, I thought about telling him how nervous I felt and I thought about asking for some sort of advance on the five thousand.

'None at all!', I replied, returning his grin with one of my own.

We headed through Paddington towards Hyde Park Corner and then turned left along a beautiful white-stoned crescent. When we reached the end Hans asked the cab to stop.

'We'll walk from here', he said, adjusting his long black leather coat as the wind whipped round from the east.

Belgrave Square was not somewhere I would normally go, and I'd never been to the German embassy. The entrance was pillared, as were all the other houses on the square, and a man in a black uniform opened the door for us, clicked his heels and bowed.

I followed Hans through into a large marble-floored lobby with potted plants everywhere. There was a large framed portrait of Adolf Hitler above a Robert Adam fireplace and suddenly a man was walking quickly towards us, his arm outstretched.

'Bosendorf! How the devil are you old man?', he asked in clipped and unaccented English.

'Very well, Schultz', replied Hans.

'You look like you've been in a fight!'

'I have. Meet the young man who saved me.'

'Bernhard Schultz. Delighted to meet you, Mister…?'

'Julius Schiller', said Hans quickly. 'Julius Schiller. He needs his documents. They were stolen by the thugs that did this to me.'

'How perfectly dreadful.'

'Yes, isn't it?'

'Please come upstairs with me, Herr Schiller. We'll have it sorted out in no time. Anything for Hans Bosendorf. He's one of our greatest cultural ambassadors. Have you seen his studios? Not far from Berlin, are they Hans?'

'He will see them, Schultz. He will. He's going to star in one of my films.'

'Perhaps some champagne then?'

It was not yet nine o'clock in the morning.

We walked up to a grand office on the first floor, an enormous sash window at one end, under it a magnificent desk and a high-backed chair almost like a throne. A chandelier hung from the ceiling, a hundred nymphs and cherubs clustered round it in gold leaf. The walls were lined with leather-bound volumes. I noticed that this room had no portrait of Adolf Hitler. Instead, a painting of a large castle hung over the fireplace.

'It is my family home', said Schultz, watching my eyes resting on it. 'Rather cold in winter, I'm afraid. So many rooms to heat.'

Bernhard Schultz was a robust man of fifty or so with a square forehead and round glasses. His black hair was swept back from his face and he had well-developed laughter lines. He seemed a charming sort of fellow, even more so when he pulled out a wad of blank passports from his desk.

'You have a photograph, I presume?', he asked politely.

'Yes, yes of course', I mumbled, pulling out my wallet with the two black and white photographs I'd had done outside the British library at Russell Square station.

There was a knock at the door and a waiter brought in a bottle of pink champagne and three glasses. Schultz waved him towards a side table and studied my photograph.

'Excellent!', he said. 'And Hans will vouch for you?'

Hans nodded. Schultz quickly pressed the photograph into the passport, stamped it in red and filled in the name Julius Schiller.

'I haven't done one of these for a while', he said. 'Sign your name and our business is done. Fill in Hans's details as your referee. Then we can relax while we drink. You will need to put down your address in Germany and then I'll pass a duplicate to central records.'

'Leave the address to me', said Hans.
I signed the name with a gothic flourish. It was the first time I had seen it on paper. I wasn't sure if I should be proud or not. I handed it to Hans who filled in the rest of the details.

'Congratulations!', said Schultz, standing suddenly. Hans and I stood too. 'Herr Julius Schiller!'

'Herr Julius Schiller!', I found myself repeating along with Hans.

I looked around the opulent room, glass of pink champagne in hand, straight through the window towards an immaculate Belgrave Square. All thoughts of Hitler vanished. All I could see was the splendour around me, champagne bubbles and five thousand Marks.

Only five days after I'd dragged Hans off the street and into the *Prince Regent* we boarded the plane at Elstree airfield. We took off, I looked out of the window and thirty seconds later I was violently sick in a tiny bathroom nine thousand feet over Hertfordshire. I had never been on an aeroplane before and the twists and turns of the twin-prop, the dips, the bumps and the disconcerting rattles were making my stomach turn green. The swaying wasn't unlike that of an underground train, but the trains didn't have all the long ups and the long downs. The trains just moved from side to side. Oh God – I had it all over my new shirt, the one Hans had bought on Jermyn Street, along with the shoes, the suit and the ties. I don't think I could ever get used to flying. It was such an unnatural activity. If God had meant us to fly, I remember reading, man wouldn't have invented aeroplanes.

I wobbled slowly down the aisle and back to my seat, my face a graying yellow-green, my shirt damp and unbuttoned at the collar and my tie loosened. I bent down and shifted into it slowly. Hans was busy looking out of the window.

'That is Berlin below us now.'

I looked past him and out of the window. A mass of houses and factories and churches and parks stretched out below me. Cars moved like ants along arterial roads and then the whole ant's-nest seemed to turn slightly, then more and then the horizon suddenly angled off onto a grey sky. We turned sharply and I reached for the paper bag in front of me.

'When you see her', said Hans to me on the tarmac, 'you won't want the money.'

'She'll have to be some girl, Hans.'

With five thousand Marks, exchanged at the right rate, I could buy a house in England. Maybe a Georgian rectory somewhere on the outskirts of town, with a little land. For three months work, and every extra day at an even higher rate, I could own a little piece of England which meant no more renting. I could entertain guests properly, maybe find a nice girl who wouldn't mind being my wife and not have to settle for a damp single roomed basement. And with one film behind me, maybe more would follow. I tried not to think about staying in Germany after this one. I'd have to play it by ear.

For a country priding itself on military precision and discipline the entry procedures seemed a little haphazard. Once we got off the plane we entered a maze of prefabricated corridors. At one point, there was a left branch and a right. To the left, two grim-faced men in black with pencil-thin necks sitting at a desk. To the right, a pretty blonde woman in a tight-fitting uniform. Hans grabbed my arm and propelled me towards the pretty blonde.

Her name-badge read *'Helga Braun'* and she smiled as she looked up at me. Germany looked promising.

'Reisepass', said Helga.

I removed my brand new German passport from my jacket pocket, watching her eyes watching mine. She opened up the passport quickly and made a note in a tiny book on her desk. I turned round and saw Hans standing behind me, looking at her. Helga held up a large black stamp, inked it on a large black pad and brought it down swiftly onto the fresh blue page leaving the imprint of an Eagle's Head and a swastika. I looked up relieved as she smiled at me again.

'Welcome back to Germany, Herr Schiller.'

I touched my hat deferentially.

'Thank you. It's been a while.'

I walked past her and stopped, waiting for Hans. He placed his passport in front of her and studied her face as if he were looking for blemishes. She opened up the passport and stamped it quickly. Hans suddenly grasped her hand.

'Mein Liebchen! You have lovely eyes', he purred as he removed a business card from his jacket pocket and placed it in front of Ms Braun. 'Call me'.

He tipped his hat and joined me.

'Everyone wants to be in the movie business,' he whispered. 'That girl certainly does. Even Hitler does.'

'Hitler?'

'Ja. You know those little hand-movements?'

I cast my mind back to the pictures I'd seen in the British Library of Adolf Hitler, a small man with side-combed black hair and a tiny moustache, addressing cheering crowds at the Brandenburg Gate. He made those little waves, with the palm raised, the small gestures of power that Hans was making now, small and effortless, an indication that greater power lurked within, capable of grander gestures.

'I taught him to do that', said Hans proudly. 'I advised him to show a little and leave them begging for more.'

'I wish you'd told me that before'.

'Yes', said Hans, 'I'm quite proud of it myself.'

The Mercedes limousine was smooth and quiet and I sat back watching the streets of Berlin slip by me, the sound deadened by the thick glass. We passed a butcher's shop, where enormous sausages were chopped by a blood-spattered arm on a large wooden block. A poster of Adolf Hitler adorned every spare wall or hoarding, beckoning Germans to work hard and vote National Socialist. Large numbers of men and women marched about in quasi-military uniform. I knew from the papers that Hitler had annexed Czechoslovakia but that Neville Chamberlain, the British Prime Minister, had said it was not worth fussing about. Peace in our time, or some such. And then I saw the sign.

I pressed my face to the thick glass. It stood outside a cinema in bold black letters, underneath a glowing neon assemblage of letters for a horror film:

'Juden verboten!' No Jews!

As the Mercedes slipped by, I couldn't take my eyes off it. Only once we turned the corner of the busy street did I turn to look at Hans who was busy studying a screenplay, heavily annotated in a jumble of different colours. The sign screamed at me. *Juden verboten! Juden verboten!* No Jews! No wonder he told me Abe

Goldstein wouldn't work in Germany right now. I asked Hans but he didn't look up.

'Ja ja', he said 'Jews can't go to the cinema.'

'No Jew will see the film we're going to make?'

Hans finally looked up at me.

'Not in Germany', he replied. 'Not at this current time. But it will change. Things will get better.'

I looked away from him and exhaled slowly.

'Do you think England is any better, my boy?', he asked. 'Do you see Jews in your London clubs? There may be no signs, but it's the same. No blacks, no Jews. That is why you are Julius Schiller, no?'

I felt in my pocket for my British passport in the name of Abraham Goldstein. I'd brought it with me just in case, despite Hans telling me I wouldn't need it. I'd thought it would make things easier on the way back home to England, a country where Jews *could* visit the cinema.

It crossed my mind that maybe five thousand Marks wasn't enough.

2

The spring sun blazed orange in the sky as the large black Mercedes pulled up outside the tall iron gates for Bosendorf Studios. A wall with smart metal grilles wrapped round the enormous expanse of land beyond them. It was the first time I'd been anywhere near a film studio. Two men in white overalls ushered us in and the Mercedes glided inside. Ahead lay six imposing grey buildings set on a five hectare lot. Men and women rushed about on film business, which to my untrained eye looked to be a very tiring business.

'Does everyone run around here?', I asked Hans.

'I never run', he replied.

The car swept up to the largest of the grey buildings and came to a halt. The chauffeur got out and I took a good look at him. He was a small man with a large grin, hardly any teeth and a limp.

'This is Jerry', said Hans. 'The best stunt man I had, but after thirty concussions he retired.'

'Thassri' sir', said Jerry, grinning. 'Thirty!' I wondered how that qualified him to drive a car, but despite the thirty separate concussions and his slight build he still managed to pick up my heavy suitcase.

'You can show Mister Schiller his trailer now and take him round the lot. Let him see what all the fuss is about.'

'Yes…yes…Mister Bosendorf…Bosendorf, sir!'

'Then you can bring him to Studio Three, to meet Miss Wendt'.

Jerry stopped grinning. *Miss Wendt* was the woman Hans had told me would make money irrelevant, that I'd be glad to work for nothing just to be near her, that she was the best, most famous, blondest, most beautiful film star in the whole of Germany.

'My co-star?', I asked. Hans winced.

'Best not to tell her you are a star or even a co-star, my boy', he replied. 'She can be, how do you say...' Hans searched for the right word, but couldn't find it, so he shrugged and walked off towards the main building. 'Just follow Jerry', he shouted back.

I turned to Jerry and smiled but he was already gone, heading quickly towards the side of the large grey building to our right.

'You had a good...good trip, sir?', he asked. I was just about to tell him about my first time on a plane when suddenly from somewhere a woman screamed and a gun fired a second afterwards, making me jump.

'What was that?'

'You get - get used to it round here, see Mister Schiller sir'.

Jerry walked on eagerly, holding my suitcase like it was a light parcel. I tried to see where the gunshot had come from.

We turned another corner and onto the edge of a simple film set done out like a main street somewhere in America. A pipe-smoking director in Lederhosen and a small camera crew were ready to roll, stationed over to the far side. In front of the crew, with two cameras pointing at them, stood two men dressed like Laurel and Hardy, one tall and thin, the other short and fat with a moustache. They were holding a large plate glass window in the middle of the street expectantly. Jerry gazed wistfully into the distance.

'I used…used to do this sorta thing, Mister Schiller, sir. Before the accident.'

'What accident?'

'Quiet on set!', shouted someone before Jerry could reply.

The Lederhosen-clad director held a pipe in front of his face and called out to a small wiry man on a bicycle positioned twenty feet from the large plate glass window.

'Ready?'

The man on a bicycle gave a thumb's up sign. Jerry walked by them quickly and headed round another corner, leaving me struggling to keep up with him.

'And….action!'

We rounded the corner and then I heard a huge crash of breaking glass behind us.

'*Nein! Nein! Nein!*'

There were a few seconds silence and then someone called for a doctor. Jerry smiled toothlessly.

'Just like the good old days, Mister Schiller sir', he said, heading for a silver trailer at the side of the lot. There was a metal sign by the door and on it I could see emblazoned the words *Julius Schiller*. This huge gleaming beast was mine.

I found my way into Studio Three about thirty minutes later. It was mid afternoon and it felt very hot inside. There was a stage bathed in light at one end containing several rooms in a baronial house. There were three people standing under the lights in one of the rooms around a long dining table. Hans waved his arms at a middle-aged woman in a blue trouser-suit and a man in a pink shirt with wild hair. Cigarette smoke was rising up from somewhere behind them.

I edged forward in the darkness until I got to a row of metal chairs. I sat down on the one at the end and leaned forward. The man in the pink shirt looked close to tears and he was wiping his eyes with a handkerchief.

'I tell you again, I cannot work with this, Hans!', he said in a high-pitched voice. 'She won't let me even *touch* her precious hair!'

'Please Marty, calm down', said Hans. Plumes of smoke rose from somewhere behind him.

'She doesn't wear what we ask her to, Herr Bosendorf!', piped up the blue trouser-suited woman.

'She's mean to me. Calls me names', said the pink shirt. 'The queen of bad hair, mincing minnie, the gay cavalier, the eunuch with scissors. You know what Hans? I just can't do this anymore today. You'll have to call Ramone!'

He threw his head back and stormed off the set, walking past me as smoke continued to rise from the cigarette in its long holder and a husky, sexy woman's voice punctured the silence.

'Has it gone?'

Hans and the woman in the blue trouser-suit turned to look at the girl I was now looking at, an outrageously beautiful platinum blonde in a figure-hugging black dress holding a long cigarette holder. She stood up from her seat and smoothed down the material over her curves.

'Darling...don't listen to Marty. He's having a bad day', cooed Hans, kissing her hand theatrically.

'You're the only one I listen to, Hans.'

Blue trouser-suit rolled her eyes, shook her head and walked off-set straight past me.

'Good luck, deary', she whispered, leaving me with a clear and uninterrupted view of Eva Wendt.

I loved Hans at that moment. I was going to be spending at least three months of my life with the most beautiful woman I'd ever seen and be paid more money than I'd ever made for the privilege.

'Darling, you must try to get along with the others', said Hans.

'I know what everyone calls me behind my back', she replied. 'I may be the youngest, beautifullest, blondest movie star in Germany but to them I'm just a blonde bitch who screwed her way to the top.'

Another long plume of smoke rose from her cigarette, which rested in a long silver holder. Hans scratched his head.

'Maybe we should rest today.'

'No Hans. The sooner we go through the script the sooner I get paid.'

'You were always the philosopher, my love'.

'So tell me about the new man'. I edged forward on my seat. 'Is he nice? He's not a sap like Herman is he?'

'No no, my darling.'

'He better not try and stick his tongue down my throat'.

'He's a professional, my sweet'. I leaned closer.

'Is he good-looking at least? All these asshole German actors look like farm-labourers, thick-set plodding Neanderthals, with no kind of manners.'

I walked into the blinding lights and cleared my throat. She turned and looked straight at me, but it felt like she was looking straight through me, as if she could see Abe Goldstein and not Julius Schiller.

'Have you been there long, *Julius*?', Hans asked nervously.

'Long enough.'

'*Julius*?', she said cagily. 'What sort of a name is *Julius*? You sound Roman. Are you Roman?'

25

'It's a very good name', Hans replied quickly. 'Julius Schiller, this is Eva Wendt. Eva Wendt, this is Julius Schiller.' I bent down to take her hand and she exhaled a long plume of smoke directly into my eyes.

'I prefer to be called *Miss Wendt.*'

'Got those prints for you Herr Bosendorf!', shouted a skinny man from the open door of a sound booth. Hans turned towards us, relieved.

'Excuse me just a moment', he said, bounding up the steps towards the sound-proofed room, leaving the two of us alone.

The spotlight moved over from her to me, leaving her in the dark. Someone was watching in the lighting booth and I thought I could hear giggling. I looked up into the light and squinted. It was bright before, but this was blinding. I was sweating and I wasn't doing anything apart from breathing. Eva looked up at the lighting booth dispassionately.

'At least they have a sense of humour', she murmured, looking up and clicking her fingers. Quickly, the light expanded to flood us both and the giggling stopped. I watched her put out her cigarette into an ashtray on the large dining table.

Her skin was flawless, the sort of skin you see on women in glossy magazines. She was quite tall, with blue eyes and platinum blonde hair that reached down below her shoulders. Her eyebrows were arched and pencil thin. She wore bright red lipstick and not much else, which meant her face looked almost white under the studio glare. The face itself was strong but beautiful, high-cheekboned and proud. She was a little like how I remembered my white-blonde German-Polack mother. I had no idea what to say to her.

'You remind me of my mother', I blurted out, suddenly realizing how that sounded. She arched an eyebrow and rolled the cigarette-holder in her hand nonchalantly.

'Really, Herr Schiller?', she enquired. 'I am meant to take this as a compliment?'

'Yes, yes you are Miss Wendt. My mother was very beautiful.'

'Well that's alright then. Tell me', she began, leaning against the table so the split in her dress reached all the way to her upper thigh, 'what films I would have seen you in?'

'I've done mainly theatre.'

'Oh? Where?'

'Dusseldorf, Hamburg, Munich', I said, the first towns that came into my head.

'Dusseldorf? Tell me about Dusseldorf. I know it well. The *Altstadt*'s not bad. Which plays? Who was your director?' Where was Hans when I needed him?

'I'd rather hear about you', I said, 'and *your* films.'

'How flattering', she replied, making me feel even more uncomfortable. 'This is your first film, isn't it?'

'Yes. Yes it is.'

'It's my fifteenth. Let me give you some advice.'

'Please do.'

'I don't like liars, I don't like fakers and I don't like tongues'.

'Excuse me?'

'And if you fall in love with me I will have you fired'.

'I haven't signed my contract yet. You can't have me fired.'

'Make sure you read the small-print. I think you'll find the only person I *can't* fire is Hans.'

She moved away from the table and my eyes couldn't help following the curves of her dress and the split that now revealed nothing. She puffed another plume of smoke my way and posed majestically in the light.

'And now, *Julius*, I want to be alone', she said.

I looked up towards where Hans was standing next to a technician looking through some prints. He smiled and looked down towards me.

'It is going well, yes, Julius?' he asked. I didn't reply. I didn't want to disappoint him. I just wanted to check the small-print.

Hans said we'd sort out the contract that day because Eva needed to rest. His office was on the first floor of the main studio block, a hundred yards from Studio Three. It was large and loft-like, thickly carpeted and full of glass display cabinets containing awards in a variety of shapes and sizes. I remember there was an eighteen-inch-high bronze director's chair in one of them, in another a large silver rhino with a man sitting on it and in another a set of scales held by three wise men, presumably the jury for some film festival. I remember my shoes sinking into the thick carpet. The walls were full of photographs of Hans with German movie stars. A photograph of Eva on Hans's arm was positioned in the middle of the room. They were smiling and waving in front of a cinema.

'That was her first film', he said, walking over to me. 'Can you believe she was only sixteen when they took that?'

I stared again at the picture. I'd have put her nearer twenty or twenty five.

'Women', sighed Hans, watching me carefully as he pushed a contract across the desk towards me.

'What about them?'

'Don't you like them?'

'The delightful Miss Wendt told me I should read the small-print carefully. Maybe I should take this away with me and let you have it back tomorrow?'

'No no', he said, 'I want to start filming tomorrow and I need all contracts today. You must sign *today*.'

'Can't I give it to you tomorrow morning first thing? I haven't had a chance to read it'.

'Trust me, Julius. Just sign on the dotted line'.

He pushed a pen into my hand and I looked down on the desk in front of me at the thick document.

'It's all there on the first page', said Hans.

I looked at the first page. Three months, five thousand Marks and a hundred Marks per day overtime including weekends.

'Then what's on the other hundred?'

'Look Julius. I had exactly the same conversation with Eva Wendt. She came to me here five years ago from nowhere and now she's made fifteen films with fifteen leading men.'

'*Fifteen* different leading men?'

'At least. Maybe more. Don't ask. Welcome to the film business.'

'Won't you let me read the contract at least? Give me a couple of hours?'

'Alright alright. I'll pay you double what we agreed. Now will you sign?'

'*Double*?'

Hans nodded and scribbled out the word *five* in the contract and inserted *ten* instead, initialing it. My hand was shaking. Ten thousand Marks was a fortune.

I signed in a state of shock, realizing afterwards, as Hans shook my hand and ushered me out, that perhaps I should have asked what sort of film it was.

***

The heavy beat of tom-toms wafted through the jungle set in Studio Five. Suddenly, two cavemen appeared, carrying Eva over their heads through a flurry of *papier mache* rocks and plastic foliage. Eva screamed, helpless in their muscular arms. In the background, the string section of an orchestra worked hard to create mood music, in this case, *Action! Adventure! Romance!*

Eva turned to camera, in close-up.

'Gogo! Gogo!', she wailed from somewhere in the bushes. This was followed by a rustling and the appearance, to a dramatic fanfare, of me dressed in a skimpy Tarzan outfit. Someone in wardrobe had no sense of proportion, I thought, as I felt the leopard-skin tighten. I beat my chest like an animal, roared and chased after the two cavemen and their prize, a screaming Eva.

'Aaaaargh! Aaaargh!', I bellowed like an idiot, chasing them through the plastic plants and across the dirty studio floor in bare feet as the cameras rolled. The two cavemen turned round at my approach, and I beat them both with a club until they dropped Eva unceremoniously to the ground with a loud thud.

'Owww!', she wailed, unscripted. And then I, her hero, scooped Eva up in my arms. I couldn't help noticing that she was dressed in delightfully little. She looked up lovingly into my eyes.

'Oh Gogo...', she whispered, as I kissed her passionately, her body melting in my arms. The kiss went on, and on, and on. I was enjoying it too much to stop. That was Hans' job, to tell us when to start and when to stop.

'And....cut!', came Hans's voice over the top of the music, the kiss and the foliage. Eva broke away from me and wiped her mouth. She spat onto the ground and looked at me disgustedly. I smiled and then she slapped me hard round the face, in front of everyone.

'I said no tongues!'

She slapped me again. It hurt. I could hear the camera crew laughing in the background until Hans turned to them sharply. The orchestra were sweating heavily, as Eva had asked for the heat to be turned up so she wouldn't freeze in her skimpy costume.

'Oh Gogo, Gogo!', mimicked first violin to second.

'Aaaaargh!', retorted second violin, beating his chest like Tarzan. The whole string section burst out laughing. Eva turned away, lit a cigarette and found herself a space to sit atop a *papier-mache* rock.

'It's terrible, Hans', she said. *'Totalsheisse!'*

I walked up to Hans rubbing my face and thinking that no-one in England would see this film anyway.

'How was it?', I asked, trying to smile. 'I didn't put my tongue inside Eva Wendt's mouth Hans. I swear.'

Hans lit a cigar with an enormous flame-thrower of a lighter, held it open, picked up the jungle script and set fire to it. It burnt into a small ball of flame and he tossed it into a metal bin on the side of the set.

'They were laughing', he shouted. 'Laughing! It is not a comedy. It is shit. Eva is right. Burn all the scripts.' Hans turned towards a quiet man in glasses, Peter Keppel, a man of about forty, who was standing behind him calmly.

'Keppel - where's your damned screenplay?'

Keppel shrugged.

'Don't hold out on me, now, Keppel. I'll pay you double if you get it to me by the end of next week...you Jews like that sort of thing, don't you?'

'Doesn't everybody?', he replied, catching my eye. 'You'll have your script, Herr Bosendorf, you'll have it by the end of next week'.

31

I watched him go and suddenly a *papier-mache* rock came down hard on my head.

'It's an improvement', I could hear her say coolly while I stumbled about like a blind man, crashing into the set and tumbling over, sending the crew into paroxysms of laughter.

I pulled the rock off my head, took a couple of deep breaths and closed my eyes. Ten thousand Marks floated into view. It would take me ten years in England to make that sort of money. Hans kept swigging from a silver hip-flask. I hadn't seen him drink like that before but then I also had no idea of the sort of pressure he was under.

***

The clock ticked its way towards midnight, but the lights shone brightly in Hans's office. He looked around him at the awards and the photographs that adorned the cabinets and the walls, the faces of famous friends and prominent politicians staring back at him. If only they knew. All they saw was the public face, the director with a holiday home off the coast of Hamburg and a large townhouse in central Berlin. There was no Mrs Bosendorf and the faces on the wall had no idea how lonely he really was, or how broke.

The knock at the door almost came as a welcome relief. Hans downed another schnapps and filled two more glasses as a man in his early fifties walked in, a blaze of medals covering his broad chest.

'Heil Hitler!', he barked, clicking his heels and saluting as he walked through the door. Hans smiled nervously at *SS-Obersturmbannfuhrer* Wilfred Keller, an ex-actor.

'Please feel at ease here, Keller', said Hans. 'Would you care for some Schnapps?'

'Very civilized of you, my dear fellow', replied Keller, picking at his words like *petits-fours*. Hans walked to the drinks cabinet by the side of his desk, removed a half-empty bottle and poured out two small shot glasses with the pinkish liquid. He handed one to Keller and raised his glass.

'*Prost!*', he said, half-heartedly. It was so difficult to smile, but Hans did his best, his arm trembling.

Keller removed a set of accounts from his briefcase and placed it on the desk in front of him. He leafed through it languidly.

'Dear, dear, dear', he tutted. He shook his head. 'Oh dear', he lamented. Keller turned twenty more pages in silence. Hans shifted uncomfortably in his chair. He always felt more comfortable when somebody was speaking and most comfortable when the person speaking was Hans Bosendorf.

'My my', said Keller lightly, turning over the final page of the accounts in front of him. 'I am afraid Herr Bosendorf that you're running at a huge loss. Everyone's salary inexplicably seems to double. You only just have enough to pay Miss Wendt and the Fuhrer's favourite *must* be paid.'

Hans blinked furiously.

'Of course Wilfred, that is how the movie business works. You've obviously gained a deep understanding over the last two years.'

'My dear fellow, how perfectly charming of you to say so'.

'Thank you and of course I appreciate the Party's equity investment but you must leave the running of the studios to me. I will obviously do my utmost to maximize your investment.'

Keller looked sniffily at the accounts in front of him, closed the front cover and placed them back in his briefcase.

'The Party may be forced to increase its stake, Herr Bosendorf, without further notice'.

'Really? Can it do that?'

'Of course it can. The Party can do whatever it pleases.'

'I see. How fortunate for it. Less so for me.'

'You are very fortunate Bosendorf. You are a wealthy man.'

Hans poured himself another glass of schnapps and took a large gulp. It came down to cash-flow and the cash wasn't flowing at the moment.

'Please be patient', pleaded Hans. 'I have our top screenwriter working on a wonderful script right now. The last project was a misjudgment, you understand? A simple misjudgment. We are doing well with our *Laurel and Hardy* comedies. The public loves slapstick.'

'I also love slapstick', said Keller stiffly.

'Good. Good. You will be patient, won't you? There's no need to do anything rash'.

Keller looked at him measuredly over his glass of schnapps and took another sip.

***

It was my third night in the trailer, my third night in Germany, and I couldn't sleep. Out of the window, framed with art-deco patterned curtains, I could see a single light glowing in the main studio building, in what could have been Hans's office. I was getting used to the trailer, but not to everything outside it.

Under different circumstances I would have been in love with Eva Wendt but she obviously despised me.

Maybe she would tell Keppel what to put in his screenplay to make it even worse for me. If she knew I was Jewish...I almost felt like telling her, just to see the look on her face, but then the sign outside the cinema – *Juden verboten!* – stopped me. If we weren't allowed to watch films we certainly weren't meant to star in them. I opened another bottle of beer. Ten thousand Marks was an awful lot of money.

My trailer was made of corrugated sheet metal and from the outside it looked like a horizontal refrigerator. Inside was a pull-down bed, a desk, a bench, a small fridge stocked with bottles of beer and orange juice and lastly a small built-in set of shelves which I'd filled with my books. There was a small chemical lavatory in a small bathroom, a sink, a shower and a large mirror surrounded by bulbs. Hans told me to be on call twenty-four hours a day, so I hadn't yet left the studios.

I drained my beer and took another one. I peeked through the curtains out to the studio block. The light had gone out now and I heard a car drive out through the gates. I grabbed the volume of Shakespeare's plays from the bookshelf, sat down at the desk and leafed through the index. What should I read? What would be most fitting? Eva Wendt's perfect face swam into my head, the blondest, most beautiful movie star in all of Germany, according to Hans and to Eva, of course. A picture of Aryan perfection, the Fuhrer's favourite. What would be appropriate? I flicked through the pages until I found the play I knew so well, the play I'd first read at the age of ten.

I settled *Romeo and Juliet* in front of me, smoothed out the pages carefully and began to read, imagining the two of us as Shakespeare's star-cross'd lovers doomed to a horrible end. I thought it might help me sleep but I was wrong.

***

It seemed that I was getting paid for doing nothing except reading in my trailer and walking around the studio. Hans kept telling me to be patient, to conserve my energy. A week passed, I was getting bored and hadn't seen Eva, but then suddenly Bosendorf Studios sprang to life when one morning Peter Keppel placed his finished script onto Hans's leather-topped desk and Hans handed him a large cheque.

'Thank God for the Jews!', said Hans. 'Thank you Keppel.'

'Thank God for the Germans', murmured Keppel.

Every foot flew across the lot in preparation for the feature film that would enter pre-production and principal photography on the same day and that day was today. Hans looked more relaxed and drank less schnapps but I didn't know that he'd sold a group of investors a large chunk of *All for Love* by Peter Keppel and that my salary was now effectively being paid by the SS.

Outside a tractor was pulling a silver trailer much bigger than mine across the studio lot and as far away from me as possible. It was eight in the morning and once the trailer had come to a halt, the door swung open and Eva appeared on the steps dressed as a chambermaid. I hadn't seen the script and she was already in costume. She looked over to the other side of the lot, towards me, and nodded, satisfied. She walked towards the studio buildings with the help of a young girl who carried the back of her dress to avoid dropping it in the mud.

I soon found out who I was when they brought the costume for a fitting. The girl helped me pull on the tight clothes – everything was always too tight – and then opened my trailer door for me. I must have looked quite a sight, an eighteenth century duke in rubber boots to avoid getting my costume muddy. I hadn't read the script, but anything entitled *All for Love* needed us to be on speaking terms unless Keppel had used the title ironically. I wondered how good an actor I was.

I headed to Studio One where Hans gave me a hearty *'Guten Morgen!'* and tossed me a thick bundle of white paper bound together with three metal pins. It was *All for Love*. Eva was over on the other side of the studio with two girls fussing over her. Her head was buried in the script and it looked as if she was already crossing things out with a silver pen.

'Read the last scene', Hans told me. 'We're shooting in reverse order.'

'Why?'

'Experience. Don't worry about it and don't ask me why.' I wondered if his curtness was something to do with me having signed the contract. He hadn't let me keep a copy, said I could pick one up from his office next week.

I sat down with the script, turned to the last scene and started reading. Eva beckoned Hans over, her cigarette-holder balanced delicately in her hand, looking stunning even in the old-fashioned chambermaid's uniform.

'Who is he, Hans? He told me he'd done theatre in Dusseldorf, but he's lying. Where's he from?'

'He's a good actor, Eva. Does it matter where he's from?'

'But he's lying to me, Hans. I can't act with someone I know is lying. Who is he? I've never heard of Julius Schiller.'

'An unknown, Eva darling, just like you were. Be nice to him.'

She looked over towards me and smiled with her mouth, but not with her eyes. I returned the favour.

Three hours later the rehearsals began.

I sat at a grand piano in my eighteenth century finery in an ornately-decorated chamber, pretending to play. The door to the chamber was opened by a wigged footman to reveal Eva playing Clara, my chambermaid. She stood meekly, avoiding my gaze.

'You called for me, your lordship?'

I rose from the piano and moved swiftly over to her.

'Yes. The ambassador tells me that I am foolish and that I must marry the Infanta.'

'She is very beautiful, sir', she replied, her voice quivering.

'Yes, she is, and if I do not marry her, the King will strip me of my title, my lands and my inheritance.'

'Oh sir!'

'But I love another, another whom I am forbidden to love. So different, and yet...'

I dropped to my knees and bowed my head.

'Oh sir! Are you not well? Shall I fetch the apothecary?'

'No, Clara'.

'You know my name!'

'Of course I do. Every second without you is eternity. Every touch against your skin paradise. I love you Clara, I love you with all my heart.'

Clara wrenched herself away from my gaze.

'No!', she exclaimed, 'This cannot be!'

'I renounce my heritage', I said, taking out a fine gold ring from a waistcoat pocket and holding it up to her.

'Will you marry me, Clara?'

She fainted to the floor. I bent down and revived her with a kiss. She lay in my arms, wide-eyed, looking up at me as I looked down on her.

'But sir! I do not understand how a servant girl can ever be good enough for a duke.'

'Darling - my love - underneath we are the same. The same flesh, the same bone, the same heart, the same soul. Marry me Clara. Say yes. Say yes and you'll make me the happiest man in the world.'

Clara's lip trembled, her hands shook. Her lips formed a word.

'Yes!'

I kissed her passionately and music seemed to come from nowhere, swelling to a crescendo. The kiss went on, and on, and on.

When I kissed her, which the script demanded that I must do, I forgot that she was Eva Wendt and I imagined her to be the love of my life, the woman I was going to wed and spend the rest of my life with. I'd never kissed a woman like *that* before in front of thirty people only inches away. It wasn't like theatre because everyone was so close. It was a little perverse, but I still enjoyed it.

'Cut!', cried Hans, turning to his cameraman. 'Did that work?'

The cameraman nodded as Eva stood up and slapped me hard round the face. She folded her arms and looked at me imperiously.

'I said no tongues', she purred.

But I bloody hadn't! I held my hand to my face and looked at the red spots dripping onto it. Was she trying to get me fired?

A make-up assistant dabbed my face gently with cotton wool to staunch the blood.

'Don't worry, sir. She does this to everyone. It's not personal', she whispered. 'You know what they call her?'

'Yes', I replied, 'the blonde bitch.'

I looked over towards Eva, languorously smoking a cigarette from a long holder and wondered if Hans had told her I was Jewish, that my real name was Abe Goldstein. Maybe she didn't like Jews.   I got the filming-in-reverse-order thing now. Best to get the kissing over with at the start with Miss Wendt, as things were bound to deteriorate. Well, that was fine. I'd done some shitty jobs in the past like wait tables in Stepney and carry old ladies' suitcases at a hotel in Frinton. For ten thousand Marks she could slap me every hour on the hour for all I cared.

She was walking towards me now, looking at me coolly.

'That was good for me, Schiller', she said, blowing smoke into my eyes, 'apart from the fact that you're a terrible kisser.'

I smiled. At least now I knew I wasn't the only one lying.

***

One day flowed into another and then another. The routine of early morning starts, hours spent under bright lights and script revisions made the time go quickly. I'd counted six weeks before I knew it, which by my reckoning was nearly five thousand Marks-worth. Working in film was completely different to theatre. We never needed to learn more than a scene at a time, and even then we could have large cue cards positioned wherever we wanted them to help us remember our lines. The discipline of the theatre, where

I'd had to learn a full two hour play, meant that I almost never slipped up on the film-set and I got the feeling that Hans was pleased with me, even though he seemed preoccupied with other things, so rarely gave me a compliment. He reserved those for Eva.

We were together for only about half the scenes and we barely spoke to each other. I wanted to kiss her again but it wasn't in the script. Although she was aloof, there was something about her that always made me want to scoop her up in my arms. I could see why she was the Fuhrer's favourite. She was blonde, slim, smart, strong yet vulnerable and very very beautiful. It was a shame she couldn't stand the sight of me but to be honest I'd stopped caring why.

I got into the habit of playing cards at night with Jerry and some of the other guys, usually in my trailer. Jerry always lost but we always let him off the money. He just liked to be there with us and I felt sorry for him after his thirty concussions.

Peter Keppel - the writer - played a few times, officially the only Jew unofficially on the studio payroll. He bet small amounts and kept the conversation moving quickly. He gave me tips on how he thought I should play the duke, or what changes Hans had in store for the next day's filming. I liked Keppel but I saw no point in telling him I was also a Jew, so I never did. He looked like he didn't belong with Hans, wasn't flamboyant enough, kept himself to himself. I hadn't read a newspaper since I'd been at the studios and the only radio was in Hans's office so I didn't really know what, if anything, was going on. Keppel helped us fill in the blanks.

'Hitler's recruiting again', he said, 'and I'll raise you five. The radio's playing non-stop propaganda telling everyone about increased pay and rations.'

'What's he planning?', I asked. 'I'll keep with your five and raise you five more'.

Keppel looked at me over his glasses.

'If I knew', he replied, 'believe me, I'd tell you. But after Czechoslovakia, who knows what he's got his little beady eyes on.' Jerry raised his hand.

'Scuse me everyone but I think…I think I've got to raise five more too and see everyone.'

We all looked at him and shrugged. Jerry couldn't bluff so he must have a good hand. We folded and watched him take the money.

'And the last will be first and the first will be last', said Keppel, watching Jerry smile toothlessly.

I liked that. I'd started last, so maybe I'd end up first. I opened another round of beers for everyone whilst we watched Jerry shuffle the cards and deal.

The first time I left the studio Jerry drove us. We went to a small town twenty miles from Berlin where Eva and I opened a new cinema. We didn't say a word to each other. The people there looked the same as they had done when I arrived, and there were a lot of military style uniforms. A disciplined group of boys in long socks and brown uniform cheered our car. It felt quite good to be the centre of attention, but the one they all wanted to meet was Eva.

Hans carried a bundle of publicity photos that she'd signed, and he'd had some done for me too. Hers ran out after a few minutes, but I was surprised to see that mine all went too. And then, as we stood outside, Eva cutting the red tape and telling everyone how pleased she was to see them, I saw my first tank.

At first I heard a rumble and thought it might be rain, what with the grey sky and skittish wind. But it was the sound of huge tracks grinding onto the cobblestones of the main street. A thick-faced man poked out of the top giving the Nazi salute, looking like he expected us to salute back. Some people did. All the little boys in their shorts and brown shirts saluted. They seemed well-behaved enough. It was the discipline I'd read about. They certainly weren't like the ill-mannered lot I remembered from the East End, near my uncle's house. They used to nick apples from carts and pelt boys with them, steal bread and jam from unlocked kitchens and ride their bicycles into pedestrians. It was 1939 and Germany looked a lot more together than England did.

I'd nearly forgotten that Jews were forbidden to go to the cinema when I looked inside the foyer and saw another *Juden verboten!* sign. Hans saw it too and turned me away from it, his hand on my shoulder.

'It's a passing phase', he whispered into my ear.

Eva seemed to stare at me more coldly than usual. She'd also been looking at the sign in the foyer. I avoided her gaze. I suddenly missed London and the men selling marshmallows on street corners. I suddenly missed all the girls in London who didn't treat me like a piece of shit. Maybe someone would have a timetable for the boat from Hamburg, maybe direct to Hull or Newcastle. A plane was out of the question and it made me ill just thinking about it. I reckoned six weeks more, maybe eight, should do it. I could keep myself going for just a while longer with thoughts of the ten thousand Marks and in the meantime maybe Hans knew where I could buy marshmallows.

3

It was a dark clear night in Hitler's Berlin in the summer of 1939 and the flashbulbs outside the cinema lit up the sky like fireworks. A crowd of photographers and film-fans looked excitedly towards the three black limousines that were pulling up at the foot of a long red carpet that led from the cinema entrance to the street. Up in neon lights above the main entrance blazed the sign *'Alles fur Lieb'*, and beneath it in big letters *'mit Eva Wendt'*. In much smaller letters, almost as an afterthought, you could just read the words *'und Julius Schiller'*.

There was a large poster of us in an embrace on the wall next to the foyer, headed by a large banner with the Bosendorf Studios logo. I hadn't read in my contract the bit which stated that all payment was conditional on attending the premiere, and at last, on a warm night in July 1939, premiere night had arrived.

We finished the film months ago and so I had to hang around in the studio, playing cards, eating at the canteen or in my trailer and reading and re-reading all my German books because Hans had told me not to bring the English ones, apart from the Shakespeare.

The door to the first limousine opened slowly and the paparazzi went mad, hollering and waving frantically. The crowd screamed in unison. One word, one short word that summed up why they were here.

'Eva! Eva! Eva!', they chanted as she stepped out of the limousine wearing a glittering silver dress. The crowd roared with approval. Eva smiled broadly and posed for them, blowing kisses between each pose.

'Eva! Eva! Eva! Eva!', they chanted again, the shouting reaching inside the second limousine, chauffeured by Jerry. In the back, I sat with Hans, both of us peering out at her.

'*Mein Gott* she's good', said Hans, proudly.

I was just looking for that bloody sign - *Juden verboten!* - but I couldn't see it. Hans placed his hand on my shoulder and gave it what I guess he thought was a paternal squeeze.

'Who would have thought it?', he said. 'There I was, lying in the gutter in London and you saved me. One good turn deserves another, no?'

'We were both in the gutter, Hans', I replied.

On the red carpet Eva was posing for the cameras, throwing dazzling smiles out to the clutch of photographers like alms to the poor. God she was beautiful, I thought for the thousandth time, despite the fact I didn't like her. I'd had relationships with women I'd acted with before in London. Isabel Robinson had been *Ophelia* to my *Hamlet* in Clerkenwell and we'd been together on and off for a couple of years. What a shame, I thought as I looked out at her, what a shame. I'd seen something in Eva's eyes a couple of times that hinted of a softening, but she always drew back and the icy drawbridge came clattering down.

'*Sheisse!*', said Hans suddenly. '*Sheisse und Doppelsheisse!*' He clasped his hands together nervously. I was sure the bead of sweat on his forehead hadn't been there a moment ago.

'What is it, Hans?'

'My investors', he replied, after a pause, 'are being difficult, putting pressure on me.'

On the street a brown-shirted Nazi raised his arm in a rigid straight-armed salute and posed next to Eva, a huge grin on his face. Three other brown-shirted Nazis joined him, swastikas on pins and swastikas splashed across their shoulders. They surrounded Eva and lifted her up so she lay horizontal across their brawny arms, posing for the cameras.

'*Ja! Ja!* Again, again!', cried a photographer, snapping away with his Hasselblad. Eva smiled majestically as the flashbulbs popped like party crackers, framing her with four grinning Nazis. Someone unrolled a large flag plastered with an enormous swastika and held it up behind them.

In the limousine, I turned away from the swastikas to Hans and we stared at each other for what seemed like a long time. Hans forced a smile and tapped me on the knee.

'Don't worry', he said softly, 'all you need to do is smile and wave. Just smile and wave.'

Jerry went round to the limousine door and opened it, releasing an explosion of sound. I clambered out, smiling and waving like Hans said, blinded by flashbulbs and cries of '*Julius! Julius!*' They were calling my name. It was intoxicating. They were chanting my name, the crowd and the men in uniform, over and over.

'Julius, Julius, Julius, Julius!'

I joined Eva on the red carpet, a little nervously. She melted into my side and gave me a beaming smile, her eyes twinkling for the cameras. I think she saw the nerves in my eyes. I tried to look behind her smile but I couldn't. She was a very good actress. We linked arms, *d'engagee*. She kissed me on the cheek. The flashbulbs went wilder than before. I started to relax a little, to try and enjoy the moment, everything was happening at once, so fast, so many smiles and the adulation, the adulation. I turned round, towards another chorus of *'Julius! Julius! Julius!'* and was confronted by six burly SS officers standing in a line. They grinned at me and saluted.

'Heil Hitler!', they cried in unison and then started singing *'Deutschland, Deutschland, uber alles'*, in deep gravelly voices, spurred on by the flashbulbs. I carried on smiling and waving, not knowing what else to do.

Photographers were racing over to me now from across the street, begging for more shots with the SS. An SS captain stepped forward, clicked his heels and shook my hand firmly. I couldn't hear what he said to me. More flashbulbs popped. I could see Eva watching me out of the corner of her eye. I must smile and wave, I thought, don't let anything crowd your mind.

A hand slapped me hard on the back. I turned, smiling and waving, to a jubilant Hans, both his arms raised, being snapped by a dozen photographers. Hans joined arms with me and Eva, grinning wildly, turning us round to please every section of the crowd. Families with their children were there, adoring men shouting Eva's name, a large number of brown-shirted Fascists and SS.

Behind them all, at the back, *SS-Obersturmbannfuhrer* Wilfred Keller watched the proceedings studiously as our entourage headed slowly into the cinema, cheered by an adoring crowd. Keller took out a small Leica from his pocket and held it up to take a picture of us. A souvenir, perhaps.

All this, I thought as I headed out of the bright lights and into the large old cinema, a former opera house, all this and they haven't even seen the film yet.

The lights were dimmed as we took our seats in the middle of the stalls, the applause fading quickly now in expectation of what was to follow. Hans bounded up onto stage and took a microphone, a single light on him.

'*Meine Damen und Herren*, members of the armed forces, my wonderful cast', he smiled down at Eva.

'I would like you to forget for tonight that you are in Germany. To forget that you are hungry, tired, or hot.'

Hans wiped sweat from his brow.

'I want to suspend disbelief for you. Please give us two hours of your time, and judge us on what you see. I give you...*All for Love!*'

The audience applauded, Hans bowed and the large red curtains drew to reveal a flickering black and white screen, the audience's faces lit by its reflection. The music, a flurry of violins, was dramatic. Eva's hand, which until this point had rested in mine, was curtly removed and she folded her arms. I gulped and stared ahead of me, wishing that Isabel was sitting next to me and not this beautiful Nazi. I tried to forget about her presence and concentrated on the screen. I hadn't seen any of the rushes after each day's filming, and doing it in reverse order, with all the script changes, made it difficult to work out exactly what it would look like. I was about to find out.

One hour fifty minutes later, the film was nearing its climactic ending. A number of handkerchiefs were already on display in the audience, driven by the romantic music and the figures on the screen. In an ornately-decorated chamber I sat at the grand piano dressed in my eighteenth century finery playing Mozart, which I found amusing, as I couldn't play a note. The door to the chamber was opened by the footman to reveal Eva, dressed as a chambermaid. The music over was soft and romantic.

'Marry me Clara', I heard myself say, my voice sounding deeper. 'Say yes. Say yes and you'll make me the happiest man in the world.'

Clara mouthed a yes and we kissed passionately, the music swelling to a crescendo, masking the sobbing in the audience. The kiss went on, and on, and on. The audience clapped their hands to tumultuous applause as the credits rolled against the backdrop of our passion.

I stroked the side of my face, remembering the pain that had followed the kiss. I turned to Eva beside me. She smiled up at the crowd, who were on their feet, giving us a standing ovation. Hans had watched the film from the back of the cinema but ran down to join us. A spotlight from the projectionist's booth fell on the two stars of the movie.

Eva took my hand the second the light was on us and smiled at me. She leaned over as if to kiss me.

'Don't get too excited, Schiller. It's not real life,' she whispered.

'You could at least pretend', I whispered back.

'I'm not that good an actress'.

Hans appeared suddenly and kissed us both floridly on the cheek.

'Listen to that', he gasped, fighting back tears of joy. 'Listen to that!' Thundering applause deafened us. Hans turned to me. 'I think all of our troubles may be over', he said and winked. The crowd gave a huge cheer. Eva smiled up at them and waved happily, her long platinum blonde hair turned away from me.

I looked up at the crowd, focusing on the group of black SS uniforms and next to them the brown-shirts. The baying, the salutes, the German national anthem now playing. Hitler's face, projected onto the screen behind us. But no Jews. *Juden verboten!* Only the one on screen in the duke's costume. Only the Jew that

49

changed his name, that didn't look Jewish. Only he was allowed to be here and he was the one everyone was cheering. I think I made the right decision to come to Germany and critically the film looked to be a success, but that night it was very clear to me that they wouldn't be cheering so loudly if they knew who I really was.

**

A week passed and I was ready to go. I picked up the two leather-bound volumes of Shakespeare's Plays and *Turandot* by Friedrich Schiller, looked at the spines and tossed them in my suitcase. The bookshelf in my trailer was now bare and on the table was my boat ticket from Hamburg to Newcastle. I was going home. I'd said goodbye to Jerry. I walked to the door and pulled on the expensive coat, camel-haired, that Hans had bought me. Ten thousand. That was the number written on the cheque I placed safely inside my wallet and then inside my jacket pocket. I took one last look around the trailer. I could afford something bigger now. A lot bigger.

Just then there was a knock at the door and I looked up. It opened and Hans walked in holding a bottle of champagne, a thick bundle of papers and two glasses. He stopped as he saw me in my coat, holding my suitcase. I watched his eyes as they darted towards the table and the boat ticket lying on it. He shut the door behind him and I swear he started to shake.

'Where do you think you're going?', he blurted out. 'Are you insane?'

'No', I replied.

'But the film! *Mein Gott!* The film was a huge success! We are in all the papers - tipped to be the biggest box office success in Germany this year!'

'Everyone's asking when the next Julius and Eva production is going to hit the big screen. I've got Keppel working on it right now.'

Hans slapped the thick bundle of papers onto the table on top of the boat ticket.

'You know what this is?', he asked. It looked too thick to be a script. 'That, Julius, is a five film contract at twenty thousand Marks a film' he said triumphantly.

I stared at the contract. *Five* films. *Twenty* thousand a film. I could retire.

'A hundred thousand Marks. Think about it', he said nonchalantly, heading out the door.

'No – wait!', I could hear myself say. Hans turned.

'So?'

I put down my suitcase. Hans smiled.

'I'll even refund you the boat-ticket', he said, pointing to it. 'You stayed the course, my friend. Under this contract no-one can have you fired.'

'Including Eva?'

'Especially Eva. This puts you on the same level.'

'A hundred thousand?'

'Yes. Shall I open the champagne now while you sign?'

I took off my coat and sat down at the desk.

***

We drank not just one bottle of champagne but three between us and Hans staggered out of my trailer at two in the morning together with my signed contract. I didn't feel like sleeping because I was too excited. No-one earned this kind of money. I calculated that I'd be in Germany for maybe two years, and then, when I went back to England, I could start my own film studios if I wanted to. I found myself on my knees outside the

51

trailer, in the mud, giving thanks to God. I'd moved onto a beer now, to wind down, and the summer night was cool and clear. I was savouring the moment and I needed someone to share it with.

I stumbled across the studio lot looking for lights. Jerry was asleep and Hans' office was dark. I looked out across the wide expanse of open ground and there was the large silver trailer, parked on its own, with a light blazing inside. I gripped my beer tightly and headed towards it, not thinking about the time or who was inside. I was a single guy, I was rich and no-one could fire me. I got closer and I tripped, falling into the mud.

'*Sheisse!*'

When I looked up, the light in the large silver trailer had dimmed, like someone had pulled down a set of blinds to mask it. I was drunk and I was happy and so I went right up to the door and yanked it open.

'*Guten abend!*', I cried, and bowed in the doorway. When I looked up, I opened my mouth to speak but nothing came out.

In front of me, seated at the table, was Eva, tears streaked down her face. She looked up at me guiltily. In front of her sat a large wad of banknotes, tied with a rubber band. Next to her, dressed in black, was a Hassidic Jew with graying hair, a large hat and a beard. He had his arm round Eva. I looked from Eva to the Jew, then at the money, then back to Eva. Eva and the Jew looked down, not meeting my gaze. I turned round without saying a word, walked out of the door and shut it behind me.

I stumbled across the muddy lot. I needed to get back to my trailer, quickly. I still had more beers left in the fridge and I needed another drink.

4

Hans Bosendorf was simmering only a few degrees from boiling point. It was eleven o'clock in the morning and he was sitting at the desk in his office on the first floor of the studios bearing his name, gripping the legs of his high-backed chair. He blinked again at the letter on the desk and he looked up at the man sitting opposite him.

'Seven years', mused Hans, 'seven wonderful years.' Peter Keppel, the author of *All for Love*, nodded his head in agreement.

'Then why end it?', said Hans, a little louder.

'All good things come to an…'

'Bloody Hollywood!', Hans shouted, banging his fist onto the desk. 'Why?'

Peter Keppel cleared his throat.

'I don't think Germany is the right place for me now, Hans. Hitler's crazy, and now this pact with Stalin…I just don't like the way it's going.'

'What are you talking about Peter? You're safe here, aren't you? Happy?' Hans's eyes narrowed. 'Well paid?'

'It's all in the letter, Hans.'

Hans reached over to his cigar box and his flamethrower of a lighter. He lit his cigar slowly, calming himself down. One puff, two puffs.

'I'll pay you double', he said deliberately.

'You're already paying me double'.

'So what? You can double anything.'

'It's not the money, Hans'.

'I don't know how you can say that, Keppel.'

'Listen Hans, it's not the money.'

Hans opened a drawer of his desk and looked inside.

'Alright, Keppel', he said, smiling, 'you're as good a negotiator as you are a writer. What's it going to take?' He removed a cheque-book from the drawer.

'Ten thousand? Fifteen thousand? Twenty thousand?'

Keppel looked away as Hans waved the studio cheque-book at him.

'Please, Hans, stop it. Look – the boat leaves tonight. The Government's paying my fare to Hamburg. They're as keen for Jews to leave as I am to get out of Germany.'

'You're making a big mistake.'

'I've really enjoyed working with you and everyone at the studios.' He held out his hand, but Hans did not take it.

'You see – you'll miss us. It's a big mistake.'

'There are other writers.'

'Really? And where am I going to get another writer from? The military's got them all and I can't take on any more Jews, you know. You were lucky I took you on in thirty-two, before the edict.'

Keppel had nothing more to say. Hans stared at the letter once more, re-reading it slowly. Keppel turned slowly and walked towards the door. He lingered for a moment.

'Goodbye Hans', he said calmly, *'und Alles Gute.'* Hans didn't look up.

As he walked out of Hans's office for the last time he could hear the words *'You'll never work in Germany again!'* ringing in his ears down the corridor. He thought of a wonderful riposte but didn't turn round to deliver it. He just kept going, down the steps and out into the lot towards the car waiting for him.

Keppel got in and they pulled away from the studios. He'd told no-one else he was leaving apart from Hans, whom he'd been contractually bound to tell. He watched the last seven years of his life fade into the distance behind him as the car headed towards Berlin. This was no time for guilt or regrets.

He wondered if there really were palm trees on Sunset Boulevard.

***

I was in the bathroom of my trailer, shaving, when there was a knock at the door. It must have been about one o'clock in the afternoon and I wondered if it would be her.

'*Herein*!' I shouted, and poked my head out, my face covered in foam, to see who it was.

She stood in the doorway, icy-cool, cigarette-holder in hand, immaculate.

'Am I disturbing you, Herr Schiller?'

'No', I replied quickly, wiping off the white foam from my face with a towel.

She glided in and studied me.

'Rough night?'

'I was celebrating with Hans. He brought some champagne. The new contract. I had too much to drink.'

'Yes I know. You broke into my trailer.'

I didn't reply. She sat down on the bench and crossed her legs alluringly, exhaling a long plume of smoke.

'I have some news for you', Eva said, 'about our screenwriter. Peter Keppel.'

'What's happened? He's OK is he?'

'He's going to Hollywood', she replied, 'and Hans is furious.'

'I'll bet.'

'He's a Jew, you see', she said nonchalantly, but I could see her watching me closely.

'I see.'

'Does it bother you?', she asked slowly.

'Does what bother me?'

'That he's Jewish.'

I moved over to the table, sat down opposite her and lit a cigarette.

'Like the old man in your trailer last night, you mean?', I asked. She looked away, not meeting my gaze.

'Oh, that', she said languidly.

'Yes, that. What were you doing with him? And come to think of it, what're you doing here now? This is the first time in six months you've spoken to me like a normal person, that we've actually had a conversation.'

I stared at her, waiting. She tried to form a reply, but stared at me so coldly I could feel stalactites pressing into my eyeballs. She stood up abruptly and put out her cigarette quickly in the pewter ashtray on the table.

'I've made a terrible mistake', she blurted out. 'I told you *no questions*. You're all the same. You're like all the others. You think you rule the fucking world. You think the sun shines out of Hitler's ass. You think you're the master race. Good day, Julius Schiller.'

She walked briskly to the door and opened it.

'My name is not Julius Schiller', I said firmly. She paused by the door. 'It's Abe Goldstein.'

'What did you say?' she murmured.

'I said my name is Abe Goldstein. And I don't think the sun shines out of Hitler's ass, as you put it. Who was the man in your trailer? You were crying, he was consoling you. There was money on the table.'

'You're a better actor than I thought you were,' she said as she turned to face me.

'Is there something you want to tell *me*?', I asked her, wondering.

'Like what?'

'Like...like what's *your* real name?'

'What do you want it to be?'

I pushed my chair back angrily and stood up.

'Stop playing games with me!', I shouted. 'I'll play straight with you if you play straight with me!'

We stood glowering at each other as Jerry popped his head round the door.

'Is everything...everything...OK...Mr Schiller sir?', he asked nervously. 'I heard...heard...'

'Not now, Jerry, everything's fine. Miss Wendt and I are rehearsing a scene from our new movie.'

Eva raised an eyebrow.

'It's going very well', I added, looking at her unblinkingly. Jerry's eyes shone.

Eva didn't take her eyes off me.

'Yes it's going very well', she purred. 'Good night, Jerry.'

'Good night Miss Wendt. Mister - Mister Schiller sir!'

Jerry doffed his cap and shut the door behind him. We stood silently, watching each other.

'From the top?', I whispered.

She sat down, took a deep breath and looked up into my eyes.

'My real name is Betty Maude Weinstein. I was born in Leipzig twenty one years ago. That man you saw in my trailer is a rabbi and happens to be my father. That money was for him, my mother and my four brothers and sisters to buy food and clothes on the black market. My accent's from the movies, my hair's from a bottle and...and...I don't know how long I can keep this all up, Abe Goldstein, or whatever your bloody name is.'

As the last words tumbled out, she dropped her head to her hands and burst into tears. I slowly moved my hand towards her. She looked up at me.

'How else can a girl earn thirty-five thousand Marks for six weeks' work?'

I raised my eyebrows and looked at her like I knew exactly how.

'He's only paying me twenty', I replied, with a smile.

Eva wiped the tears from her eyes.

'Good old Hans. He tells everyone he'll pay them double. He did the same with me. So you got ten before. Not bad for a first movie.'

'Does Hans know about Betty Maude Weinstein?'

'He doesn't know anything about me. I came to him at sixteen and he put me in a film. Does he know about you?'

'Yes. He does. He named me and the rest is history.'

'You *are* a good actor, Abe Goldstein.'

'Not as good as you. You really had me fooled.'

'I thought you were just another lumbering Nazi, although...'

'Although what?'

'Although, I must admit, you're better-looking than the others.'

'So are you', I replied, 'better than *all* the others.'

'We'll keep this to ourselves, then?'

'Perhaps it's best.'

'I suppose I better not hit you anymore, then.'

'I suppose I better sit down, then.'

I sat across the table from her and looked up at the clock. It was nearly two in the afternoon and I hadn't eaten anything all day. My stomach rumbled.

'Hungry?', she asked.

'Yes.'

'Can you hold on 'til the evening?

'What happens then?'

'Oh, nothing', she replied, cagily.

We sat and looked at each other without speaking for what seemed like a very long time.

'So what's my next line, Miss Wendt?'

'I need to get out of here', she replied.

'Good line.'

She stood up and walked to the door.

'Come by my trailer about eight.'

'For dinner?'

'You'll see', she replied as she walked out of the door of my gleaming horizontal box, shutting it softly behind her.

***

I picked her up at eight. She was wearing a simple black dress and a black coat over it. A hat was pulled down to cover her face. I was in a suit that Hans had bought me.

'This way', she said a little mysteriously, as she walked me to a large grey building that turned out to be the Bosendorf Studios' garage.

Inside – it was unlocked - we were surrounded by ancient Daimler-Benzes, large Mercedes saloons and three small black Volkswagen prototypes with curved backs just like beetles. There was no-one else around. She pointed to the Volkswagens.

'Check for keys', she whispered.

I looked inside each of them. One still had the keys in the ignition. I picked them out and waved them at her.

'Can you drive?', she asked.

'No. Can you?'

'No.'

'Then what are we doing here, Eva?'

'You drive', she said, pressing the keys into my hand and climbing into the passenger seat.

I sat in the driver's seat next to her and put the keys in the ignition. The dials in front of me looked straightforward enough. The gears were on a lever on the floor and there was a clutch pedal. I turned the engine over and it started first time. We were pointing towards the open garage door which led directly onto the path towards the studio gates. As long as I didn't have to find reverse this would be fine, I thought.

'First time?', she asked, watching me touch every switch on the dashboard, clicking them on and then off. I sounded the horn and she giggled.

'Do you want me to drive?', she asked as my indicator lights flickered on and off. She pointed towards the gates.

'Berlin's that way.'

I put my foot down on the clutch and shoved the gear-stick into what I thought must be first. The car jerked forwards and I changed gear into second. We moved in a straight line towards the gates. I braked and the car stalled. I turned the ignition key and Eva got out.

'Where are you going?'

'The gate isn't going to open itself now, is it?'

I started the car again and the engine roared into life. I turned on the headlights and could see her face reflected in them as she swung open the large gates and waved me through.

The road was dark, quiet and straight. I held the wheel firmly, concentrating on the surface, the potholes and the insects that collected on the windscreen in front of my face.

'How far is it?', I asked, after another small black beetle splatted on the smooth windshield of our large black one.

'Just keep going along here 'til I tell you to turn.'

'We'll be recognized. You'll be mobbed.'

'Don't worry. No-one will see us. It's quiet.'

'You've taken people here before?'

'No', she replied firmly. 'Never.'

The roads were strangely empty, so empty that I started to suspect that maybe there was a curfew, or a gasoline shortage or something else that meant we weren't allowed to be on the road. Hans didn't like us leaving the studios, as if he were worried we might not come back.

'Stop worrying', she said to me, reading my face as I focused on the road ahead. 'It's not far.'

At last a car approached from the other direction. I was glad to see it. We seemed to be in the middle of an enormous industrial estate, with gloomy buildings on either side of the road surrounded by wire fences. A road-sign told me we were just entering the outskirts of Berlin.

'Left here', she said and I swung the car round the corner. Ahead of us I could see houses now and proper streets, not just industrial plants and warehouses.

In the rear of the car that passed us, Wilfred Keller checked his watch and noted down our number-plate. The Volkswagen prototype was on the Bosendorf Studio inventory and he had provided the car to Hans on specific condition that it was not to be used on public roads. He wrote a little note to himself on a pad, leaned forward towards his uniformed driver and tapped him on the shoulder.

Thirty minutes later, our little black Volkswagen pulled up outside a tall nineteenth century house in a long line of similar buildings, a quiet residential neighborhood in a Berlin suburb twelve miles from the studios. I turned off the engine and looked at Eva.

'I don't see a restaurant', I said.

'Just follow me. They're in here.'

'Who's in here?'

'Come on!'

She got out of the car and walked up to the front door of one of the tall good-looking houses. I followed her. It looked like an expensive neighborhood, with nice cars parked on the road. She took a small key out of her purse, inserted it into the lock and opened the door. The hallway was carpeted and the walls were covered with maps and portraits of stern people in drab colours. She held her finger up to her mouth, signalling for me not to say anything. I listened and I could hear children chattering downstairs in the basement.

'We always eat in the kitchen', she whispered. 'Let's surprise them.'

She walked down the narrow stairway to the basement and I followed two steps behind. When she reached the bottom she slowly pushed open the door and suddenly the Hassidic Jew I saw in her trailer picked her up and hugged her.

'*Ay gevalt!* My little Betty!', he said in between kissing her on both cheeks.

'Betty! Betty!', cried more than one child, from inside. Rabbi Weinstein looked past her up the stairwell and saw me.

'*Mein Gott!* The actor!' He gripped Eva's shoulders. 'Why did you bring him here?'

'Don't worry, papa. He's one of us.'

'*One of us?*'

'He's Jewish.'

'He doesn't look it.'

'Do *I*?'

'Alright! Alright! In! In!' He waved his arms frantically. 'We weren't expecting you.'

I walked into the kitchen and a large friendly woman smiled at me.

'That's mama', said Eva.

'Hello Mrs Weinstein', I said, offering her my hand. 'I'm Julius Schiller.'

Four children, aged perhaps fourteen, eleven, eight and six looked at me warily. Eva smiled at them.

'He's Betty's friend from the cinema', she said.

There was an uncomfortable silence.

'Maybe', said Rabbi Weinstein slowly, 'we can eat *upstairs* for once?'

Mrs Weinstein nodded and handed me a large tureen.

'Up! Go up, Schiller!'

I turned round and walked up the stairs. Eva and the children giggled.

The dining room was immediately to my left and the table was already set for eight. It was a high-ceilinged room with a dark-wood table and chairs and a Chinese rug on the floor. Books and photographs adorned every spare surface. The books were a mixture of Hebrew, Russian, English and German. The photographs showed a happy family, five smiling children, two doting parents and old wedding photos of Rabbi and Mrs Weinstein. On the mantelpiece, in the centre, was a large sepia photograph in a silver frame. It was Betty Maude Weinstein at the age of about fifteen, with long dark brown hair and unshaped eyebrows.

I looked at her, six years on, as she walked into the room holding a loaf of bread and some glasses. With her blonde hair she looked more German than the Germans, more Aryan than the Nazi Party's finest poster girls.

The four children followed her in and she introduced me to them. Marcus, fourteen, tall for his age wearing a yarmulke. Ruby, ten or so, pretty in a blue dress. Baruch, a feisty little boy of eight with his shirt hanging out of his trousers and lastly Lillie, at six the youngest, and the only one tugging at my jacket.

'Excuse me, Mr Schiller, sir', asked Lillie before we'd sat down, 'but are you the duke who marries Betty and lives happily ever after?'

'I am.'

'We missed your wedding', continued Lillie. 'Hitler wouldn't let us see it.'

'Excuse Lillie, Mr Schiller', said Rabbi Weinstein, patting her on the head, 'for her forthright nature, but Jews can't go to the cinema. We just have the poster.'

'It's so wrong', I replied.

'Yes. It must make it very difficult to go into work in the morning, Mister Schiller?'

I didn't have time to reply because the rabbi immediately started singing and we bowed our heads.

'*Baruch attach adonai, elochenuh melech ha'olam, b-rei pree ha gafen*' he intoned, blessing the wine.

'Amen', we replied. He drank from the glass.

'We've got soup, we've got stew', said Mrs Weinstein.

'Thank you mama', said Eva.

'Soup, Mr Schiller?'

'Please, call me Julius. And soup would be lovely.'

Mrs Weinstein ladled out the steaming liquid to me, then to Eva, next her children and lastly her husband. I closed my eyes and let the smell of home cooking waft around my face.

'Julius is a girl's name', said Baruch, the fourteen year old.

Eva stifled a laugh and her father cleared his throat.

'Julius Caesar was a famous emperor in Rome', I said gently. 'He was a great warrior and statesman.'

'Like Hitler?', asked Baruch.

'No', I replied firmly, 'not like Hitler.'

I noticed Rabbi Weinstein smile at me. He nodded to his wife.

'Not like Hitler.'

'Will you dance with me, Julius?', asked Lillie. 'I know how to waltz.'

'Lillie! Mr Schiller only just started his soup!'

Rabbi Weinstein shrugged at his wife.

'Why not? Let them dance.'

Lillie stood and I stood with her. She reminded me of her eldest sister. I bowed and Eva placed a shiny seventy-eight on the turntable of a large gramophone resting on a side-table. She lowered the needle onto the black vinyl and the music began. It was a waltz, by Strauss.

'Stand on my feet, Lillie.'

Lillie obliged. The music began and she waltzed with me, the man in the poster, Julius the duke.

As I turned again and again in time to the music – one-two-three, one-two-three - I kept meeting Eva's gaze. She was looking at me in a different way, a softer look, not the piercing stare I was used to at the studios. We were doing what normal people did, and I hadn't done anything normal for a long time, not with a family.

We whirled faster as the music gained in volume and Eva got up to dance with Baruch. One-two-three, one-two-three. We turned and turned and the rest of the family swayed in time to the music. When it finished, I bowed to Lillie and Eva curtsied to Baruch. I bent down to give Lillie a kiss on the cheek and she looked up at me wide-eyed in her pretty floral-print dress, her long dark hair bunched.

'Remember what I told you', I heard Eva say to her.

'Oh yes!'

Lillie suddenly slapped me round the face.

'Good girl', said Eva, smiling. I looked up at her, then knelt next to Lillie.

'You have a bright future ahead of you in the film business!'

Mrs Weinstein clapped her hands, laughed and we all joined in. My eyes didn't leave Eva's and hers didn't leave mine.

We finished supper and then Rabbi Weinstein looked up at the clock.

'It's time for bed, little ones and don't forget your manners.'

'Goodnight, duke', said Lillie as she curtseyed and followed her two brothers and her sister out of the door.

'I'll come and kiss you all in a minute my little ones', said Eva.

As they left, Mrs Weinstein passed around a jug of coffee. I poured myself a small cup. The rabbi and his wife's eyes moved from me to Eva and then back again. When they looked at each other a troubled look crossed the rabbi's face.

'What's wrong, papa?', asked Eva, watching him. 'Is the money enough? It's all Hans had in the safe. He said he could give me more next month when we start filming the next one.'

'It's enough, my darling. It's enough. It's not about the money.'

He turned to me.

'You're not from Germany, are you, Julius?'

'My father was German, my mother was Polish', I replied truthfully. I hadn't told anyone I was English yet, including Eva. It would have been an unnecessary complication.

The rabbi nodded sagely.

'And, if you don't mind me asking, why do you do this, this film acting work? For the money?'

'Partly', I responded, truthfully, 'that and the chance to act with your daughter.'

'Is it solely a professional relationship?'

'Excuse me, sir?'

'Is it solely a professional relationship?'

'Well I'm here now, sir, so I suppose, um…'

'What? What do you suppose?'

'Papa, stop being a grouch', said Eva. 'He's here because I like him. And his real name's not Julius Schiller. It's Abe Goldstein.'

'Abe Goldstein?'

'Yes papa, he's like me.'

'Ah. The chameleon tribe, yes yes, I've heard of you', said the rabbi ruefully. 'Any more of you?'

'A screenwriter', I replied. 'But he didn't bother changing his name. He left for Hollywood.'

'Hollywood in the United States of America? It seems like a very long way to go.'

'Have you heard of Ehrlich Weiss?', I asked.

'Houdini you mean?'

I smiled. I'd been going to give him the speech Hans gave me back in England.

'Betty takes care of us here, Julius. We have no need to go to Hollywood. Our lives are here and I'm not transporting my whole family thousands of miles just because that idiot Hitler wants me to.'

He put his hand into his wife's and she nodded vigorously.

'Morry's right', she said. 'We're happy here, as happy as we can be. They leave us alone for the most part.'

'Eva was crying in the trailer, you know, when I broke in on you last night. She didn't look very happy.'

'She was lonely.'

'But not now', Eva said quickly, looking at me. 'I can make the films papa, make enough money to get away from this place once and for all and you'll never need to work again. Either of you. Ever.'

'But I don't *want* not to work again.'

I cleared my throat.

'Sir, isn't it a little risky to go to the studios? Surely if they see you two together someone will get suspicious. Won't it get Eva fired? Jews aren't allowed to work, are they?'

The rabbi stroked his beard.

'We have a system.'

'That's why I am the way I am at the studio, Julius', said Eva. 'No-one ever wants to go near the blonde bitch.'

'Betty! Language!'

'They're scared of me', continued Eva, 'and they're scared of what Hans will do to anyone who pisses me off.'

'Betty!'

'Sorry mama.'

'If you told Hans he'd protect you. Just like he protected me. He got me a new identity, a passport, everything, very easily.'

'I don't trust Hans a hundred per cent.'

'Do you trust me, Betty Maude?'

'You said not to play games, didn't you?'

We looked at each other for what seemed like an eternity, forgetting that Rabbi Morry Weinstein and his wife were there too, watching us closely.

'Hadn't you better kiss the little ones goodnight?' said Mrs Weinstein suddenly, a little too loudly.

'Yes, yes of course', Eva replied. She stood quickly. 'Come with me Julius. I'm sure they'd like to see you too.'

We rose and Eva pulled me out of the door before her parents had a chance to object. As we headed up the stairs to the first floor landing Eva turned, one step above me, her head at my head height and kissed me on the lips.

'What was that for?'

'That was for driving me here.'

'Do you always kiss your drivers like that?'

'Always.'

'There must be a queue then.'

'Oh, there is.'

'I hope you'll allow me to drive you back.'

She smiled and headed up the stairs.

**

The drive back seemed much quicker than the drive there. I seemed to have got the hang of it now and the car was being kind to me. I couldn't forget the kiss on the stairs. It hadn't been just a thank you kiss.

'Remember what I said about falling in love with me', she said after a long silence, reading my mind or maybe my face. I turned to her and the car swerved a little.

'I do. You said you'd have me fired.'

I steadied the wheel. She was smiling.

'We're going to be working together for a while, aren't we, Julius?'

'Yes. The five-picture deal. Hans said the German public can't wait for the next Julius and Eva production.'

'I bet', she replied, wryly. 'Right turn here.'

We headed back through the industrial estate on the outskirts of Berlin, the streets empty again. I looked for signs of life, another car or a truck or someone walking on the pavement, but there was no-one, not even a security guard standing outside a warehouse or on his way home.

It was about eleven thirty or so and I didn't think of using my rear view mirror. I was focusing on the road ahead of me, which was dark and marked by the odd pothole. If I had looked behind us, I might have spotted the same car that we had passed on our way to her parents' house, now following us with dimmed headlights.

5

We spent the next few days waiting for the new script, a follow up to *All for Love* with the same characters, five years later, on a ship lost at sea. Hans had found someone called Friedrich Denner to write it. We waited in our trailers for the next instalment of our screen lives and while we did that we fell in love. We made one more visit to Eva's parents, using the same Volkswagen as before, and I think they could tell that second time that our relationship had become more than just professional.

We were lost, blissfully lost, in a world which was as far removed from the outside world as a desert island. We visited each other's trailers discreetly and had food and drink brought to us. We had no newspapers, no radio, no post. I barely saw Hans in two weeks, other than Monday morning meetings for everyone to give everyone else an update on what they were doing. At the meetings Eva and I were careful not to arrive or leave together, and we sat apart, not looking at each other. In public, or in the studio at least, Eva maintained her frostiness towards me and Hans was the only man she smiled at.

In private, we made love every night and sometimes during the day, our siesta time we called it. It was odd to think that we were being paid all the while, the money mounting up in our studio bank accounts. I told Eva that I was English, and she was very interested to hear everything about London, the King and West End theatres. I told her about my plan to earn enough money to buy a wonderful house, maybe produce films in England when our five films had been made in Germany. I also told her about my plans to marry, to find the right girl who loved me as much as I loved her. I told her that she was the girl for me.

Perhaps I was rash, or foolish, or sensible, or mad, or a combination of all of those things, but after two weeks she must have been at least as foolish as me because when I asked her to marry me she said yes.

We decided to tell no-one apart from Rabbi and Mrs Weinstein, certainly not Eva's siblings who already found it difficult to keep it secret that their eldest sister was the film star Eva Wendt. Her parents cried and hugged us but we agreed with them that we would only marry when we could have a proper Jewish wedding, which would not be until we all left Germany. In two years, with five movies under our belt apiece and more than two hundred thousand Marks between us, we could go wherever we wanted and could afford to take Eva's family with us.

It was now late August 1939 and Rabbi Weinstein told me that things might be looking up for the Jews in Germany. Hitler had made a non-aggression pact with Stalin which meant both countries, he reasoned, would converge in their treatment of their respective peoples. Russians, he told me, weren't averse to Jews, in fact there were two or three in Stalin's government. Hitler would never make a pact with the Jews unless he was prepared to soften his stance towards them, he said.

I remembered *Mein Kampf*, the book I'd read in England, the rantings of an angry young man. People changed, I thought, and obviously Rabbi Weinstein thought so too, because he'd read it as well.

***

Elsewhere that night another man was reading *Mein Kampf* for inspiration. He put the book down and said a prayer to his wife, sleeping alone in her bed in Berlin like she had done every night for the last three months. The man was Horst Weber, an *Untersturmfuhrer* in the SS. He had a low Nazi Party number, meaning that he had joined very early on. He was a trusted, loyal man of about thirty-five or thirty six with fairish hair, a bulbous nose and a thick neck.

In 1933 he had helped with the rise of Hitler to Chancellor. Quelling disturbances had been his speciality, despite his university education, and until the National Socialists took control he had seen the inside of a jail cell four times. Miraculously, after 1933 his past offences were quickly banished from the books in furtherance of the rehabilitation of Party offenders. By the thirty first of August 1939 Horst Weber was a man of exemplary character, possibly a man deserving promotion.

His unit was stationed on the border between Poland and Germany, waiting. He had traveled since early that morning with a battalion to which he had been assigned as a special adviser. His job was to make it look as if the Poles had started it first. He helped arrange for the theft of four hundred Polish uniforms which he distributed to five special Wehrmacht assault groups. They were to create border incidents, inflammations, provocations that would threaten the very safety of Germany. Once these provocations had taken place, albeit engineered by four hundred Germans pretending to be Poles, then Germany's only course of action would be to protect itself. An animal, if wounded, struck back. A nation, a different kind of animal, must do the same.

He gave a signal to move forward and his tank crushed the wire fence easily as it rumbled into Poland. He could hear shots being fired, grenades detonating. Men would be killed tonight, he thought, and Germany would have its excuse to fight back, to protect itself.

The build-up required the full might of the Wehrmacht, the ingenuity of the SS and the ego of Hitler. With the three 'H's - Hitler, Himmler and Heydrich - they could not fail. *Lebensraum* must be created, to make room for a thousand German farmers to tend the barren soil and create order in the lands to the East. No-one gave a shit about the Poles. Or the Jews.

'Ship them to Siberia!', his commanding officer used to say and Horst agreed with him. Jews had poisoned the banking system in Europe and deprived the German people of the prosperity they so richly deserved. He stood in his tank looking out through a pair of binoculars as the tracks rumbled beneath him, crushing the barbed wire of another border fence.

'Welcome to Poland!', he shouted into his field radio to the tanks behind him.

'Heil Hitler!', came the response crackling over the airwaves.

***

Hans Bosendorf sat grim-faced at his desk on the first floor of the studios which bore his name. Next to him was a large, silver-fronted radio with big round dials for tuning and volume. He stared ahead, listening to the voice on the radio as it crackled out. The unmistakeable tones of Adolf Hitler, Supreme Commander of the German Forces, Chancellor of the Third Reich and protector of the German people cut through the static.

74

Hitler was apopleptic. *How dare they question the might of Germany? We must fight to protect our children! The Poles deserve everything they get! They need the strong leadership of the sort I, Adolf Hitler, can provide!*

Hans wondered if the speech was fooling anyone.

Helga Braun sat opposite him. She had worked in passport control for three years and she hated it. Some days her face hurt so much from smiling that she went home after work and straight to bed with sliced cucumbers on her eyes and a black sleeping mask. She smiled at Hans. She wasn't listening to Hitler on the radio. She was more focused on what Hans had said on the telephone about casting and actresses and money and fame. The last two were really interesting, especially as the passport control job was mindless and badly-paid. Hans's business card lay in front of her on the desk. She crossed her legs seductively, getting ready for her screen-test.

Hitler finished, Hans turned the dial and the radio crackled into life again. He was tuning into the BBC, which he knew was illegal. A calmer voice than Hitler's, an English voice, rose above the static. It was the voice of Neville Chamberlain, the appeaser of Hitler's annexation of Czechoslovakia, a mild-mannered man, not a warrior.

'This morning the British Ambassador in Berlin handed the German Government an official note', Chamberlain read somberly.

Helga Braun unbuttoned her jacket slowly.

'Stating that unless they withdrew their troops from Poland, a state of war would exist between us.'

Helga removed her jacket.

'I have to tell you now that no such undertaking has been received, and consequently this country is at war with Germany. You can imagine what a bitter blow...'

Hans turned off the radio with a click. He remembered the last war, the miserable years between 1914 and 1918 when every young man seemed to vanish. He'd been too old even then for conscription but his contacts had already promised that he wouldn't have to die on a field in Flanders like most of the men from his home town. He stared ahead grimly, motionless, at the pretty blonde with the lovely eyes in front of him.

Helga watched him focus on her and smiled, raising a leg and resting it gently on the desk. She reached up under her skirt and found the top of her garter. She loosened it, ensuring Hans got a long look at her long leg. She slowly removed a stocking. The telephone rang. Hans looked from her leg to her face.

'Just a moment, *mein Liebchen*.'

He picked up the receiver.

'Bosendorf, *kann ich Ihnen helfen*?'

'This is Wilfred Keller on the line, I hope I'm not disturbing you.'

'Good morning, Wilfred. No, not in the slightest. Have you heard the news?'

'Why do you think I am calling?'

'What can I do for the Third Reich, Wilfred?'

'This war, Bosendorf, invokes section four sub-section seven of our agreement. You do remember section four sub-section seven?'

'I'm not sure I do, Wilfred.'

'I suggest you look it up now then.'

Hans cupped his hand against the receiver and scribbled the words '*section four, subsection seven*' on a pad in front of him.

'*Ein moment, bitte*,' he said into the telephone.

Hans rested the receiver on his desk, stood up and walked quickly over to a filing cabinet. He pulled out a file. On the other side of his desk Helga Braun removed her other stocking. Hans sat back down grimly at his desk with the file. He opened it up, pulled out a large document and leafed through it quickly. He picked up the telephone receiver.

'I'm sorry about that, Wilfred', he said quickly as Helga unbuttoned her skirt, 'but we're very busy this morning.'

'It will get busier', Keller replied coldly.

Hans looked down at the file in front of him. A large Eagle's Head was stamped on the cover, and the document inside was decorated with little red Swastikas down the margin of each page.

'Do you understand what you have to do?', Keller asked down the 'phone.

'Yes', replied Hans as Helga slipped off her skirt. 'I understand.'

***

Inside the trailer my clothes were on the floor and Eva's were on the back of a chair. We lay asleep on the bed in each other's arms, covered only by a white sheet. I opened my eyes and turned my head slowly towards her, to her beautiful bottle-blondeness, child-like and vulnerable, curled up asleep in my arms. I stared at her for a long time and kissed her cheek tenderly. It was eleven in the morning.

She finally stirred and I got up to make us both a coffee using the gas-ring next to the fridge. She came over and kissed me on the cheek.

'Shall I be Mrs Goldstein, or Mrs Schiller?'

'We can let the rabbi decide. Black or white?'

'Black today', she replied.

'Sugar?'

'No.'

I handed her the coffee and we clinked mugs. I put on my summer suit, a lightweight linen one, and my brown brogues. We normally planned it so I'd go out first and walk around a bit. If the coast was clear I'd go back in and let Eva out, re-emerging a few minutes after. It stopped people asking questions, kept our private lives private. I looked out of the window. It looked as if they'd finished the script because there was a lot of movement.

'You better wait for a bit, darling', I said, kissing her. I opened the door of the trailer and stepped outside.

A group of men in white overalls, maybe twenty of them, were carrying large rolls of barbed wire to the perimeters of the studio lot. Three men were carrying ladders. I walked as nonchalantly as I could, pretending to be learning lines, holding a script in front of me. I watched them as they unrolled the barbed wire and started fixing it above the studio fence with iron rails at six feet intervals. Another single wire, a thick one, was wound carefully around the whole lot and connected to the generator building by two electricians.

A small van arrived through the gates, and another. Men wearing thick gloves unbolted the rear of each van and I could hear dogs barking. They were Dobermans, proud, sleek and muscular. The men with thick gloves started walking them around, letting them mark their territory.

I avoided them and headed towards the main gate, where a little crowd was gathering. A lorry had stopped outside and a group of men I'd never seen before were arguing about its contents, a number of advertising hoardings or some such covered in white sheets. Two sentries were patrolling, armed with pistols in black leather holsters and rifles slung over their shoulders.

They hadn't been there yesterday. I approached the gate. A wooden sentry box had been assembled and I could see there was a man inside in military uniform. One of the Dobermans barked at me and I turned away from it, walking away from the gate and quickly to my trailer.

Eva was already outside, by the door, waiting for me, immaculate in a polka-dot blue dress, smoking a cigarette.

'What's happening?', she asked.

'I don't know, but I don't like the look of it.'

'Then look behind you, look what they're putting up.'

I followed her gaze. My eyes rested on the main entry gates, now patrolled by the two armed sentries. They would make our evening trips into Berlin a little bit more difficult. I looked up above the gates and there, above the Bosendorf Studios sign were two new signs each proudly displaying an enormous black and red Swastika and an Eagle's Head.

'Hans. We've got to speak to Hans right now', I said quietly.

'It's nearly twelve. Let's check his schedule with Jerry.'

'We're a strong team, aren't we?', I said to her as we headed quickly across the studio lot.

'Yes, but there's only two of us.'

She lit another cigarette with the one she still had in her mouth and passed it to me.

Our pace was hurried, the corridor at the back of Studio One seemingly endless. We walked quickly, nervously, hand in hand towards the door at the end where Jerry had told us Hans would be. She took her hand away from mine as we got to the end of the corridor.

'For now', she murmured, smoothing down her dress.

I nodded, pushed open the door and walked out of the shadow of the corridor into the bright lights of Studio One.

We walked quickly through a new set, what looked like a medieval torture chamber. A painter daubed splashes of red strategically over the grey metal.

'Blood', he grinned.

Hans looked up from the script of a horror film. He looked pleased to see us, almost bullish. There was an advertising hoarding next to him covered in a black sheet.

'Ah. Good afternoon, Eva, Julius. Please, take a seat. I'll be with you in just *ein Moment.*'

He motioned to a row of metal chairs and Eva and I sat leaving a chair-space between us. Hans handed his script to the writer Friedrich Denner and came over to us. 'Well?' he asked finally.

'We're a little concerned about the additional security arrangements', I replied.

'Ah, yes. I made a general announcement at nine this morning. You were both... unavailable...at that time.'

'What announcement, Hans?'

'Our military was forced to invade Poland. As of this morning we appear to be at war with Britain, and I believe France. And Poland, no doubt'.

Eva lit a cigarette and I could see her hand shaking. I took one from her and she lit it for me.

'I heard Hitler on the radio this morning', continued Hans, 'and he sees it as a great opportunity. *Lebensraum* for the German people.'

'What?', we both said together.

'Living space. You needn't worry. This is the safest place in Germany. No-one can break in.'

'Or out.'

'We can talk about that later. But now I have something very exciting to show you. Just back from the printers'.

Hans turned to the blackboard set up next to him.

'Ladies and gentlemen, I give you our next little project together!'

He raised his arm theatrically and pulled off the black sheet to reveal a poster. It was large and damp, as if it really had just come back from the printers. It depicted a man, obviously me, kissing a woman, obviously Eva. Our lips were locked together and our eyes closed. I was in SS uniform and Eva was also in military uniform. Beneath us, in darker colours, was a Hassidic Jew who looked like Rabbi Weinstein and a trio of British officers pointing rifles at me.

'Good, isn't it?', puffed Hans, lighting a cigar. Eva reached nervously for another cigarette, her hand shaking more noticeably.

'That was quick.'

'Yes, everything's moving quite quickly. Just right to catch the mood I think.'

'What exactly is the mood, Hans?', asked Eva, coolly.

'Isn't it obvious?', he replied enthusiastically.

We both shook our heads.

'War is going to save this studio. You, Julius my dear boy will play the character of Wolfgang Blitzkrieg, a handsome SS officer who saves Germany by defeating an Anglo-Jewish plot to assassinate the Fuhrer.'

'You're not joking, are you?'

Hans raised his eyebrows.

'No', he said firmly and he turned beaming to Eva.

'My precious Eva. You will play Greta Battenburg, Wolfgang Blitzkrieg's feisty and beautiful Intelligence contact with whom he falls in love and who helps him save the day.'

'Charming', she said.

'It's a change of genre, but as from this morning, our future is secure.'

'How does this make our future secure, Hans?'

'My dear boy. How secure can you get? Our contracts have been taken over by the Third Reich.'

The colour drained from Eva's face and I could feel it draining from mine.

'Just read the script', pleaded Hans as he tossed two bound sets of papers towards us. 'It's not at all bad.'

'Who wrote it? Denner?'

'The *All for Love* follow-up is on hold', he replied. 'This one's by a talented writer called Josef Goebbels.'

'Goebbels? But isn't he…'

'There are some good moments. Just read it.'

Eva and I exchanged nervous glances. I turned the first page and lit another cigarette.

It took me two hours, but Eva stopped after the first few pages and sat there, smoking, waiting for me to finish. An ashtray on the floor between us was full of spent cigarette-ends.

'You smoke too much', I said, looking at the over-flowing ashtray.

'It's not going to kill me.'

'Neither is this script.'

'What are you saying, Julius? That we do it?'

'Have you considered our alternatives?'

'What do you think I've been thinking about?'

'I need a drink', I said, standing up sharply, making the metal chair screech on the studio floor.

Back in my trailer Eva sipped a vodka-tonic while I swigged a bottle of beer, my eyes on her. We had managed to get hold of today's copy of the *Volkische Beobachter* and it was spread out on the table in front of us.

'It says here there's a curfew now, Julius. What about my family? How do I get money to them? They're going to need it more than ever now. And look at this.'

I looked at an article about the redenomination of currency. A hundred thousand Marks, as of today, was not worth nearly as much as it had been when I'd signed my contract.

'They're recalling the old money.'

'Exactly. Where are my family going to get more money from?'

'We'll get some to them', I said.

'How?'

'We can go in the daytime. Hans can give us an official driver.'

'Yes but they'll find out about me and then they'll have nothing.'

'I won't let that happen.'

'And if they find out about *Abe Goldstein*?'

'They won't.'

'So you can trust Hans, can you?'

'I think so. It's not in his interests to have me out of a job or denounced as a Jew, considering his name's on my passport as Julius Schiller's next of kin.'

'That was clever of you.'

'He thought of it, not me.'

Eva sipped on her vodka. She lit us both a cigarette. I got up to open the window as the trailer was getting a little muggy.

'Maybe we can ask Jerry to get money to them', I suggested, 'he'd do anything for his stars.'

'Can we really trust him, Julius? He's Hans's man through and through.'

'I think I trust Hans not to drop us in the shit. Same for Jerry.'

'He'll be followed.'

'Maybe.'

'Our money's still good', I said, 'maybe we can bribe someone'.

'To do what?'

'Get us all out of here. Go back to England.'

'Are you mad, Julius? The only Germans going to England now will be in the Luftwaffe. They won't let us in. We're at war.'

'We won't know til we try.'

'It's too dangerous!', she shouted.

I took a long drink of beer and she put her hand in mine. 'Sorry', she murmured, 'for shouting.'

'Forgiven', I said as I kissed her. 'Look – maybe we can tell Hans we need to go to Berlin to promote our film and make a quick unscheduled stop on the way...'

'Darling', she replied, holding my face in her hands, 'we both have a lot of thinking to do now. I think, just for tonight, I should go back to my trailer and you should stay here.'

I nodded. She was right. We both needed to collect our thoughts.

'Goodnight, Julius Schiller', she said in the doorway, her face half in light, half in shadow, looking more beautiful than ever.

'Goodnight, Eva Wendt', I replied softly. 'I'm here if you need me.'

'I love you, Abe.'

'And I love you Betty Maude.'

I kissed her and watched her walk out of the door and into the darkness.

6

The outside of the Weinstein house was proud and tall, the red brick and the Dutch gables complementing the porticoed entrance and flight of stone steps leading up to it. A tall thin senior Gestapo Officer in a black leather coat and glasses eased himself out of an unmarked grey saloon that was parked twenty yards away on the other side of the street. Behind the saloon was a small black van. Another man, shorter, also in a black leather coat joined him on the cobblestones and waved towards the van. A man inside waved back. The tall thin senior Gestapo officer opened a piece of paper and noted down the address written there. Yes, yes the address was correct. The paperwork was in order, Keller's signature legible.

He looked up again at the house. There was a light on. Such a big place. He didn't live in such a big house. He had a small apartment near the centre of the city which looked out onto a main road on one side and some ornamental gardens to the rear. Four rooms, two children, one wife, one cat. The salary was not good but the Gestapo promised other types of remuneration. When it was all over, when the war was won he would be one of the thousands that Heinrich Himmler envisaged beginning again, tilling the soil of the lands in the East, sipping wine at the end of the day as the sun set over a countryside paradise stretching over thousands of acres. It would all be theirs, soon enough. He beckoned to the junior officer and they walked up to the door of the large red-brick house and knocked. There was no reply.

'*Noch einmal* – again!', whispered the senior officer. His junior knocked again. The light that had been on in the basement went out and the house was dark.

'*Sheisse*', they both murmured. The senior officer removed his pistol from a holster inside his coat, fitted a silencer quickly to it and shot out the lock on the door. His junior drew his pistol out and the two men nodded at each other. The door swung open and they walked into the hallway softly, wedging the door shut behind them with a heavy metal umbrella stand.

'*Darunter*' said the senior officer, pointing towards the basement. '*Bleib hier!*'

His junior did what he was told and stayed by the main door whilst the senior man took out a torch and walked slowly down the stairs and into the Weinsteins' basement kitchen to find the whole family standing in the dark. He turned on the light-switch by the door and, seeing the children, put his gun back in his holster.

'*Guten abend*', he said politely, bowing and clicking his heels together. 'I am sorry to disturb you but I must ask you to pack your things, only what you can comfortably carry, while I wait with the children. Perhaps your living room might be slightly more comfortable?'

Rabbi Weinstein looked at the man.

'On whose authority do you do this?'

'*Bitte.* Quickly now.'

Ten minutes passed and Rabbi and Mrs Weinstein packed up two small suitcases together with some small bags for their children. They brought them down to the living room, relieved to see their children still there.

'Open the suitcases please', asked the senior Gestapo man politely. He used a knife to slit the lining of both of them and hidden inside were tight bundles of banknotes, the ones from Eva. He picked out the banknotes and slipped them into the pockets of his black leather coat.

'*Vielen dank*', he said to the rabbi. 'Searching the house would have taken hours.'

The officer gazed at the children in front of him.

'You're going on holiday', he said gently as he walked up to the photographs in silver frames dotted around the mantelpiece and the sideboards. Six pairs of eyes watched his every move.

'What a delightful family you have, rabbi' he said, picking up a photograph and kneeling down next to Lillie, the smallest. He smiled at her. 'Would you like a holiday little girl?' he asked. Lillie smiled and nodded. His black-gloved hand rested on a framed photograph of Eva at sixteen with brown hair.

'Four children, or five?'

He looked round quickly at Mrs Weinstein. She looked away, but before anyone could answer, a toilet flushed and the junior Gestapo officer walked in shaking his hands dry. He gazed at the photograph of Eva. He scratched his head. Mrs Weinstein looked up worriedly at Rabbi Weinstein.

'Morry', she whispered, 'the poster'.

Rabbi Weinstein gripped her hand tightly. Lillie looked up at her worried parents.

'Mummy, don't we need to tell Betty we're going on holiday?'

'Hush, dear.'

The junior officer looked up.

'Betty? Did I hear you say Betty? One moment please.'

He went back into the bathroom and returned holding a poster. He passed it to his senior, who knelt next to Lillie, a large smile on his face. He held out the film poster for *All for Love*.

'What's your name, little girl?'

'Lillie.'

'Thank you Lillie. And is this girl in the poster Betty?'

He pointed to Eva's picture. Mrs Weinstein shut her eyes and prayed. Lillie nodded in reply. The officer exchanged a satisfied look with his junior and pointed to my face in the poster.

'And who, my little one, is this?'

Lillie smiled, remembering the dance.

***

I was having a terrible dream. I'd managed to get to sleep after twelve small bottles of beer and countless cigarettes, but now I wished I hadn't. It went like this, my dream. I imagined I was arriving at Bosendorf Studios for the first time. I walked past a film set and suddenly Laurel and Hardy stood in front of me, holding a large pane of glass. Hans suddenly propelled me towards it at fifty miles an hour and Stan and Ollie's grinning faces loomed closer and closer. My head hit the glass with a boom and then thousands of shards flew into the air and into my flesh and eyes. Eva ran out towards me, barefoot in a flowing ball-gown, screaming like a madwoman.

'You've killed him! You've killed Goldstein!'

A line of a hundred SS officers clapped their hands and turned to Hans, who was stationed by the camera.

'Keep filming!', one of them ordered.

Hans gave him a big thumb's up and turned to me grinning.

'I want you to die very slowly, please now Julius. Make it look good.'

'I'll try', I found myself replying, mimicking Hans's thumb's up sign.

A large bloated face loomed into view and pointed a pistol right between my eyes.

'Faster!'

I could hear laughing, hollering, cheering and applause and then the sound of a gunshot.

'That's what the people of Germany want!', gushed Hans.

The poster for *Blitzkrieg against the world* appeared in front of me. My face had been swapped with the Hassidic Jew's. He was in the SS uniform and I was dressed as a rabbi.

***

I woke up in a sweat and found sunlight filtering through the slits in the blind over my window and onto my face. My sheet was damp and I almost had to peel it off me. I walked slowly to my little bathroom and turned on the shower, set it to cold and walked in. The sharp tingling water bounced off my skin and made me feel better. I brushed my teeth quickly and looked over to the table in the sitting area with the *Blitzkrieg* script on it. I would rather Eva had been here last night. I went over to the blind and tilted it so that I could look out and see if there was any movement from her trailer. I froze and rubbed my eyes. Her trailer was gone.

I walked quickly out onto the studio lot. I went round the perimeter, making it look like a morning constitutional, but there was no sign of the trailer or her, just the dogs, the barbed wire and the sentries. I spotted Jerry coming out of studio six and called over to him.

'Jerry? Have you seen Miss Wendt this morning? Her trailer seems to have moved.'

Jerry mumbled something and headed straight back inside the studio, shutting the door quickly behind him. Two workmen painted a set nearby and I could swear that as I passed them I could hear one of them say to the other something like *'Poor bastard.'*

Hans. Bloody Hans. I had to see Hans right away.

I ran towards the main studio building, up to the first floor and walked in without knocking. Hans's facial expression stopped me dead. He was at his desk, looking lovingly at a pretty blonde in a short skirt next to him. He was showing her how to light a cigarette from what looked like one of Eva's elegant cigarette-holders. He looked up, surprised, but composed himself quickly.

'Ah Julius! Just the man! I want you to meet your new leading lady, Helga Braun.'

Helga nodded towards me and smiled but I could feel the sweat prickling the back of my shirt.

'New leading lady? Hans, this is the girl from passport control! Where's Eva?'

Hans didn't answer.

I ran down the long corridor, breathing heavily, flinging open doors as I passed, desperately looking for her. Out of the corridor now and into the light, I ran to the middle of the studio lot and turned around full-circle, scanning faces. Marty the hair stylist walked past and avoided eye-contact. A cleaner wheeled a trolley quickly across the lot, studiously avoiding me.

I was facing the main gates now. If Eva had gone anywhere, the sentries would have seen it. I marched up to them briskly and they turned lazily towards me as they watched me approach.

'Have you seen Eva Wendt?', I demanded. 'Did she leave the studios?'

A dead-eyed sentry stared through me, almost nose-to-nose. I jumped back a few steps and then took a run at the gates. I clambered up quickly and started to climb over.

'Get down, Herr Schiller!'

'You can't stop me!'

'I said get down Herr Schiller!' The sentry unfastened the safety catch on his rifle with a click. 'This is your last warning!'

He fired a shot into the air.

'Stop or I shoot!'

Suddenly Hans came running towards us, his braces flapping behind him.

'Don't shoot him! Don't shoot him!'

The second sentry jumped up onto the gate and climbed a few feet, grasped my ankle and threw me to the ground. I hit the earth with a thump that winded me. The first sentry straddled me and pointed his rifle right into my face.

'I told you to get down Herr Schiller.'

I could see Hans now, peering at me.

'Hans?'

The sentry raised his rifle butt towards my face.

'Not the face! Not the face!', Hans cried.

The first sentry lowered his rifle and whacked me in the ribs with the butt. I couldn't move, all the breath had been knocked out of me, so I just lay there on the ground, looking up at Hans.

***

91

'Not the face?' I said angrily to him in his office fifteen minutes later, nursing my bruised ribs.

'I have to protect my investment.'

'What the - ? What about Eva? She not a good enough investment for you?'

'Now Julius - '

'Where is she?'

Hans poured two glasses of schnapps from the bottle on his desk and handed me one.

'Unlike in your case, I did not know she was Jewish. you must remember, I just run a film studio. I do not run Germany.'

'This isn't a studio. It's a prison. Where is she?'

Hans looked down at his nails, subdued.

'You do not want to know.'

'Yes I do.'

'You can do nothing about it. Nothing at all.'

'We'll see.'

'Very well then. The Gestapo will have passed her and all her possessions to the SS. I believe they deal with the Jewish question.'

'The what?'

I stood sharply and grabbed Hans by the collar.

'You can hit me Julius if it will make you feel better.'

I raised my fist but then lowered it again.

'No. I just want you to get Eva back.'

'I'm afraid that is out of my control. You'll need to speak to the SS, which I strongly suggest you do not do.'

'Why not?'

'Because they might ask you questions. Questions about you. And questions about me.'

'I see.'

'You will not be able to leave the studios. And if you do, I'll find you', he said icily. He looked up at the poster on the wall of *All for Love*. 'You have an instantly recognisable face, I'm afraid.'

I felt my collar tighten. My ribs were hurting, throbbing constantly.

'I didn't want to have this conversation', said Hans, leaning forward, 'but I've lost one star and I'm not losing another.'

'So - so *what*? So she's not coming back? That's it? We just forget about her? Forget she even existed? I go on happily with the new girl? She's from the airport Hans for fuck's sake!'

'That is my understanding of how the whole thing operates. I have been instructed to dispose of all the master copies of Eva's films.'

He stood up and walked round to my side of the desk. He rested his hand on my shoulder. I looked at the hand, then up at the face and wondered what was going to come out of the mouth.

'You would do well to remember who you are, how I found you, that there's a war going on.'

'Oh I do, Hans, I do remember.'

'I will continue to protect you, Julius Schiller.' The last two words lingered. 'We'll make some movies and we'll both get paid handsomely for it.'

'By the Third Reich.'

'It's still good money. You Jews like...'

Hans stopped himself, embarrassed at his own words.

'This is not about money and you know it! I'm not *negotiating*, Hans. We have to find Eva! I have to know she's safe!'

Hans looked at me quizzically.

'You are very concerned about her all of a sudden, my boy, if I may say so? Has anything happened between you I should know about?'

I paused for a moment.

'Nothing has happened', I replied. 'I just want to know she's fine. I don't want to hear about how much money we're going to make'.

Hans reached into a drawer of his desk.

'What about if we doubled it?'

I looked at him in disgust. I'd thought I could trust him. I got up, turned round and headed back out the door clutching my ribs.

He stood up and waved the studio cheque-book at me.

'Julius. Julius! Did you hear me?'

***

Rabbi Weinstein, Mrs Weinstein and their four children stood in the early autumn heat at a train station milling with thousands of displaced people, most of them Jews. A red-faced SS officer walked up and down the platform and smiled at the children. He kept checking his watch.

'They're late', he murmured. 'Always late.'

Suddenly, all heads turned due north. In the distance, puffs of smoke rose into the blue sky and the sound of a steam engine, pulling a heavy load, drew nearer. Mrs Weinstein hugged Lillie close.

'We'll be fine, dear. We'll be fine', she whispered. 'Did you remember Betty?'

Lillie nodded and pulled out a little doll with blonde hair from inside her coat pocket.

'She's tired', Lillie said. 'Tired and a bit hungry'.

'We'll get her something to eat soon, Lillie. Then she can have a nice rest.'

'Yes mama', Lillie replied, stroking the doll's long blonde hair.

The train drew up to the platform and the assembled passengers looked at their new transport. Cattle trucks. Large cattle trucks with slits for windows and heavy metal locks on the doors. Rabbi Weinstein and his family joined hands and prayed in Hebrew. The red-faced SS officer watched them and shook his head sadly. Around the Weinsteins, others joined in the prayer. It was a prayer for a safe journey across the desert to the promised land, the land of milk and honey. That they would have food and water and clothing and beds to sleep in.

The Rabbi did not pray that they would live, at least, not out loud.

***

I was alone again. It was five in the afternoon and I was alone in my trailer with my beer, holding ice against my ribs, just like a stuntman, except that trying to climb out of the studios had been no stunt. I took another swig of beer, emptied the bottle and threw it against the side of the trailer wall, smashing it into pieces. I let my head fall to the table with a bang. And another. I was a coward. I looked up at the thick contract with Swastikas in the margins, my new five-picture deal. My new masters were Hitler, Himmler and Goering, my new producer and screenwriter Josef Goebbels, head of Nazi propaganda. I'd be expected to play my part, again and again and again whilst Eva lay in some Nazi prison or camp or worse. Next to the contract was a ten by eight black and white publicity shot of her. As I reached for another bottle of beer I heard someone knock on the door.

'Mister...Mister Schiller sir?'

'What is it Jerry?', I shouted drunkenly.

95

The door opened and Jerry walked in holding a stack of thirty-five millimeter film canisters.

'I brought you this...this film...I managed to save it...they were...they were gonna burn it, like the rest...'

Jerry placed the canisters carefully on the table and I stared at them. On the side of each reel I could read *'All for Love, dir. Hans Bosendorf/mit Eva Wendt/Julius Schiller'*. I looked up at Jerry's smiling face, eager for recognition, and dropped my head to the table with a bang. Jerry looked alarmed. He gulped and sat down.

'Please don't be angry with me...I couldn't bear...bear to tell you Mister Schiller, earlier, when...'

'It seems I'm always the last to know round here'.

Jerry scratched his head.

'I ain't no genius or nothin' Mister Schiller sir...but sometimes, sometimes the answer to your troubles..is...staring you right in the face if you get what I mean, Mister Schiller sir. You know what I mean, sir?'

I didn't look up. I just stared at Eva's photo on the table in front of me.

'All my troubles?', I said finally.

'All of 'em, sir.'

'Good night, Jerry.'

Jerry could take his cue and he sloped to the door.

'Good...good night Mister Schiller sir'.

I turned my head away from the publicity shot and to the thick contract next to it. It was so thick it was more like a large book, with a hundred tiny swastikas printed in the margins of every single page, a reminder of who the contract was with in case I was tempted to forget. I turned over the first page and stared. If anything could send me to sleep this would. I read it very slowly. I turned another page. And another. I stopped and stared at paragraph seven-fifteen. I read it through again. I took a swig of beer and read it through a third time. Just then, there was another knock on the door. My eyes were fixed to the words on the page. I could hear the door open.

'Not now, Jerry! Not now!'

I turned round to face a middle-aged man in full SS uniform with medals splattered across his chest. I dropped my beer and I think my mouth must have been hanging open.

'This is a bad time, Herr Schiller?'

'Come in', I said, composing myself. 'Come in. Would you like a beer?'

'I prefer schnapps, but I suppose one beer won't hurt me.' He pointed to my contract lying on the table. 'Reading your contract I see.'

'Yes, Herr…?'

'Wilfred Keller. Please call me Wilfred and I will call you Julius.'

I sat down and opened a beer for him. He took it, sat down opposite me and held his beer to mine.

'*Prost!*', he exclaimed, and took a long drink.

'Yes, *prost!*', I replied and took an even longer one. He put his beer down on the table, opened his attaché case and smiled at me.

'I've come about your contract.'

7

Two weeks passed, night fell and the mist settled over Bosendorf Studios. There was a distinct chill in the air. The sentries now numbered six, the barbed wire around the perimeter seemed to have doubled in density and the Dobermans were barking. It was a big night for the Studios and an endless stream of black cars filtered through security at the main gates, flashing passes scanned by sentries' torches. The whole of Germany's press had been invited to the announcement of the next Bosendorf Studios production, due to begin filming the following week. It was to be the first production under the Third Reich's control, the first script produced by Josef Goebbels and his team of assistants.

The handsome hero *Wolfgang Bliztkrieg*, in other words, me, was in a classic tuxedo, a wing-collared shirt with gold pins holding the collar in place, gold studded buttons down the front and a red and black bow tie. I felt like an idiot, but this time I didn't mind feeling like an idiot. I looked at myself again in the dressing room mirror behind Studio One. I had to be strong tonight.

Hans adjusted his tie next to me. Our faces caught each other in the mirror and Hans smiled. I could see what he was thinking, that I'd come round, seen sense, agreed to do the film, that Eva had been lovely but also a pain and now we had an equally lovely girl who was infinitely cheaper, a girl whose salary could be doubled five times until it got to what he'd been paying before. We shook hands firmly, warmly. After all, I didn't want him to suspect anything, and I was a good actor.

In the ladies' dressing room all was not quite so calm. In an effort to mimic the look of Eva Wendt, Helga Braun had had her hair styled, a dress made and had taken elocution and deportment classes. She wasn't a star yet, but you wouldn't know it from the way she ordered everyone around.

'Get me that hairbrush...no! Not the blue one, the grey one you numbskull!'

The young assistant handed it to her.

'What are you waiting for? Brush! Brush! I want that backcombed full-bodied look, you know, like *her*.'

An orange light went on in every dressing room above the door. Through the loudspeaker next to the mirror Hans's voice came crackling out.

'Two minutes, please! Two minutes to corridor!'

The corridor was the assembly point, a twenty yard walk to the rear of the main stage, beyond which two hundred people would be waiting for us with cameras, note-pads and questions. I smoothed down my lapels once more and checked the side-parting in my hair which was slicked down flat. I rehearsed my answers over and over in my head, the answers to the inevitable questions. And I must remember to smile and wave, just like Hans taught me.

Almost in slow motion, one by one the doors opened onto the central corridor in the depths of Studio One. Hans, Helga, the supporting cast and I stepped out from our respective dressing rooms and looked each other up and down. The moment was nigh. I had butterflies in my stomach. I took another quick look at Hans, who was kissing Helga's glove and staring up into her eyes. No doubt what was on *his* mind. Hans turned and shook hands with me. He clapped me on the back yet again.

'I'm proud of you', he said. I smiled back, as best I could. He linked arms with me and Helga Braun and we walked grinning towards popping flashbulbs and the excited murmur of a crowd.

A roar greeted us in Studio One. The bulbs were dazzling and the noise immense. The three of us sat excitedly at a table facing a barrage of chattering from the press and a thousand flashbulbs. Hans stood and signaled for quiet. His voice was booming and he didn't need a microphone, but he still used one.

'Quiet please! Good evening *meine Damen und Herren*! We welcome the press to Bosendorf Studios and to our latest film! In conjunction with the Third Reich we give you...*Blitzkrieg against the World!*'

A projection of a movie poster appeared on a large white screen behind us to a fanfare of dramatic music and some pyrotechnics. All eyes looked up at the screen and I turned to it as well. It showed me in an SS uniform and Helga in a dirndl, locked in an embrace. Above us, in a clear blue sky, Luftwaffe planes flew, the pilots signaling a big thumb's up sign out of the cockpit windows. More flashbulbs popped.

'Thank you, thank you', said Hans to the ripple of applause. 'We'll take questions now. One at a time.'

'What's it like working with Julius Schiller, Miss Braun?', asked an eager young reporter. This was good, thought Hans. Planting questions always worked. Everyone turned to Helga for a reply. She smiled nervously. She'd forgotten what Hans had told her to say.

'Simply divine', she replied, reaching for my hand, which I gave to her willingly. I even smiled at her.

'And you, Julius, do we win the war? Beat the English?', asked Bert Gertz, a seasoned supporter of

Bosendorf Studios and staff-writer for the *Frankfurter Allgemeine.*

'Oh, you know the answer to that, Bert', I replied, to laughter from the crowd, 'but when you're about to make a film like this, you think of the real men and women whose lives are at risk just so we can walk about here on set, so you can publish your papers and Hans can count his money.'

More laughter erupted from the journalists. Hans smiled at me.

'Very good. You have a keen sense of humour my boy.'

'And on that note', I continued, adopting a slightly more serious tone, 'I wonder if it's right.'

The room went silent. Hans turned to me, warily. This wasn't scripted. All eyes were on me now. There were murmurs of approval from the press. A flashbulb popped. Hans stood and clapped his hands.

'Thank you, Julius', he said, but I didn't sit down.

'I was looking for something', I continued, 'and the answer was staring me right in the face.'

At the rear, Jerry's eyes shone.

'I was looking for a way out, an honourable way to do the right thing.'

Hans looked extremely worried.

'I'm under contract to the Third Reich and under that contract there is only one avenue open to me, one path that I must now take.'

I looked out into the sea of faces. I had them right where I wanted them.

'Discussions have taken place', I continued as Hans looked at me in amazement, 'and I am here to make an announcement that may interest you.'

The press leaned forward in their seats, the television cameras rolled and Hans started sweating. I paused for dramatic effect, two hundred pairs of eyes locked onto my face.

'Under section seven-T of my contract with the Third Reich, I will cease work as an actor and start fighting for my country.'

The crowd gasped but I barely paused.

'I confirm that as of tomorrow morning I will be joining the military.'

There was a moment's silence, but then the flashbulbs went crazy and a rousing cheer erupted from everyone bar Hans. His head, held high a few moments ago, fell slowly to the desk in front of him. It paused there for a few seconds and then resurfaced, phoenix-like, covered in a fixed grin. I even saw him wave, pretending that he was in on the decision. He was a smart man, Hans, and I hoped I was being smart too. Helga didn't know what was going on but as she couldn't think of anything to say she simply smiled and waved. Bert Gertz from the *Frankfurter Allgemeine* stood again.

'That's a great propaganda statement Julius. Which part of the military were you thinking of? The Luftwaffe?'

I slowly turned to look behind me at my image projected on the giant poster, the man in SS uniform. I turned to the press and smiled.

'The one where he gets the girl, of course!'

The crowd erupted into laughter.

'You cannot do this!', Hans hissed at me. 'You cannot, you know who you are!'

'Yes I do Hans and I'm sorry.'

In front of us the press were giving me a standing ovation.

'Julius! Julius! Julius! Julius!', they chanted.

I stood and looked out again over the sea of heads. I could see at least two television cameras rolling, which made it even more real.

This wasn't just for me. It wasn't just for Eva. They thought I was doing this for Germany. Well, they could think what they liked. I raised my hand and gave the crowd an understated, Hitleresque wave, straight arm, only the palm raised.

***

Horst Weber's tank unit was pushing west. The combined armies of the Third Reich had conquered Poland in a matter of days, and Hitler had told them not to stop there. The tanks rolled quickly through Holland, Belgium and France. There did not seem to be much resistance. The might of the *Wehrmacht* and the guerilla tactics of the *Schutzstuffel* - the SS - were an indomitable combination. *Einsatzgruppen* cleaned up behind the marching troops and tanks, sweeping up the remains of resistance and taking no prisoners.

However, despite the victory celebrations that he and his fellows had almost daily, Horst Weber was very depressed. It was not the foot-rot or the lousy frankfurters they had for every meal. It wasn't the lack of sleep or the foul smell inside the tank. The reason he was depressed was as a result of reading the contents of a telegraphic communication from his wife, received in encrypted form that day.

Before he had left he had built a fine wooden cot and painted the dressing room next to their bedroom, which was to serve as a nursery. They had prepared the whole house for the baby. His wife had rested for six hours a day and seen the doctor every week. Everything had been planned and he had hoped to conquer Europe before the year was out so he could be there for the birth. He looked at the short telegram he held in his hand as he sat inside his Panzer tank. He read the transcript again.

'Attention: U/Stmfr Horst Weber
From: Frau G. Weber
Message: Lost baby this morning. Stop. Am coping. Stop. Hope you come home soon. Stop. Love. Stop.'

What good was land that stretched out as far as the eye could see if you had no-one to leave it to? What good was it? No-one to send to school, to watch grow up, to play catch with. No one to read stories to at night. This was the third time. The third miscarriage. Horst wished he was home now with his wife. He remembered the last time. They'd been younger then, but with his wife approaching thirty-four, things did not look quite as optimistic.

He lifted his head out of the tank. It was night, and the flares ahead of him signified what they had all been waiting for. In a giant pincer movement, the tank units and infantry battalions were meeting up, closing off any and all resistance in between. The enemy would be squeezed to death, quickly and relatively painlessly in the arms of the giant crab's claws. His unit had already killed three thousand in the last week. It had been necessary. *'To achieve our goals'*, Hitler had said, flailing his arms about wildly, *'we must never falter. Never!'*

Horst Weber watched the spattering of light against the night sky and the silhouettes of the tens of Panzers in front of him, their guns reaching out into the darkness, but he could think of nothing else other than the solitary soul somewhere up there looking down on him that could and should have been his first child.

***

104

The cinema was crowded with women of all ages and men too old to fight. It was the old *Kino* in an outer Berlin suburb, five miles from Bosendorf Studios. All faces turned to the crackly, jump-cutting black and white newsreel on the screen. The loudspeakers played out an SS marching song. The music dropped in volume and an announcer's voice boomed out over the top as my face filled the screen.

'Here's Julius Schiller! What courage, what an inspiration to all Germans. Not for him the cosseted world of the film studio. There'll be no champagne and caviar where he's going. Our man's volunteered for the Waffen-SS, one of our top fighting units and here he is, greeting his fans as he boards a train, on the way to serve his country.'

On screen, two men in SS uniform saluted me. I wore a smart suit and waved at a crowd of press and fans. A lady passed me her baby. I kissed it. Another lady handed me a bunch of flowers. I smiled and waved. A train whistle sounded.

'We wish him good speed in our fight against the Allied forces and international Jewry!'

My face filled the screen. A hand patted me on the shoulder. I smiled and gave a big thumb's up sign to the camera.

Hans shifted uncomfortably in the red velour seat of the cinema. He could not bear to look. Helga Braun sat next to him chewing gum. She looked up at the screen wistfully.

'He's so brave, isn't he Hans?', she whispered.

Hans could not think of anything to say. He looked up at my black and white image receiving the adulation of the German people and walking voluntarily into the open arms of the SS. He had to agree with her. I was brave. Very brave indeed.

Either that or something else.

8

Clank clank clank clank clank clank clank was all Eva could hear. The noise was deafening. She didn't know where she was, but what she did know is that they would all suffocate to death if no-one opened the doors soon. They'd been traveling for hours and hours with no break. The smell was now unbearable. The cattle truck had those tiny thin slits at the top, intended for cows, not human beings. Whatever this contraption was, she thought, it was going to kill them all. She stood on a suitcase and tried to peer through the slits but all she could see was fleeting glimpses of green and brown fields.

She looked around at the women in the carriage. There were no men and no children, just women aged from eighteen to forty-five. It was uncomfortably hot and sweaty and many faces were streaked with dried tears. *Clank clank clank* went the cattle truck against the rails. An insidious sound. The clanking drowned out the sobs of the pretty dark-haired young woman who stopped to touch Eva's long blonde hair.

'You're that actress' she said, wide-eyed. 'I didn't know you were Jewish.'

Eva looked down at her from her position up by the air vent. She hadn't the energy to smile. She clambered down from the suitcase and looked at this girl. A nice girl. Good-looking. An honest face with good bone structure.

'My hair's Eva Wendt, the rest of me's Betty Weinstein. We're both dying for a cigarette.'

'Sarah Bloom.'

The other women looked towards Eva suspiciously. Eva stared coolly at them. She would have preferred to stare with a cigarette in her mouth, but at present she was simply grateful to be breathing.

'They don't seem to like me much', said Eva, nodding towards the five or six scowling faces. 'I tried to get a ticket in first class but they said no'.

Sarah tried to smile. Eva wiped the sweat from her forehead. Today she was Eva Wendt, she kept saying, Eva Wendt. Only Eva Wendt would get out of this mess. She must be strong.

'Where we headed, Sarah?'

'Not the hospital', she replied. 'The other train was going there. They took all the old men, old women and children.'

'All of them?', Eva asked, surprised. 'To *hospital*? Were they all sick or something?'

Sarah scratched her head. It had been a huge platform. So many people. That red-faced Nazi walking up and down putting people into lines, trying to keep families together, he said, as he led her parents away to another line. Her father had limped there slowly.

'My father has a bad hip...and...I thought...'

Her voice faltered.

The two women sitting next to Sarah shook their heads. Eva watched them and then Sarah's face. The unblemished skin wore a frown now and Eva gently took her hand. Sarah looked around her at the silent bowed heads and she burst into tears, sobbing into Eva's hair.

'They're dead, aren't they? They're dead!'

'Shhh, Sarah', said Eva, stroking Clara's arm softly. *Clank clank clank clank.* They weren't slowing down.

'They were there', Sarah sobbed, 'on the platform. With hundreds of others. A rabbi prayed as they walked to the carriages.'

She wiped her eyes, taking solace in the memory.

'A nice man, the rabbi. He had a lovely voice. He had his children with him. They were sweet children. All four of them.'

Eva's mouth opened slowly but no words came out. A rabbi with four children? What were the odds?

***

Inside a gas chamber at a brand new concentration camp in Eastern Germany, hundreds of faces stood waiting. They did not know they were in a gas chamber, an experimental one, built to take the place of mobile extermination vans. They thought they were taking a shower. They looked up and what they saw were normal shower heads, positioned at regular intervals in the concrete ceiling.

Rabbi and Mrs Weinstein and their four children stood naked, hair shorn, hand in hand. Lillie was crying. Mrs Weinstein hugged her. Lillie had been allowed to keep her doll Betty with the blonde hair. She held her tightly.

'That was a nice prayer, Morry', said Mrs Weinstein as a tear rolled down the rabbi's face. There was a loud banging noise above them. Hundreds of heads looked up as the shower heads began to rattle.

***

Inside a dark grey block in an SS training camp somewhere in Eastern Germany, large twelve-pronged metal-headed showers shot out freezing cold water onto hundreds of new recruits. They shouted and screamed as the icy blasts hit them. Most turned away, protecting themselves from the blasting.

I stood near a wall, hiding my circumcision and avoiding the bulk of the icy water. I was shivering bitterly and my lips were blue. It took my breath away the water was so cold. Keller hadn't mentioned this.

I looked behind me, away from the wall and two men a few yards away pointed at me. They waved. I blinked. They waved again. One of them gave me a big thumb's up sign like I'd done for the cameras at the train-station. I forced a smile and cursed the movie business. Even here I couldn't escape, but maybe I could get what I wanted.

Just as suddenly as the water had started, it stopped. There was a pile of black towels to the side and the shivering men raced for them, desperate to get warm. I edged over and grabbed one. I rubbed myself down quickly, trying not to catch anyone's eye. The two men who had waved at me appeared next to me. They peered at my face and the thicker-set one, who must have been close to six foot six tall, slapped the other on the shoulder.

'I told you it was him, you asshole.'

'Yeah well...'

'Say something to him.'

I edged away slowly. They looked like criminals, both with broken teeth, scars and strange tattoos, conscripts, by the look of it.

There seemed to be some movement towards the door we'd entered by. Someone was shouting at us to move our tiny little pricks. I kept my head down and headed towards the shouting. *'Do what you're told'*, Keller said to me in my trailer. *'Just do exactly what you're told.'*

I was now being told to march across a freezing courtyard wrapped only in my towel and into a large white-tiled room full of syringes and nurses. One of them motioned for me to approach her. She held up a large needle, squirted some greenish liquid out of the top so that little droplets cascaded onto the tiled floor and grabbed my arm.

'Hold still!', she ordered. I did what I was told and looked warily at the large needle.

'What's it for?'

I looked at her grim face as she squeezed a tourniquet brutally around my upper arm. She wasn't listening to me. She picked up the needle and plunged it into my arm and my knees buckled from the pain. I could swear I saw her smile as droplets of my blood joined the greenish drops on the floor. She covered the hole in my arm with a sticking plaster and turned to the next man in line behind me.

'In there, next room!' she barked.

I did what I was told.

The barber was a small man with wire-framed glasses and he handled his electric razor like a weapon, cutting deep grooves into my skull, the hair tumbling off quickly. He put it down, picked up one of the cut-throat variety and held it to the back of my neck. I suddenly saw a flash of light to my side and heard the unmistakeable pop of a flashbulb.

'Can you smile this time, Mister Schiller?'

I looked round as a photographer prepared his Hasselblad for another picture. I thought I recognized him from the premiere of *All for Love*, one of the men outside the cinema on the red carpet. The flashbulb popped again and again, the barber grinned for the camera, his hand rested on the back of my neck and he sunk the blade deep into my flesh. I put my hand to the back of my neck and felt the blood dripping out, a long cut. The blinding flashbulb popped again as the barber staunched the flow with a towel that was soon red.

'Six stitches should do it. Tell them Walter sent you', he said to me, nervously. I stood and pressed the towel against the wound.

'Thank you', I said, doing as I was told.

An hour later, with six stitches in the back of my neck, I was spitting out mud. I crawled flat on my stomach underneath barbed wire in fatigues holding a rifle in both hands. I fell again into a filthy pond, submerging completely, pulled myself up and spat out more earthy water. Ahead of me the other recruits were already stripping off as three SS instructors assembled them into lines. I ran as fast as I could towards them, threw down my rifle and tore off my mud-drenched clothing. I didn't want to be last.

They set us off in our vests and shorts, barefoot, to toughen our feet. They marched us up and down the makeshift parade ground and out of the corner of my eye I could swear I saw that photographer again, holding his Hasselblad out in front of him and grinning. *'Two weeks'*, Keller had said. *'Do what you're told and be patient.'*

That night I just thought of Eva and the pain from my neck. The rough stitches were coarse and pinched my skin. The nurse had laughed when I'd asked for painkillers.

'You're a soldier now, not a movie star', she said. 'Painkillers are reserved for officers.'

I turned my head towards the other men, all sleeping. It wasn't difficult avoiding them, in particular the tattooed six foot sixer. Everyone was exhausted and there was a five o'clock start tomorrow morning. I looked out again at the stars. Orion's Belt glowed brightly. It was a very clear night. I wondered if the Luftwaffe were bombing London, if the glistening Thames would light their way. I knew, whatever happened, that I could never go back to England now. I was the enemy, a traitor. They'd have me shot, like that Lord Haw-Haw on the radio. They'd get the both of us and we would hang by the neck until we were dead.

***

Two weeks could be an awfully long time, especially when you were just doing what you were told. Sit, stand, run, jump, shoot, shoot again and a third time for luck. But two weeks did pass, it was autumn 1939 and I'd finished my Waffen-SS basic training. It was now time for Keller to keep his side of the bargain and this he did with impeccable punctuality, calling me into his office for a three o'clock appointment, precisely two weeks from my arrival.

I knocked and entered, standing to attention in my new Waffen-SS uniform, the silver insignia shining on my shoulders as Keller walked round me, inspecting me closely.

'Well, well, well. I'm very impressed Schiller. Very impressed. You came eighth out of your class of three hundred.'

'Thank you, sir'.

I couldn't help feeling a little proud of myself, despite the uniform I was wearing.

'Herr Bosendorf was disappointed to see you go', said Keller, watching me carefully. 'We had a long discussion about you.'

'Did you?'

I wondered if Hans had been smart or if Hans had been stupid.

'He was a terrible businessman. Such high overheads he had. Some of the salaries you movie stars were picking up...' Keller shook his head. 'I can only dream about such funds.'

'I was never in it for the money, sir.'

'I'm glad to hear it. That's exactly what Hans said.'

'Oh?'

'Yes. He said you'd want your accrued fees to go to a good cause, so we've donated them to head office, to Himmler's SS headquarters. He thought you'd like that, seeing as you volunteered to serve him and the Fuhrer.'

Bloody Hans! I was bothered by the thought of bankrolling the SS at least as much as I was by the fact that they'd stolen my money, but I just wanted Eva back. They could keep the bloody money. Keller picked up a large contract with the tell-tale Swastikas scrolled down the margins.

'We must take care of you, Schiller. You are a valuable asset. I will do my best to ensure I do not waste you.'

He pushed the contract and a pen towards me.

'Could I trouble you for an autograph? It's for the Third Reich. Your commission as lieutenant in the specially-designated propaganda division of the Waffen-SS. You will find all the terms are as previously discussed. The SS and Waffen-SS always adhere strictly to the terms of their contracts, as I'm sure will you.'

I held the pen and flicked quickly through the pages of the contract to find what I was looking for. There it was, in front of me in black and white:

Subject: Eva Wendt, otherwise known as Betty Maude Weinstein, Jewess, aged twenty-two, born Leipzig.

'You sign just there, on the last page. Next to my signature.'

He picked up the ten-by-eight publicity photo of Eva from his desk.

'This has already been distributed', he said smiling at me, 'as a mark of our good faith. This is your copy'.

He handed me the photograph. My pen hovered over the page. I flicked through the contract one more time. It certainly looked like the one I'd seen before, that Keller had shown me in my trailer. The list of propaganda chores above and beyond the normal call of duty went on for at least six pages and they expected me to fight as well.

'It's not as bad as it looks', said Keller, gently. 'Lawyers, you know, always have to put everything in.'

I felt the sides of the thick silver pen in my hand, gritted my teeth and signed my name next to Keller's. I wrote the two words out carefully, finishing with a flourish. *Julius Schiller.*

It was, I kept repeating to myself, the only way. Eva would understand. Her family would understand. Everyone would understand.

***

A large metal sign read *Arbeit Macht Frei* - work will set you free. It hung over the entrance to Kithausen Concentration Camp in Eastern Germany. Kithausen was a camp solely for women and Captain Gerhard Metz, a tall thin-lipped man in his mid-thirties, was its commandant. The camp was new and relations with the locals were dreadful. They did not want thousands of skeletal women walking through their villages, reminding them of the reality of what it took to fuel the great German war effort.

115

Despite being surrounded by women, the only woman in Gerhard Metz's life was his mother, with whom he had lived until his commission into the SS. Gerhard Metz was not married. The SS files noted that he was a homosexual and a misogynist. His superiors had had these two factors in mind when they made him commandant. They reasoned that he would have no distractions and would be able to mete out justice more effectively. He would feel no guilt when forced to do his duty, whatever that duty might be.

Beyond the black metal sign at the gates and the electrified fence lay a set of grim grey prison buildings and barbed wire, much like a disused barracks, even though it was brand new. The skeletons of the workers who had built it lined the foundations. Two lines of women now stood in the courtyard. Their train had arrived this afternoon, a long jumbled collection of cattle trucks pulled by an ageing steam engine.

Gerhard Metz walked up and down the lines of women. They looked of poor quality. He inspected their hands as he passed, looking for signs of manual work, which would signify potential.

'Dear, dear', he sighed, 'dear, dear'.

He held a photograph in his hand. It was a photograph of a woman that Gerhard Metz expected most men would find very appealing. To him, however, she was no more than his first task of the morning. He was under instructions to identify this Jewess and deliver her to the location that he had been given, together with six others. He studied the photograph again. It was the standard ten by eight publicity photograph of Eva Wendt. Her blonde hair shouldn't be too difficult to spot, he thought, as he stopped right in front of her.

'Step forward!', he barked. Eva didn't move. She looked him up and down disdainfully. The man was ugly – a Nazi stick-insect.

'What is your name?'

'What do you want it to be?'

Metz slapped her hard across the face and the women near her watched disbelievingly. Metz pulled out his pistol. If there was one thing he could not tolerate it was insubordination.

'You ungrateful little bitch!'

He hit her on the cheekbone with the butt of his *Luger* and she dropped to the ground, clasping her face. Metz took the publicity photograph and screwed it up into his hand. He took out a lighter from his pocket and set fire to it, letting it fall to the ground where it swiftly turned black. He kicked it away, throwing up dust onto his boots. He pointed to the next woman, who happened to be Sarah Bloom, another pretty face.

'You! Polish my boots!'

Sarah nodded subserviently, kneeled and polished the boots with her skirt.

'You'll do. I need six more like you. Get in there.'

He pointed to a small open truck waiting by the gates to the camp.

'Now!'

Sarah got up quickly and walked towards it. She opened the tailgate and hopped into the back. Metz took out a cigarette and lit it calmly. He looked out over the faces in front of him. He placed the cigarette into a long holder, not unlike the ones Eva used to have. He quickly selected six more girls of the obedient sort. The girls, all aged between eighteen and twenty-five, ran towards the open truck to join Sarah as Metz stood over Eva and held his shaking pistol out towards her head. It was within his power to do what he liked with any

117

prisoner if she displayed disobedience or insolence. Everyone would understand.

***

The rumble of tank tracks was deafening. Keller was shouting something into a field radio in front of me, but I couldn't hear what it was. The landscape around us was bleak and starved of life. Our unit had been on the move for five days as part of a convoy east, to consolidate the Polish invasion of a few months before. Armoured cars seemed to have no suspension and I sat on a folded blanket to cushion the bumps in the road. I was, Keller assured me, not far from Eva. I had no idea what I would do with her when I got to her, but my contract promised me that she would be safe and could accompany me on my propaganda duties. My thoughts were disturbed by a large explosion.

'Mine!'

I heard a man scream.

'What are mines doing here?', bellowed Keller as I covered my head to protect me from the earth which flew up around me. Bodies and body parts flew up into the air.

'They're ours, sir!', shouted back a corporal.

'Fuck! Stop the convoy!'

Our armoured car and the rest of the convoy ground to a halt, somewhere near the Russian border.

Keller pointed in the direction of the village about half a mile away which we'd just passed.

'Find some mine detectors!'

Two jeeps drove off towards the village and twenty minutes later they returned with ten frightened villagers, a mixture of old men and women. I couldn't bring myself to look at them. I assumed that they were the mine detectors.

The convoy proceeded slowly, following the line of three villagers who walked as slowly as they dared with their arms stretched out in front of them like divining rods. In the back of two jeeps, the remaining seven villagers were being held in reserve. I could see their faces. Not frightened any more. They were beyond that.

'Grenade!'

I heard it bounce into my armoured car. The two men and Keller in front of me jumped out and I dived into a ditch next to them. The car exploded and the six foot six tattooed recruit next to me, the one who'd smiled at me in the showers, took the full force of the blast. My ears were ringing from the explosion and suddenly we were under attack.

I looked round at the dead Waffen-SS man lying open-eyed next to me, another man's blood dripping down my forehead. The seven human mine detectors in reserve had been detonated by a grenade. The three at the front had run off. Blood trickled from my ears. I heard another mine explode. I fumbled with the buttons on my tunic, gasping for air, when suddenly a hand grabbed my collar.

'I'm a fucking idiot, Schiller!', shouted Keller right into my ear. 'Walked straight into a minefield and an ambush situation. If I pull a stunt like that again I'll let you shoot me yourself!'

I couldn't reply, the dull ringing in my ears obscuring everything else and making me feel detached. Keller reached over to the dead man and pulled a cigarette case out of his tunic pocket. He offered me a cheap Polish cigarette and I nodded nervously and took it. We lay back in the trench, smoking, the sound of gunfire and artillery behind us deafening.

119

'Don't want you blown up!', Keller shouted at me. 'Not now!'

I think I said thank you to him.

'The Luftwaffe will be here in a minute. We'll be fine unless of course they have the wrong coordinates, in which case they'll probably blow us all up.'

'We should radio in the *right* coordinates, sir.'

'Too late.'

'Too late? How far away are we?'

Keller pulled out a map and pointed to a tiny dot.

'We're here, Schiller. And we need to get here.'

He pointed to another tiny dot on the map three inches from the first dot. 'Take it. I have to pee.'

Keller handed me the map and unfastened the buttons of his trousers. I looked away as he emptied his bladder into the ditch, a cigarette dangling from his mouth. Another explosion threw more dirt up and over us like a filthy grey blanket. I covered my ears and got down flat on my stomach. Keller didn't flinch, finished peeing and calmly re-fastened his buttons.

'Don't move', he said as he grabbed his rifle and looked over the top. I lay still, breathing heavily, my hands shaking. I reached inside my jacket and pulled out the crumpled publicity photograph of Eva. Two days, if we could get out of this ditch, two days until I saw her again, until I could hold her and protect her from all this madness.

Suddenly a plane screamed overhead. The Luftwaffe were right on cue. I lay flat against the earth and Keller dropped down next to me.

'Our air support is arriving, thank *Himmel*!'

He looked swiftly at Eva's photograph.

'Don't waste your breath on her, my boy. Has nobody told you?'

The long whistle of a bomb falling to earth made us both stop and listen. I looked at Keller, horrified.

'Told me what?'

But Keller could not answer, or at least I couldn't hear what he said because I was rocked by a huge explosion and then everything went black.

9

Inside the cavernous space of a German armaments factory, Eva Wendt nee Betty Maude Weinstein sat in a long line of women fitting firing pins to pistols. She had a black eye and facial bruising. Her blonde hair had been shaved off her head and she wore a blue cap like all the other women. They'd been going since six in the morning and she'd never done anything as boring or repetitive or as badly paid. She held out a pistol to the young woman next to her.

'Have I got this right?', Eva asked. 'You see, I wouldn't want to kill anyone.'

The young woman took the gun from her and frowned.

'Where's the firing pin?'

Eva pointed to her apron pocket.

'But the gun won't work without it!'

'Exactly', whispered Eva. 'Those are the only ones I've worked with. They always used to remove the firing pins. I watched them do it.'

'Have we met before?'

The young woman stared hard at Eva's face.

'I used to be in the movie business'.

'You're not *that woman*, are you?'

'I probably am.'

The young woman scratched her head. Even with no hair she still had lice.

'What were you saying about these pins?'

Eva leaned over.

'They seem to box them up so fast...maybe no-one will notice if we leave the pins out of the equation. I don't want to be responsible for anyone's death, and I'm not helping these bastards kill anyone.'

The young woman nodded slowly. She handed the gun back to Eva.

'We're on bullets later', she said.

'Then I think I know how we can get rid of these firing pins.'

Eva winked and the young woman next to her dropped a firing pin into the front pocket of her apron just as Eva had done. Eva smiled.

'Spread the word', she whispered. They nodded slowly at each other. The young woman turned and tapped the one next to her on the shoulder.

'Listen', she said, 'you'll never guess who I've got sitting next to me...'

***

Inside a small bivouac tent in a field somewhere in Europe, my eyes flashed open. I was sweating. I put my hand to my head and felt a bandage there. The stitches on the back of my neck were gone. I remembered the explosion. Everything had gone black. Outside I could hear someone humming and a sizzling sound. Something was cooking. I managed to ease myself up and I opened the flap of my tent to look outside.

It must have been five or six in the morning. In the field were a number of other small bivouac tents. They were all closed apart from one that was larger than the others. My eyes turned towards the sizzling sound. In a clearing surrounded by two stoves, Wilfred Keller stood in a white vest and long underpants breaking eggs expertly into an enormous frying pan. He threw on twenty strips of bacon and the pan flamed and spat out fat. Keller hummed happily to himself, turning the bacon with a long metal spatula.

I closed the flap of my tent again. I looked down at the bloodstains on my uniform. I shook my head, trying to wake up. I stared at the pistol which lay by the side of my bed. And then I remembered what Keller had told me, just before everything had gone black. Eva Wendt was dead. I wasn't thinking straight but I remembered exactly what he'd told me. She was dead, and someone was going to pay for it.

I picked up my gun and looked outside. Keller was throwing sausages into an enormous pan. A large flame rose and Keller prodded a string of sausages with a skewer. He looked happy. I stumbled out unsteadily, waving my pistol, not thinking. I held it up. My head hurt. Keller's face swam into my sights. The pan sizzled. What was I doing?

'Ah. That sounds like Schiller', said Keller without turning round. 'I cannot offer you champagne and oysters, but a few slices of bacon and you'll feel better. You had a nasty bang on the head.'

I suddenly felt dizzy and I fell over. One of the sausages on Keller's grill banged and I fired my pistol by accident. It clicked. There was no bang. Keller looked round. I squeezed the trigger again and again, pointing the gun at the ground. Click click click.

'I took the liberty of removing the firing-pin, Schiller, you were in such a state. I was worried you might hurt yourself. Put it down now there's a good fellow and come and have some breakfast.'

Around me, my fellow Waffen-SS rose from their tents. I replaced the gun in my holster. I sat down on a metal chair at a makeshift table and Keller thrust a large steaming plate of food in front of me. I stared at it.

'Pig's stomach, sausages and bacon. You're going to need your strength today, do you hear, Schiller?'

'I'm not hungry, sir', I replied.

'Suit yourself', said Keller with a mouthful of sausage. 'But you'll need to clean yourself up and make yourself presentable for our visitors.'

I stared at him. We were in the middle of nowhere, three inches from the little dot on the map. Eva was dead. I didn't need any visitors. I didn't need anything any more.

***

Hundreds of boxes of bullets moved down a conveyor belt. Eva sat behind the machine in a line of women. It had been a long day and she winced. They hadn't had much to eat and she felt sick with hunger. She held her stomach for a moment and took some deep breaths. Next to her a woman was packaging up bullets into a box with a little Swastika stamped on each side. Eva grabbed a handful of bullets from the belt in front of her, looked around and dropped the bullets into the drains that ran along the length of the large factory. The drains stank of God knows what. She took out the firing pins from her apron that she'd saved from that morning and dropped them into the box in front of her. She quickly packed the rest of it with straw. She lifted the box to test its weight, fitted the top and placed it on the conveyor belt.

The woman next to her watched Eva closely. She nodded her head and grabbed a huge handful of straw. Eva smiled. What they all needed now was a distraction, something to make them forget where they were. She opened her mouth and started to sing a Hebrew song her father had taught her a long time ago. She was sure the others would know it.

'*Hevenu shalom alechem!*'

A dozen hands filled boxes with straw and firing pins instead of bullets.

'*Hevenu shalom alechem!*'

The woman next to her joined in the singing. And another. And another until the chorus grew to match the volume of the conveyor belts.

'*Hevenu sha- a - lom alechem. Hevenu shalom! Shalom! Shalom alechem!*'

Up in the factory office behind a glass partition, Captain Gerhard Metz surveyed the women working from on high. Next to him lounged a senior SS officer and a frumpy fat Fraulein, also in SS uniform. The senior officer was there to inspect the work Metz was doing, to ensure productivity levels were met. The fat Fraulein was Metz's assistant. She reminded Metz of his mother. The sound of singing drifted through to them above the whir of the conveyor belt motors. The senior SS officer turned puzzled to the fat Fraulein.

'Is that *singing*, Fraulein?', he asked, spitting the words out. The Fraulein, alarmed, looked to Metz for help. Metz ignored her and stood by the glass searching for Eva amongst the crowd. He found her, sitting near the end of the third row of women. She appeared to be working quickly, packing up boxes of bullets. She also appeared to be singing heartily, her body swaying to the unfamiliar tune filtering through the glass. He addressed the fat Fraulein without removing his eyes from Eva.

'How many units have you shipped today, Fraulein?'

She checked a manifest hurriedly.

126

'Fourteen thousand boxes of cartridges, Sir.'

The singing seemed to get louder. Metz didn't take his eyes away from the window.

'And what is normal for this period?'

'Approximately eleven thousand.'

'Then let the Jews sing!' boomed the senior SS officer.

Metz turned.

'More cartridges, less Jews!'

The two men laughed, looking out of the window down to the women workers below. Metz opened a bottle of Schnapps and found two glasses. He poured out the sweet liquid slowly.

Down on the factory floor, Eva was almost enjoying herself. They were now on *'David, melech Israel!'*, a different song whose chorus was as repetitive as the task they were performing. But it meant everyone knew the words and the tune. They'd even started a round.

Eva stuffed more straw into an empty box of cartridges and dropped in a firing pin to make up the weight. She looked up quickly at the factory office high above them. Standing in the window were three figures looking down on her. The two men, one of them Metz, raised their glasses of Schnapps. They were smiling. Just for a second, a flicker of doubt crossed Eva's face. She rested her hand on her belly. The sickness was returning.

***

I had my eyes firmly shut. Strains of some obscure national anthem wafted over to me across the large field next to Wilfred Keller's makeshift Waffen-SS camp. Six guerillas stared down the barrels of a six-man Waffen-SS firing squad.

127

'On my command', a sergeant cried. The firing squad aimed.

'Fire!'

They pulled the triggers of their rifles and the singing stopped.

Two Waffen-SS footsoldiers hauled six steaming corpses one by one across to a pile of thirty or forty more guerillas. It had been a busy morning. Twenty yards away I stood to attention with Keller and Corporal Kretzmar. Keller's chest swelled with pride.

'They don't show you this in the movies, do they, Schiller?'

I opened my eyes and promptly shut them again. I shook my head slowly. Keller swiveled on his heels and turned to Corporal Kretzmar.

'Why aren't they here yet?', he barked. 'They're late!'

'They're arriving now, sir', replied the Corporal dourly.

I looked towards the edge of the field as a black Mercedes ploughed swiftly across it, throwing up dust and mud. It pulled up in front of Keller, little Swastika flags flying from the wing-mirrors. The doors opened and out stepped a Waffen-SS General, followed swiftly by a three-man film camera crew. The General walked swiftly over towards Keller and saluted.

'Heil Hitler!'

'Heil Hitler, Herr General!'

The General whispered into Keller's ear as the crew set themselves up.

'*This* is Julius Schiller?'

'Yes, Herr General.'

'And he's a lieutenant now, you say?'

'Yes, Herr General.'

I watched the crew as they set up a large movie camera, tested the light with a large meter and unpacked two microphones from an aluminium box. I was feeling sick. They pointed the camera towards me. The director, a young man with a harassed look about him, shook his head.

'I don't want those bodies in shot!'

The cameraman shifted so that he had an oblique view of me, Keller and the General. The General summoned Corporal Kretzmar to him and pointed to the car. Kretzmar walked slowly towards it, reached inside the window of the Mercedes and pulled out a black metal container about the size of a shoe-box. He brought it round to the General who grasped it firmly in his hands.

'Everybody ready?' shouted out the director. Keller looked at me and the General. Everyone was there. They could begin. 'OK...roll it!'

The camera pointed at me and the director mimed a huge smile but I was in no mood to perform.

'Smile!', hissed the director at me. 'Smile!'

I stared haggardly at the camera. I'd have preferred the firing squad at this precise moment.

'And...cut!', said the director, looking weary.

The camera stopped rolling and he walked quickly over to Keller. He whispered, agitated, into his ear. Keller turned to me exasperated.

'Smile, you idiot! It's in your contract!'

The television director walked back to his crew. He stood by the camera.

'And...action!', he cried for the second time.

Inside the cinema the air was thick with cigarette smoke. Tobacco manufacturers were doing very well out of the war. Sales had tripled. The large screen, framed by red velvet curtains, was filled with a crackly black and white German propaganda newsreel trailer with news from the front.

My grinning face filled the screen, standing in a field next to Keller. In front of us, the General held a metal box, which was open. Uplifting propaganda music blared out as the General removed a medal from the box. It was an Iron Cross. A narrator's voice filled the cinema.

'And look who's a happy boy! Only three months with the Waffen-SS and already our man Julius Schiller has seen some action, battling hand-to-hand with the enemy, sustaining minor injuries but ready for action again!'

On screen the General saluted me and then Keller and he pinned Iron Crosses on us both.

'Here he is receiving his Iron Cross with his commanding officer, Obersturmbannfuhrer Wilfred Keller, a former actor who once graced the stage in Berlin...'

Keller grinned broadly at the camera. Keller and I stood to attention and saluted the General. He returned our salute. The image on the screen suddenly vanished. A second later it was filled with footage of Messerschmitts and Spitfires fighting it out in a smoke-filled sky.

'Other news now. Yesterday the Luftwaffe shot down three hundred Allied planes for the loss of only two...'

Hans Bosendorf shifted in his seat. He hated these newsreels. The production quality was so poor. He sat in the middle of the front row staring grimly up at the screen. Next to him Helga Braun lay fast asleep, draped over two seats. You could fool all of the people *some* of the time, he mused.

Back in the field, I still had a fixed grin on my face. The Iron Cross glinted on my chest. Keller and the General stood as in the newsreel, holding their salutes.

'And...cut!' shouted the director.

Keller relaxed. My grin vanished instantly from my face as the film crew packed up quickly. The General clicked his heels and marched off to his car leaving me alone with Keller.

'You're very good, Schiller', he said proudly. 'Iron Cross, my boy', as he fingered his own.

'How did she die?', I asked suddenly.

Keller froze and looked me up and down.

'It was an industrial accident. She probably didn't feel a thing. Chin up, we've arranged for replacements.'

'Replacements?'

'Yes. We're allowed replacements under the contract. It's in there somewhere. Excuse me a moment, Schiller, the General's going now.'

Keller marched off towards the Mercedes as my knees gave way for the second time that day. I threw up on the ground and stood, bent over, breathing heavily. Keller's words rang in my ears. The film crew finished packing up behind me and the youngest man on the crew approached me nervously.

'Excuse me Herr Schiller', he said timidly, 'but can I have your autograph?'

10

Hundreds of women stood in lines in the courtyard of Kithausen concentration camp. It was a cold day but the sun was shining. Gerhard Metz paced in front of them, seething with anger. He held a pistol casually in his hand and an open wooden cartridge box from the factory.

'After all we've done for you', he spat out, bitterly. He emptied out the box on the ground. Three bullets fell out, some firing pins and a big lump of straw. Every woman in camp stared at it in silence.

'Three cartridges. When there should be at least one hundred. And firing pins.'

Metz was furious. He pointed his pistol at the woman who happened to be in front of him and shot her in the head from feet away. She slumped to the ground, dead. The other women tried not to make a sound. Metz looked approvingly at his pistol.

'This one works', he said.

In front of them were twenty large full sacks on the ground, flies hovering over them. Metz waved his gun at them.

'These were recovered from the sewage system. These are *my* cartridges. They are covered in *your* shit.'

Three SS wheeled in barrows filled with empty cartridge boxes.

'You will clean them and box them' Metz continued, 'After we've tested them.' He stopped in front of a woman at random.

'You! Pick me six cartridges from a sack. Clean them and give them to me.' The woman raced to a sack, screwed up her face against the smell, picked out six cartridges and wiped them quickly on her prison uniform. She handed them to Metz. He emptied his gun of existing cartridges and handed it to the woman.

'Load the gun', he ordered. The woman's fingers trembled as she loaded the cartridges one by one. She held the gun out to Metz.

'No. You will test it.' He pointed to Eva. 'Test it on *her*. Shoot her with the gun.'

Eva stared at the woman in disbelief. She was only six feet away. The woman shook and dropped the gun in panic. It went off with a bang.

'One out of one. Excellent. Five more. Try again.'

Eva closed her eyes and shook uncontrollably. If she ran, Metz would kill her for sure. Her mind raced. She held the woman's gaze. She looked down and tapped her hand against her leg, a desperate signal. The woman's hand shook. She looked at Eva down the barrel and took aim. She pulled the trigger and fired. A wisp of smoke spread from the end of the barrel. The shot rang out and Eva felt her leg go numb. She couldn't stand on it. She sank slowly to the ground and looked in shock at the bloody mess below her right knee. A wave of nausea overcame her.

'Excellent! Two out of two!'

The woman holding the smoking gun was also in shock. She looked at Eva on the ground and then back to Metz. Her hand trembled uncontrollably. She raised the gun into the air and fired four more times high over the heads of the women in front of her.

'Six out of six. Well done!'

Metz raised another pistol at point blank range, pulled the trigger and blew off the back of the woman's head.   He looked up at the hundreds of bedraggled figures in front of him, their faces stunned and their bodies numb. Eva lay on the ground, the blood soaking her blue uniform. She had her fist in her mouth to stop herself screaming. Metz pointed to the twenty sacks.

'I want all those cartridges cleaned and in those boxes by the end of today.'   Everyone stared at him, frozen with fear.

'Now!', he screamed.

The women raced for the bags. Metz stood over Eva, the blood forming a puddle on the ground next to her. She could see his shadow on the ground next to her, the pistol in his hand.

'And there better not be any singing', she heard him say, just before she blacked out.

***

A week later Eva opened her eyes. Up above her was a white ceiling. To the sides, white walls. She raised her head slightly. She was lying on a metal bed with white sheets. A nurse walked by. She turned her head to one side. Six women lay in beds, all in a row, three on either side. The face of a handsome young man loomed over her. He was wearing a doctor's coat, he had straw-coloured hair and he wore gold-rimmed glasses. Everything seemed covered in a delicate haze, softened somehow, but there was a dull throbbing in her right leg.

'Where...where...?' she mumbled to the doctor.

The words seemed to come from somewhere else and not from her.

'Don't move'.

The doctor reached down and examined a bandage on Eva's right leg. He nodded briskly.

'No significant blood loss. Just as well.'

He made a note on a chart, looked up at her and smiled.

'You're breech.'

'*Breech*?', she could hear herself ask. What's...*breech*?'

'Your baby is in the breech position, which means it is facing the wrong way.'

Eva blinked several times.

'The baby?'

'Yes. I think you're maybe six or seven months gone, even though you'd never tell it from your bump. It is small, you see, because you have been undernourished. We'll feed you up.'

'I'm pregnant?'

Eva moved her hand to her belly in shock. Six or seven months? There could only be one father. The doctor moved away to the next bed and began examining the patient's eyes. He called over for a nurse. Eva turned over on her side, away from him.

'I'm pregnant', she whispered excitedly to herself and then the realisation of where she was slowly hit her. Her face fell.

'Oh God. I'm pregnant', she said in horror as she looked around. She was in a hospital ward somewhere. She'd been shot. She reached out her arm to the woman in the bed next to her.

'Where are we?', Eva asked desperately, her leg starting to throb more painfully.

'Sick bay.'

'Which sick bay? *Where*?'

'Kithausen'.

She'd hoped it would be somewhere else but Eva hadn't moved and she was still under the control of Gerhard Metz. She stared at her neighbour's face and then lowered her eyes until they rested on her belly. She appeared to be heavily pregnant. Eva turned slowly onto her other side, towards where the doctor was making his rounds. Lying in bed chewing a carrot was another heavily pregnant woman. Eva looked closely at the others. All seven women, including her, were pregnant. Eva frowned.

It was more like a maternity ward than a sick bay.

***

Anticipating the war and the bombing that would inevitably follow, Hitler had ordered the construction of a number of bunkers underneath the streets of Berlin. Underground bunkers housed many of the Third Reich's governmental offices. The bunkers had been sunk hundreds of feet into the ground, lined with steel and cased in concrete. They were hot, depressing places to work with no natural light.

Siegfried Knabel, a civil servant grade four-eight-two, was glad that he had been assigned satisfying work. He was working in furtherance of one of Hitler's government's most inspired programmes, a programme that Siegfried Knabel, although only a mid-level clerk, actually believed in. He liked to think, as he read through his files under the phosphorescent lights, that he was working towards a better tomorrow, today.

The file he had in front of him was thick and heavy and it contained countless statements, letters and photographs. He turned another page and pulled out one of the photographs from the file. It was a largish print in black and white. The photograph was of a man and a woman, standing stiffly for the camera, hand in hand, the man in SS uniform. They looked sturdy people. Strong people. The backbone of Germany. Siegfried sighed. He could almost feel their heartache.

136

He turned to his left and took a sip from a cup of instant coffee. It tasted dreadful. He picked up a shortcake biscuit and popped it into his mouth to try and take away the foul taste of the coffee. Now, where was it? He reached inside a large file index of small passport-sized photographs, packed together in alphabetical order. *Adamski, Arter, Buckowski, Cohen*...they blurred into one. He turned to the back of the file. The SS man in the photograph had a low Nazi party number. He'd give him the best he had.

Siegfried worked his way from the back of the alphabetically-ordered photographic index and in a few seconds, found what he had been looking for. It was a recent addition to his data and he was proud of this one. He looked down at the small photograph in his hand. It was a prison mugshot of a pretty woman with blonde hair, although brown roots were starting to show through, he noticed. Very pretty. Very pretty, he thought. He turned the photograph over. The name on the back in meticulously-produced handwriting read *'Wendt, Eva – seven months'*.

Siegfried Knabel placed the mugshot on top of the photograph of the SS man and his wife, a Mr and Mrs Horst Weber. He looked again at their letter. Three miscarriages. Dear, dear. He checked the number, picked up the telephone and dialed. The telephone rang once, twice, three times and then he heard a woman's voice on the line, tired and hopeful.

'Horst? Horst, is that you?'

Siegfried could hear the desperation in her voice.

'No, no, it's not your husband Mrs Weber', he replied gently. 'It's Siegfried Knabel.'

'Siegfried Knabel?'

'From the adoption office.'

He paused and smiled. He always liked this part.

'I have some very good news...'

***

The pain came between inhaling and exhaling the stale musty air tinged with ammonia. It was unbearable. It wasn't in waves, like a bullet wound, the dull sensation and numbness spiked with a searing bolt every few minutes. This was constant agony, the feeling of being ripped apart, of torture that would continue unabated until death or unconsciousness, whichever came first, until the captors had prised their mewling subject from its safe, warm womb.

She felt like running, running fast away from the pain, away to a small lake where she could drown in peace, where the pain would stop. She knew there were drugs that lessened the pain, but there was no epidural here, no air and no gas. The ammonia smell was intoxicating her, making her retch. She could not run anywhere because her feet were in stirrups. The doctor's head loomed over her and he was shining a bright light into her eyes. She hadn't the energy to scream anymore.

Surely it was too soon? Her bump was so small that she would never have known she was pregnant. How could a baby survive in a world like hers, a world controlled by Captain Gerhard Metz and the Third Reich? What would they do to her baby? Experimentation, she had heard from one of the other girls. A doctor called Josef Mengele injected little boys' eyeballs with blue dye and petroleum into their veins. Was this why she was enduring the agony? So that her baby would live a few days longer until subjected to such vile tampering at the hands of madmen? She would rather die now and take her baby with her.

If Abe Goldstein were here now, she was sure he would want the same as her. Maybe, maybe if Abe Goldstein were here now, maybe he could save her, maybe he could carry her off in his arms and out of the concentration camp to a nearby wood where he could deliver their child away from these murderers. But that was not going to happen. That would take a miracle and her faith had been wrecked beyond repair.

He would never know she was pregnant or how she had died, for which she was grateful. Apart from this nurse, this kindly nurse who was mopping her brow with a damp towel and urging her to pant to control the pain, there was no-one. Things had never been more clear to her than at this moment. Pain had sharpened the awareness of her own expendability. She could feel no self-pity because things had passed beyond self-pity. Only the feeling that death would have to be the release, the end of this suffering.

The nurse looked worriedly at the doctor.

'She is nearly ten centimeters dilated,' she ventured nervously.

The doctor calmly checked his watch. The seconds ticked slowly. The nurse bit her lip. Eva Wendt was passing in and out of consciousness. Soon she would not have the energy to push. They were going to lose both mother and baby because of the refusal to use pain-relief on grounds of cost and for fear of halting the delivery process. It had happened last month and the horrible memory still lingered in the nurse's mind. The doctor was simply obeying his orders and the level of wastage, although regrettable, had been factored into the programme. She picked up a set of forceps and a suction pad but the doctor shook his head.

'No forceps, Nurse. No suction. We don't want marks on the baby's head. Get her to push.'

The nurse replaced them sadly. She leant over Eva and whispered into her ear.

'Just push now dear...push...for the love of God push!'

She wasn't sure if her words were getting through or not, but then the nurse heard Eva whisper something, one word, over and over again, feverishly.

It was my name.

11

Four years passed. It was now 1944 and it had been four years since Keller had told me that Eva Wendt had died in what he called an industrial accident.

Even though things were going badly for Germany I still had my job to do. Newsreel followed newsreel, my progress tracking that of Germany's. In 1941 when we fell out with Stalin I was filmed shooting a Russian soldier, but what the camera didn't show was that the Russian soldier was already dead. If I'd have refused they were going to make me shoot one that was still alive. When the Japanese bombed Pearl Harbour in December of that year things started to get very complicated because we couldn't find any Americans for me to shoot.

Hitler started to overstretch himself, and the more worried everyone became the more jolly I had to look in the newsreels, the more sure I had to look that Germany would win. The winters of 1942 and 1943 had severely dented Hitler's Eastern forces and we had no way of knowing that come 1944 things would get a whole lot worse, except that is for me, for whom everything had hit rock bottom so long ago that every time I thought of Eva or the word *'replacement'* a sickening wave of nausea enveloped me.

I kept asking, over and over again, what had happened to her, what they meant by replacement and what would happen when the war was over.

I didn't want to be Julius Schiller any more. I didn't want a replacement for Eva. There was only one original. My sorrow would be recorded by Goebbels' cameras for the edification of the German people. I sat alone in the back of a jeep, retching into my hand, my Iron Cross flapping in the wind. I certainly hadn't deserved the medal. Another of Goebbels' ideas. The jeep swerved again and I threw up over my boots. Corporal Kretzmar was driving brutally over the potholes in the country road, and next to him sat Keller, in bullish mood.

'*For he is an Englishman, he-ee, i,i,i,i is an Englishman!*', he sang tunefully, appearing not to have a care in the world.

'You don't know this song, Schiller?', he asked.

I wiped my mouth and shook my head. I'd appeared in three Gilbert and Sullivan operettas in London but I didn't feel like boasting. Keller faced forward.

'What a beautiful day! We're in for a special treat, courtesy of the Third Reich, in gratitude for our bravery in the field.'

I wasn't sure if he was being ironic or not. We'd got the Iron Cross when our three-hundred-strong unit overwhelmed forty-three guerillas and then shot them all in groups of six. '*Smile and wave*', I could see Hans saying to me, '*smile and wave*'.

Our jeep approached ornate wrought iron gates at the end of a bumpy country lane. Beyond the gates lay a large white-stuccoed country house with domes, spires and large windows. It was enormous, maybe thirty-six windows across spread over three wings. The manicured grounds swept into view and a warm smile greeted us at the gate. The driveway beyond was at least a hundred yards long and lined with plane trees. To the left a beautiful lawn stretched out under a blue sky. A tall man with a swimming cap performed a

142

wonderful dive into a glistening pool. Horses rode through, the riders in full SS uniform. We approached the main house and a footman ran out to greet us and take our bags. I looked around. At least there were no cameras.

I slung my kit-bag over my shoulder and walked slowly over towards the swimming pool. I sat down on a wooden bench. The cool blue water was empty of people now and it twinkled in the sunlight. I rested my head on my hands and tried to calm myself down. I had felt sick for four years now, ever since the news about Eva had sunk in.

I was the only British Jew in the Waffen-SS, not just a quiet foot-soldier but a role-model for Germans with my own newsreels. My name was probably sitting on a list somewhere in Whitehall, a list of British subjects who would be tried after the war was over. Maybe they would send someone to assassinate me now. With Eva gone I was nothing more than a traitor, furthering the German war effort. Perhaps I should have killed myself or tried to desert and have them do it for me. I had betrayed my country and my religion, a decorated Nazi war hero and propaganda weapon.

I raised my head slowly as I heard someone dive into the pool and in front of me Keller was swimming lap after lap, his slow but powerful crawl scything easily through the blue water.

Ten sun-loungers lay in a row next to me, each with a freshly-folded white towel with a black SS symbol on it. Keller climbed out in his black bathing costume and picked up a towel.

'You wouldn't know there was a war on, would you, Schiller?', he said as he rubbed his hair. 'You must cheer up, my boy. This moroseness helps neither you nor me for that matter. I'm your sponsor after all. Ah! There they are!'

A film crew walked towards us. They pointed at me and gave me a big thumb's up sign. Keller waved at them. I looked towards the pool, ripped off my uniform and dived into the pool in my underwear just as the film crew started to roll their camera. The water parted quickly and then closed smoothly behind me, leaving the crystal clear blue surface now flat again. Ten seconds passed. Twenty seconds. Thirty seconds. I thought I could see the director peer down at me in the water.

I was sitting on the bottom, little air-bubbles escaping slowly from my mouth. I stared blankly ahead and watched the little bubbles float gently a few feet ahead of me and then disperse. This was the first time I'd been alone for a while and the first time I'd seen a swimming pool in five years.

As my blood became less oxygenated, my mind started to wander. I closed my eyes and slipped back to London, back to the bright lights of the West End and to the glaring spotlight on centre stage in a packed theatre. The spotlight flooded the middle of the stage with a bluish light. In the midst of its beam I stood in full uniform with an Iron Cross pinned to my chest. I looked up slowly, powerfully, to the Gods.

'To be or not to be, that is the question.'

'No it's not, you fool!', said Keller, appearing next to me on stage dressed as Polonius.

'Whether 'tis nobler in the mind to suffer the slings and arrows of outrageous fortune or to take arms against a sea of troubles, and by opposing end them?'

'End them! End them! End them!', chanted the audience.

I swam quickly towards the surface, my lungs bursting, towards the afternoon sun as it shone hazily through the ripples in the water above me. My head punctured the smooth blue surface and I took in a large lungful of air. I blinked droplets away from my eyes and looked around, treading water. A director and camera crew were filming me.

'And cut!', said the director smoothly. I took another gulp of air. The director whispered to his cameraman, knelt by the pool and beckoned me over.

'Can we do that again?', he asked me.

***

It must have been in Josef Goebbels' mind that the country house with its pool and manicured lawns made for the perfect movie location. After a couple of hours filming by the pool, the director and his camera crew trailed me all day.

'We won't use all the footage at once', the director kept saying to me, as we moved about the grounds under Keller's watchful eye, 'we'll release it in little chunks.'

The material consisted of me swimming, horseback riding with Keller, playing croquet on the lawn with three other Waffen-SS officers, writing a letter to my non-existent parents – God if they could see me now! – and eating lunch in a canteen. I had to sing the German national anthem and an SS marching song. The only place I managed to escape was when I went to the bathroom, and even then I wondered if the director in his zeal had set up a camera by the little window to watch the marvel of Germany taking a leak.

Goebbels ordered newsreels depicting a daily diary of events, a life in the day of a model SS officer. He chose me to be the subject of this documentary. Keller worked out a schedule for me that was straight out of a military academy. Eight am, cavalry drill on horseback. Nine am, target practice, rifle range. Ten thirty, swimming competition, which I was expected to win. Twelve, hand-to-hand combat training, *und so weiter*. The only good thing about all the activity is that it stopped me thinking about Eva, because whenever I stopped, I started thinking about her again. It was eating me away from the inside. The physical exercises, without the stress of actual combat, were the best thing for me. They stopped me worrying about how I might end up, how I would get out of this mess and how she died.

By the time evening came, I didn't feel like doing anything much. I'd done so much for Goebbels' propaganda machine that I just felt like sleeping. And I cried, too, but only when I was alone in my room on the second floor of the main house. I cried for Eva and, I must admit, I cried a little for myself too.

No-one would believe I joined the Waffen-SS to escape from a five-picture deal worth a hundred thousand. No-one would believe I got an Iron Cross without doing something to win it. If they knew how much I loved her they might understand, but then again they might not. I was fighting for the enemy, very publicly. I took a shower to let the hot water pound my skin and soothe my aching limbs, but not unfortunately my tormented mind.

I toweled down and pulled on my uniform. There was a special event tonight and all decorations were to be worn. I picked up my Iron Cross and fixed it to my tunic. I caught a look at myself in the mirror and saw a lieutenant in the Waffen-SS with an Iron Cross, fair hair, two scars on the face and one on the neck. The face was weather-beaten and lined.   Abe Goldstein was gone forever. This replacement was his antithesis. I blinked and stared at my reflection, at the Nazi in the mirror.

***

The dining hall was wood-panelled and high-ceilinged. The floor was highly polished and three ornate chandeliers hung from three large hooks, similar to the ones I'd seen at the German Embassy on Belgrave Square in what was like another life. At one end of the room was a set of double doors inlaid with gold leaf. Four long buffet tables were set up along one side and a hundred chairs were lined against the other walls, leaving the floor clear for mingling.   The furniture was antique and the paintings on the walls equally so.

'That is a Rembrandt', said Keller to me, pointing to a Rubens. 'Herman Goering has earmarked it for his personal collection.'

I nodded and sipped from a glass of champagne.

'Do you not love the irony of it all?', Keller continued, eyeing me carefully over his glass.

'Irony?', I asked, 'how so?'

'The irony of you being here, and of me being here, in this house drinking French champagne looking at a Dutch painting.'

'Yes. The irony', I replied.

'You know, Schiller, after each final curtain in Berlin, before my days in the Waffen-SS, I shared a bottle of champagne in my dressing room with Werner Hoffman, the great producer.'

'That must have been very special.'

'Yes it was.   More champagne!'

The drinks party was in full swing, a hundred or so men were mingling, Waffen-SS, SS and Gestapo.   A

147

string quartet played in a corner. Keller stood over by the drinks, chatting to a small group of officers. I headed for the other side of the hall and stood next to a buffet table. I looked down at the copious quantities of rich food. A huge suckling pig seemed to stare at me, an apple wedged in its mouth. I felt like killing myself.

Just then the double doors opened again and seven maids walked in with yellow Stars of David sewn onto their blue uniforms to make me feel even worse. Seven reminders, and these girls were no doubt just the lucky ones, young and pretty. I turned back to the *hors d'oeuvres* on the buffet table. I did feel like killing myself but I was also ravenously hungry. I chose a satay stick of beef dipped in ginger. It was delicious. I took another bite and Keller placed his hand gently on my shoulder.

'You've seen the replacements I take it?', he asked me.

'The replacements?'

'Don't sound so surprised, Schiller. I did say we would be giving you replacements under your contract.'

'That was four years ago.'

'Rome wasn't built in a day.'

I looked at the serving girls in their blue dresses and yellow Stars of David.

'You can have one as your assistant for propaganda duties, but no sex.'

'No sex?'

'No. Fucking Jews is an offence, of either sex, especially for the armed forces.'

Keller winked at me and I nodded.

'Good man.'

He picked up a carving knife and expertly sliced the suckling pig on the table. He laid three slices of gleaming juicy pork on a plate, added some potato and cabbage with a set of tongs and handed the result to me. I looked at the suckling pig next to me and then down at his plate.

'I'm not hungry, Sir'.

'I insist' he replied, 'you won't always be able to eat like this.'

I tentatively picked up a slice of pork with my fork, popped it slowly into my mouth and chewed the whitish meat slowly. Keller watched me closely.

'Well? What did I tell you?', he asked. I nodded and chewed faster, surprised at the taste.

'It's actually rather good.'

'I know my pork, Schiller. Bring your plate. There's someone I want you to meet.'

Keller led me over to a group of five SS officers. One of them was singing a song from a German opera, performing for the others. As we arrived, the group parted to let us through. I looked up at the man with the outstretched arm, his mouth wide open holding a long vibrato note. He was an odd looking man, rather ugly. He was tall and thin with angular limbs and long fingers which were outstretched as he held the note and his eyes bulged. I could tell he was a captain from his insignia, a *Hauptsturmfuhrer*, but he looked just like an over-grown stick-insect.

When he finished and bowed we all clapped our hands and Keller stepped forward.

'Captivating, my friend, captivating. Like a window to another world!', he gushed. 'Julius, this is *Hauptsturmfuhrer* Gerhard Metz. May I present Lieutenant Julius Schiller?'

I bowed stiffly.

'*Herr Hauptsturmfuhrer*,' I replied, clicking my heels.

'Call me Gerhard', Metz implored, taking my hand, his face cracking into a smile, 'and it is an honour to meet you, Herr Schiller. I saw you in that film.'

'*All for Love?*'

'Yes', he said, 'perhaps we could sing a duet together later?' I bowed.

'You were a good duke, Schiller', he continued, 'you exemplify Germany's greatness. Well done on your Iron Cross. I saw the newsreel.'

I bowed again. It seemed everyone had seen it apart from me.

'I think a toast is in order!', cried Keller and he beckoned to one of the girls in blue, a pretty, dark-haired young girl with a yellow star of David. She walked quickly towards us holding a tray stacked with large glasses of golden beer. I saw the look on her face as she approached and I hated myself even more.

Suddenly an SS officer bumped into her and, nervous already, she lost complete control of the tray which flipped up and spilled its liquid contents all over us. The glasses smashed loudly on the floor and the girl was already down there scurrying to pick up the pieces. Everyone turned to see what had happened and I heard a guffaw from across the room. Keller looked down at his drink-spattered uniform, then at the girl.

'You stupid fool!', he bellowed, 'I've just had this cleaned!'

He pulled out a handkerchief and wiped his lapel. The girl crouched down to pick up more pieces of glass, not daring to look up. The beer was dripping off me, I'd had the worst of it, and the ribbon of my Iron Cross was soaked and discoloured. Metz's hand went slowly to his pistol.

'I've shot Jews for less', he said matter-of-factly as he removed the Luger from its holster.

It was the word *Jew* which made me lose my temper. I pulled up the girl by the wrist and slapped her hard round the face. She dropped to her knees, looking up at me, petrified. Keller was wiping the beer from his face with a handkerchief. He looked hard at me.

'Not here, please, Schiller. Not here.'

I grabbed the girl's arm. The wood floor was so highly polished that it was easy for me to drag her along it, away from Metz and Keller and out through the imposing gold-inlaid double-doors of the dining hall, out along the smooth corridor. She was whimpering, petrified.

A General passed me and saluted, but my hands were full and I couldn't salute back as I was dragging the pretty brown-haired girl angrily towards the nearest doors which turned out to be the kitchen. The doors burst open as I dragged her behind me. She couldn't have weighed more than eighty pounds, if that, I thought.

The cooks saw the look in my eye and the girl I was dragging behind me. They ran out almost as soon as I entered, leaving me alone with the girl, the ladles hanging from the ceiling and the mountains of dirty dishes. I looked around and could see another door at the rear of the kitchen.

'Stand up!'

She did what I asked and stood shaking uncontrollably. I knew what she must be thinking. She was thinking she was going to die now in a kitchen. She covered her face and I dragged her through the door into the darkness.

I fumbled for the light switch and a single bulb flooded the tiny room. I moved away from it. The girl was still shaking uncontrollably, her hands still held to her face. She was trying to back away from me but the

151

room was so small that she couldn't go far. I realized I was breathing heavily, still angry, so I calmed myself down by taking slow deep breaths and looked up to see her staring at me.

'Do you understand why I had to hit you?'

She held her hand to her face where I could already see a bruise forming, swollen skin and tissue.

'I said', I repeated, 'do you understand why I had to hit you?'

She looked around her again, trembling uncontrollably.

'Because I dropped the drinks?', she whispered.

'No. I didn't do it for that', I replied.

She stared at me white-faced, like a thinner version of Eva with dark hair, not quite as pretty but pretty enough to make me remember.

'Industrial accident, that's what they said', I murmured, and then I couldn't hold it any longer. I covered my face with my hand and I slid slowly to the floor. I began to cry, for Eva and for the girl here now. Suddenly I heard a metallic scrape, looked up and she was pointing a knife which she must have found on a chopping board.

'Don't come any closer', she whispered, staring at my face.

'I won't move', I replied. 'I hit you to stop Metz shooting you, you know? I had to make it look realistic. I'm sorry if it hurt. I'm not as good an actor as I used to be.'

'I - I know you', she said, her eyes widening. 'I've seen you before.'

I stood slowly, my hands raised in surrender.

'You're the actor. *All for Love*, with Eva Wendt'.

'What's your name?'

'Sarah Bloom', she replied, wide-eyed.

'Well listen to me Sarah Bloom. Eva Wendt is dead. I can't do anything about her, but I can stop them doing the same thing to you. You can come with me and I'll get you out of here.'

'She's dead?', Sarah asked, distracted.

'In an industrial accident. Four years ago.'

'Betty's dead?'

'Betty? How do you know her real name?'

'I…I…met her.'

'Oh my God! When? Where?'

'She was a very nice girl', she stammered. 'She was beautiful…at least, when I saw her last.'

'When? *When* did you see her?'

'I - I'm not sure. It was a long time ago. I met her in thirty-nine on a train with lots of other women. There were no windows and it was stinking and hot. They took our families away. We cried for hours.'

I remembered dancing with Lillie while her brother waltzed with Eva.

'I knew she was that actress, you know, and then she told me her name was Betty Weinstein. Eva was what she called her hair. She wanted a cigarette. I couldn't understand why she was there on the train. I didn't realize she was Jewish.'

'She's a good actress.'

'We were going to a work camp. We got there and then they lined us all up. An SS officer spoke to her and she said something out of line to him.'

'That sounds like her.'

'I was in the back of a truck and when I left her she was still on the ground, and this man, I think his name is Metz or something, was standing over her. But then I went to the camp again a few months later and I'm sure I saw her in the courtyard.'

'Fucking Metz. I'll kill him!'

153

'Metz is here.'

'I know he's here! I'm meant to be duetting with him later.'

'It's called Kithausen, his camp.'

'How far is it?'

'Possibly two or three hours. It's difficult to tell.'

I shut my eyes. Metz would know. Metz would know everything. If she was dead, and Metz had killed her, I would kill Metz and then someone would kill me.

'Sarah, please listen to me. When they told me Eva Wendt was dead they said it was an *industrial accident*. Do you know what that means?'

She looked away from me.

'They did have a furnace at the camp, sir. And a big grey building with no windows.'

'You know the way there?'

'I'm – I'm not sure', she replied, hesitantly.

'I'm Jewish Sarah, just like Betty and just like you.'

'What?'

'Don't say anything. I know how I look. If there's even the remotest chance she's still alive…'

'You're Jewish?'

'Don't worry', I said to the pretty brown-eyed girl. 'I'll look after you.'

***

I rested my hand on Metz's shoulder, gave it a manly squeeze and we filled our lungs for the second verse of a two-part harmony. Metz hammered the piano keys, pounding out the base line. Keller was round the piano with a few others. When Metz opened his mouth he released a strong vibrant tenor, belying the thinness of his stick-insect body and when we finished, the applause was prolonged and hearty.

154

'Beautiful', Keller whispered to me, 'worthy of the finest of opera houses my boy! We must order more beer! That is, Schiller, if you have left us any waitresses!'

Everyone laughed, including me. I rested my hand on Metz's shoulder again, wondering how easy it would be to break his thin neck.

'A toast! To German opera!', I cried, handing Metz a glass. He took it gladly.

'To German opera!', he replied.

We clinked our glasses together and I smiled at the man I wanted to kill.

'You know, sir, I'd been meaning to talk to you.'

'Really, Schiller? Pray what about?'

'Concentration camps. I'm absolutely fascinated by them.'

'They are marvellous places, Schiller. I run Kithausen, you know.'

'Yes sir. Keller told me.'

'Did he? Did he now?' He looked at me carefully. 'What else did he tell you?'

'He told me a woman I once knew, Eva Wendt, was dead. That she died in an industrial accident. I mean, if she were at your camp you would know if she had died or not?'

'Yes, Schiller. I would know.'

'I know she is a Jew, sir, but I found her a most pleasant person. Before I knew, of course, of her background.'

'Really?' *Pleasant*, you say? Well I'm terribly sorry, Schiller, but Keller was right. Eva Wendt is dead.'

I tried to keep hold of my facial muscles but I could feel my mouth twitching. My hand edged towards my pistol. I wanted him dead, just for the way he said it. My voice was low and steady. I held my beer up again and took a quick swig.

'Is it easy to kill a woman, Captain Metz?'

'If you're talking about the delightful Eva Wendt, I wouldn't know, Schiller.'

'But you know what goes on in your camp?'

'Naturally. Everything.'

'So how did she die?'

'If you must know Schiller, she died in childbirth.'

12

Colonel Harvey Watkins stroked his moustache as he sat in first-class watching the glum suburbs of London turn swiftly into the flat fields of Cambridgeshire. British Military Intelligence was headquartered in bland unromantic places with bland unromantic names. Bletchley, for example. Fortunately for Watkins, there were also more pleasant-sounding places. Cambridge, in the fens of East Anglia in the east of England was one such place, an hour's train ride from London's King's Cross or Liverpool Street Stations.

Marjory, his wife, complained bitterly whenever he left her alone in their large house in West Hampstead.

'That man will start up the bombing again', she complained, 'and you said it would be over in two weeks'.

Marjory's eyes narrowed at this point and she would always contrive to look rather hurt. Yes, he had told the woman that it'd be over in two weeks. That had been four years ago. It was now 1944 and in September 1939 they had assumed that it would be all over in fourteen days, not long enough to disturb the shooting season. Colonel Harvey Watkins favoured grouse and pheasant. Not even Hitler could stop that. But they'd all been wrong. Watkins had been moved from counter-intelligence to something called counter-propaganda. It had taken him a few days to work out exactly what it was he was meant to be doing and when he had he still wasn't sure.

The station was crowded with young men in uniform kissing young women goodbye. He knew where the young men were going and he didn't like to think how much emptier the platform would be in a few months. He had his briefcase with three letters stamped on its worn brown leather exterior: M.O.D., standing for Ministry of Defence. Inside the briefcase he'd brought with him the materials that his superior, Brigadier Wittington, had inspected the night before. Things like this did not happen very often but when they did they had a disproportionate effect. The particular matter that Colonel Harvey Watkins had come to discuss today was particularly disproportionate.

Watkins was forty-two, medium height and build and medium everything. He looked quite ordinary, the perfect intelligence officer. He did not stand out on the Cambridge train platform, and he decided to walk the two miles to his destination, it being a fine day and first class having been uncommonly stuffy.

He walked down Hills Road and towards the centre of the university town. He passed Fenner's, Downing and Emmanuel Colleges on Regent Street and found himself on cobblestones, heading for the grandest college of them all, or at least, the one with the grandest chapel. He headed through a four hundred year old door, nodded to one of the bowler-hatted porters and crossed a small internal courtyard with a stone sundial in the centre. Quarter to eleven, Watkins mused. He was late, as usual. He walked towards a grey stoned medieval building and disappeared under an archway.

They were already waiting for him. Archibald Smethers, a corpulent London theatre-critic, Roger Pilkington, a warm smile on his face and a sherry in his hand and two others that Watkins didn't recognize. A small slide projector was set up in front of them and the curtains were already drawn. The room was lit by a single angle-poise lamp on Pilkington's large red leather topped desk.

'Good to see you Watkins', said Pilkington, a historian and senior tutor, languidly, 'I trust you had a pleasant trip.'

'Stuffy', replied Watkins, 'stuffy, hot and the food's no better.'

'No of course not my dear fellow. Perhaps a sherry?'

'Not on duty, Pilkington, thanks all the same.'

'Don't mind if I do?'

Watkins shook his head.

'This is Walther and Rudi', nodded Pilkington to the two young men in drab matching grey suits, white shirts and ties. 'They're Jews. Escaped from Germany in forty-two, been here a year.'

Watkins couldn't help noticing how incredibly thin they were.

'You know Smethers of course.'

Watkins nodded to the corpulent theatre critic.

'We thought we'd compare your material with our material and see if we both came to the same conclusions.'

'Those are my orders too, Pilkington.'

'Good', the historian mused as he sipped his sherry. 'Good show.'

Watkins unlocked his briefcase and removed a manila envelope. He opened it up and removed some acetate slides. He handed them to Pilkington who in turn handed them to the two thin Jews. They studied them in the dim light, passing each acetate from one to the other, silently. Their faces did not register a single emotion. Watkins handed over some six-by-four black and white photographic stills, some of which looked out of focus.

Pilkington unlocked a drawer in his desk and pulled out a large canister of thirty-five millimetre film. It looked slightly singed and battered, as though it had been salvaged from a bonfire. He handed the canister over to Watkins who read the legend at the side. He stood directly next to the desk lamp and turned the silver edge of the canister directly towards the light.

The black felt-tip marker pen was very faint and every other letter was missing. It was written in a Germanic script, loops and crosses virtually obliterating anything vaguely legible. Watkins read it again and pursed his lips. He looked over towards the projector. A young man who looked like a student walked in and was introduced by Pilkington as Philby. He was studying English or law or philosophy at Downing, Pilkington mumbled over his glasses. He knew how to work the projector.

Philby reached over and Watkins handed over the battered film canister. Philby set it down on the table on which the projector stood and carefully opened it with a small penknife that he fished out of a large square belt-buckle. He held the canister very close to his face as he pulled out a roll of celluloid film. He held it gingerly in front of him and pored over an eighteen-inch section, holding it over the desk lamp with a magnifying glass clamped to his eye. Philby nodded at Pilkington and Pilkington nodded towards the screen. Watkins watched the two of them silently. Philby set up the projector, placed the reel of film into the metal housing and connected the power cable. The projector hummed into life, a white light flooding the five foot high screen at one end of the room.

'It'll be a little grainy, sir, I'm afraid', said Philby.

'Don't care', Watkins replied.

Philby fed the reel of film into the gate of the projector and the screen crackled with cue cards counting down from ten to one at one second intervals.

'There's no sound', said Pilkington.

'Don't need it', replied Watkins.

On screen a beautiful country house came into view and then the film jump-cut to a swimming pool. A man swam lengths gracefully. The film jump-cut to the man sitting grinning on the side of the pool, dangling his legs into the water. He had fair hair and looked toned and physically fit, the perfect Aryan specimen. He laughed and a larger older man came into view holding up an Iron Cross towards the camera, then pointing at the perfect Aryan swinging his legs over the side of the pool who waved again at the camera and gave a big thumb's up sign.

'And hold it there', Pilkington said.

The film froze the Aryan's smile and thumb's up.

'It's him', said Watkins, looking again quickly at the acetate in front of him. 'It's definitely him.'

Pilkington looked towards Walther and Rudi. They nodded in unison. Pilkington turned to Smethers, the theatre critic.

'Smethers?'

Smethers turned his corpulent frame away from the screen.

'I can hardly believe it', he said, pulling out a theatre poster from a long cardboard tube, 'but it would appear to be the same man.'

Smethers handed the poster to Philby who placed it next to the screen, side by side with the image of the handsome blonde Aryan dangling his legs into a swimming pool, which I am ashamed to say was me.

'The question is', growled Watkins, 'what are we going to do about it?'

***

In the skies above Germany, a large unmarked British-made aeroplane banked sharply, the noise-dampeners on the four propellers cutting the sound back to little more than a light whisper. Inside the cockpit, the captain and his co-pilot checked the coordinates once more. It had been easy identifiying the location of the photo-shoot, the country house British Intelligence had visited in the past, the country house where the British Foreign Secretary had swum with his German counterpart, belly-flopped into the pool and bagged a few birds at a shoot in the grounds.

The night was cloudy and the plane was covered in non-reflective charcoal-coloured paint which made it virtually invisible. It flew out of radar range – below the Nazi radar-line, an invention which they'd copied from the British – sticking to the open wastelands and lightly-occupied areas. The fuel tank was enormous and range was not a problem. They could fly around for hours, thought Colonel Harvey Watkins as he stroked his moustache, sitting in his jumpsuit towards the rear of the quad-prop.

The plan was a brilliant one, or so they'd all thought. Pilkington had been masterful. They'd worked out that I was Abe Goldstein and had somehow become the German's Waffen-SS poster boy. I was Goebbel's secret propaganda weapon, a movie-star playing out his role in real life. Schiller, perhaps under duress it had been pointed out by Pilkington, was boosting German morale considerably. Apparently I was making heroism possible, selflessness acceptable and dying not an option. Something had to be done and Watkins was going to do it, together with the four young parachute-

162

happy soldiers that he'd been assigned. The war had been going on for too long now. Hitler was being repulsed on various fronts – the Russians in particular were not budging – and anything to hasten the fall of Germany had to be done. If they could somehow get Julius Schiller to reveal himself to be a British citizen and tell the world that he'd been spying for the Brits all along it would be a small but important slap in the face for the Germans, a small easy propaganda victory for the British.

It was much easier to get to someone like me than it was to get to someone like Hitler, Himmler or Goering. I was of no direct military importance and would not be heavily guarded, or indeed guarded at all. Harvey Watkins, like the rest of them, had been tempted to simply have me shot. I was, the possibility of duress aside, a traitor against the King and would and should be hanged by the neck until I was dead.

However, after much debate and on a unanimous vote it had been decided that kidnap was the best option. If I was working under duress surely I'd *want* to be kidnapped, which would make the operation easier. They could always try me for treason after the war was over, Watkins pondered, smoothing down both sides of his moustache. All they had to do was find the bugger.

The aeroplane passed low and to the side of the country house. Through his binoculars he could see lights in the main rooms on the ground floor.

'Coordinates match, sir', called out the captain via the cabin intercom.

'Target eight hundred yards to the East, drop conditions cloudy, wind-speed ten knots, forest cover three hundred yards north.'

Watkins gave the four parachutists a thumb's up. He slid the door of the unpressurised cabin open and looked down at the treetops and woodland clearings. There was a lot of cover. It would be an easy drop.

But then there was something above them, the searing, whining sound of *Messerschmitt* fighters approaching quickly. Watkins gripped the side of the open hatch so tightly his fingers went numb. The German fighters opened fire with their powerful guns, deafening him even through his leather ear-muffs. Bullets ripped through the fuselage and Colonel Harvey Watkins gritted his teeth and jumped just as his aeroplane exploded into a ball of fire and began a swift unplanned descent through a steep burning trajectory. It hit the ground violently and exploded, killing everyone inside instantly.

All that was left after weeks of planning and not inconsiderable cost was the lone parachutist, the one who'd been standing at the door ready to lead them off, and the wind was now carrying Colonel Harvey Watkins, Bachelor of Arts second class, miles off-course and far away from me.

Horst Weber watched the aeroplane explode from the turret of his tank. His unit had been stationed to the North but was now, like the other units, heading West. He saw a flash of light and heard a crash as the aeroplane fell to earth. It was a few miles away. He shielded his eyes from the glare. Two Messerschmitts zoomed overhead, also heading west. Horst Weber watched them pass and as his eyes followed the German fighters he saw a lone parachutist floating behind them, heading for his tank convoy. The parachutist's boots crashed into the ground and the parachute enveloped him, so close to Horst that the silk snagged in his tank tracks.

'*Halt!*', Horst cried. The driver slammed on the brake, stopping inches from the parachutist's head. Horst reached for his *Schmeisser* machine pistol and jumped out. He walked briskly up to the billowing silk and pulled it aside, trying to get to the man who would still be winded from the fall. Horst knelt down and a face lurched into view, a surprised face that was red and black from the explosion. Horst grabbed him by his jump-straps and punched him hard, aiming for his moustache. The man was out cold before he'd had a chance to say a word.

Horst quickly bound him. His driver came out to help. This was perfect, Horst thought, as he inspected the uniform. A British soldier. A senior one as well, judging by the insignia on his epaulettes. It must have been a mission of some importance for a lone British aeroplane to be so far into German territory. He pulled the British soldier into the back of his tank. He could speak good English and he had never interrogated a British soldier before. This man with the moustache who lay in the darkness bound and bruised would be his first subject.

'What is your name?'

Horst Weber looked calmly at the man lying on the metal floor of the tank.

'I repeat. What is your name? What are you doing here? What is your mission?'

Horst brought the butt of his pistol down hard onto Harvey Watkins' ribs. Watkins winced in pain but stared up resolutely at his interrogator. Weber ripped open Watkins' jacket and rifled through his pockets. Still nothing.

'If you do not talk you will be shot', he said calmly. He found a compass and a map with coordinates centred on the lovely country house with the swimming pool. He pulled out an envelope which was heavily-folded, opened it up and studied the contents.

Colonel Harvey Watkins had never been interrogated in a field situation, but he had been on enough training sessions to know never to give away anything, especially one's name. The theory, however, was much easier than the reality.

'Can you explain these to me?', demanded Horst Weber, holding up two photographs. He unfolded the white foolscap-size piece of paper that he had found with them and read it slowly to himself.

'What is *Operation Goldstein*?'

Watkins grunted as Weber hit him again, this time in the face, breaking his nose. The blood streamed down and Watkins's eyes were full of tears. He didn't want to cry but it hurt so damned much he couldn't stop himself.

'I repeat', said Weber, calmly placing the barrel of his *Schmeisser* against Watkins' leg, 'what is *Operation Goldstein*?'

Harvey Watkins was not a coward. He was an intelligent man and he knew he had to think quickly. What did he have to lose? As an officer he would be a prisoner of war, unless he was completely uncooperative. What would Marjory want him to do? Was she still there in West Hampstead, waiting for the horrible little man to drop more of those rockets on her? Was she sipping tea from the Coronation Service her mother had bought them?

'*Don't be a fool*', he could hear her say, '*and remember to tell them you're British.*'

'*Alright*', he thought, '*chin up and let's be smart about it!*' as he felt the tip of the gun-barrel press firmly into the flesh of his forehead.

'Name's Watkins, Harvey Peregrine.'

166

Weber slowly lowered the Schmeisser.

'What rank?'

'Colonel. British army.'

Weber pulled out a pencil and small writing pad.

'What is your mission? What is *Operation Goldstein*?'

Damn it. They wanted Goldstein back, but if he were dead...would it be so bad?

'If I tell you, what will happen to me?'

'I will refrain from shooting you. You will simply become a prisoner of war.'

Watkins had no option. He had no option at all. He better make it good, he thought, as Horst Weber inserted a Russian cigarette into his mouth and lit it for him.

13

A hundred and thirty eager SS and Gestapo officers settled down to watch a screening of rough-cuts of the next instalment of my war progress, filmed that week in the country house. One hundred and thirty men stood as the grainy film bounced around the white wall at the side of the room. I excused myself after performing a lackluster rendition of Wagner with Metz, on the grounds that I was feeling unwell. Actually I was feeling sick to my stomach after what Metz had told me. As I undid the laces of my boots in my room on the second floor, the curtains billowing open in the breeze, I felt very unwell indeed.

If Eva Wendt, *nee* Betty Maude Weinstein had died in childbirth sometime in the last five years then there was a possibility that I was a father. To think that the father might have been someone else was too awful for me to comprehend. Was that what Keller called an industrial accident? What sort of industry was that? I could hear cheers coming from downstairs.

Still in my uniform, the Iron Cross pinned to my chest, I curled myself up into a ball and wept. I wept not just for Eva but for the child that might have been mine. I had no tears for myself, not now. But for my meeting with Hans Bosendorf and my ignorance and greed, the lure of five thousand Marks that were now worthless, I would never have come to Germany, I would never have met Eva and I would never have made a deal with the Waffen-SS to try and save her.

I picked up my pistol. It had a full cartridge and a working firing pin. Had I lost my faith, I wondered? Could I ever think of myself as Jewish, or even human, again? I was one of *them* now. I unlocked the safety catch. If or when the war was over, assuming I was still alive, I could never live in Germany. The Nazis would find out about me sooner or later. There would be no Hans to protect me. Keller and Metz would blow my brains out. The German people would feel cheated. Cheated by a Jew from London. Hitler would probably want to meet me before he ordered my execution. I could never go back to England.

I rocked backwards and forwards. My eyes stared hollowly ahead and the pistol felt heavy in my hand, which started to tremble. It would be so easy, one quick movement and then nothing to worry about ever again. If there were a heaven, I hoped I might see Eva there, unless I was destined for the other place. And maybe our baby, too. The longer it went on, the longer the charade continued, the more I was in danger of sucking on fire and brimstone instead of milk and honey.

I stopped rocking and slowly raised the pistol to my head, a single tear rolling down my cheek. No family, no-one to mourn me. They'd have to say I died bravely in the field and award me another Iron Cross. Better, I thought, than telling the German people the truth, the simple fact that I'd blown my brains out in a second floor room over a white bed-spread. One pull. One squeeze. I could do it. I could do it.

But then, if I *knew* I could do it, why do it *now*? I had nothing to lose by waiting a day or two, and first I had to know for sure. I needed to know what had happened to her. I needed to see it with my own eyes. I needed to get out of this ridiculous country house and find

Kithausen Concentration Camp. Find Eva, or a record of her. We were still engaged. Until I saw her, dead or alive, I could not believe a word Metz or Keller had said. I could only believe Sarah Bloom. I replaced the safety catch of my pistol.

***

My hand covered Sarah Bloom's mouth as she slept. She looked up scared from her tiny garret nook which consisted of a flea-bitten mattress resting on a ledge by a circular window on the fifth floor of the country house.

'Don't make a sound. I'm not going to hurt you', I whispered. 'I need your help.'

She nodded and I handed her a woman's Waffen-SS uniform. She looked up at me with her big brown eyes and I felt a pang of guilt. Sarah Bloom was a very attractive woman. With a hat to cover her brown hair, at a distance and under cover of darkness she could easily pass for Eva.

'I think it'll fit', I said. 'You're her size. They had stacks of spares downstairs.'   She looked at me nervously.

'What do you want me to do?'

'Keller said I could pick one of the girls as Eva's replacement under my contract and I'm picking you. There's something I need to do.'

'In the middle of the night?'

'We'll be back by morning.'

'Where are we going?'

'Where do you think? You told me it was a two hour drive.'

'No!'

'Yes! Kithausen, and you're navigating.'

We walked quickly towards the rear stairwell at the end of the corridor and flitted quietly down the cold stone steps. Everyone was still in the dining hall. The rough-cut screening had finished and cheering and singing drifted out from the open windows. I looked at my watch. It was approaching midnight. I stood at the foot of the stairs and peered out. Three or four sentries were smoking and drinking, passing a bottle amongst themselves.

I walked out, head held high, towards a jeep parked out in front, a large duffel bag over my shoulder. Sarah walked stiffly behind me dressed in her Waffen-SS uniform. I hopped into the jeep and placed the duffel bag in the back. Sarah opened the passenger door and got in next to me. The gates were open. I started the engine and drove quickly through them and out into the night. The sentries barely turned from their cigarettes and bottle of rum.

The road was unfamiliar apart from the potholes which I remembered from our violent drive on the way here. Sarah held a map in front of her and passed it to me. Finding this place in the day would be difficult enough and Sarah had only been there once before. The Germans preferred to hide their concentration camps, almost embarrassed at what awful places of death they had created and you needed a special map to find one. The camp was marked on the official SS map that I had with me, but someone had taken down all the road signs and so all we could see were tracks and unmade roads in front of us with the headlights on, and nothing with the headlights off.

I checked my watch again. It was twelve-thirty. We'd been going for about half an hour and Sarah hadn't said a word. I took a quick look over to her. I could swear she looked excited rather than scared.

'I don't know what's going on, Sarah, but we're going to find out. If you saw the look in Metz's eyes you'd know what we're doing here. He's lying. Someone's lying.'

She glanced nervously at me. I tried to smile.

'Don't worry, you look fine. Look in the bag behind you.'

She reached for the duffel bag on the back seat.

'There should be everything we need. And an extra uniform, just in case.'

She uncovered the bag and the extra uniform. The bag fell open to reveal a sub-machine gun and a pistol, together with some ammunition. She looked worriedly at me.

'Just in case', I repeated.

I drove on and caught a flash of her face in the moonlight. She was staring straight ahead of her, biting her lip.

'You know, Sarah,' I said, 'you've got great bone structure.'

***

Somewhere else in Europe, a large tent in the centre of a frozen wasteland was billowing in strong wind. It was one o'clock in the morning and the tent was the site of a German field command post, deep into Russian territory. Outside sat a German army truck, a black Mercedes limousine and two shivering sentries. Inside the tent a telephone started to ring. Four senior German Wehrmacht and Waffen-SS Officers shivered. A war-games board was laid out across a map of Western Russia on a wooden card-table. There were little model German and Russian tanks and little model concentration camp markers. An Enigma machine sat next to the table on a metal stand.

A craggy-faced Wehrmacht General picked up the telephone.

'*Jawohl?*'

He listened for a moment. His face fell.

'Fine...Fine...Yes. Yes. Goodbye.'

He put the phone down and turned to the four lower-ranked generals in the tent.

'Herr General? What are our orders?', asked one of them.

The General exhaled loudly. He knocked all the model German tanks onto the floor. He gathered the cardboard concentration camp markers on an ashtray and set fire to them with a lighter. They burned very easily.

'*Those* are our orders', snapped the General.

'Herr General?'

'I need you to send this message to all our unit commanders.'

The Enigma operator sat expectantly by his machine. He took out the stick of gum he was chewing and stuck it to the side of the grey metal.

'By order of the Fuhrer, Adolf Hitler', the General began in a quiet monotone, 'all unit commanders are instructed as follows...'

***

Back at the country house the clock stood at twenty minutes past one in the morning. Keller was a unit commander and he had just received a most disturbing communication from field command. He stood now before a hundred Waffen-SS men, next to him a grim-faced Captain Gerhard Metz.

'I am sorry to report that things are not going as well as our propaganda department would have liked', Keller intoned somberly. The men murmured quietly to each other. Keller looked down at the paper in his hands.

'Our instructions are clear. The battle for Russia is not going well. We are in danger of having to retreat – perhaps I should say *regroup* – behind pre-existing German borders. However, we have been ordered to destroy all concentration camps in the East as quickly as possible. The first camp on our list is not far from here.' Keller turned theatrically to Metz.

'Captain Metz will brief you, as that is his camp. It is called Kithausen.' Keller motioned again with his hand. 'Captain Metz?'

Metz pulled a chair towards him and stood on it. Although he was tall he liked to be able to see all the men's faces.

'Now listen carefully. We must leave no traces of any of our special programmes.' Metz nodded deferentially to Keller.

'Herr Keller has just given you our orders, and this is what we're actually going to do...'

***

Trucks and jeeps were mobilizing fast. The Waffen-SS walked round carrying clipboards and shouting. Soldiers ran to their transports. The Germans were on the retreat. It was horrible news thought Keller as he watched Metz standing with a clipboard and barking out orders. An SS private walked out from the main building with six terrified Jewish serving-girls in their blue uniforms. He led them straight up to Metz.

'Sir? The Jews. I can only find six, sir, not seven.'

174

'Not good enough. We're a jeep down, too, soldier. I suggest you look for both or I'll have you court-martialled.'

'Yes sir'.

'Hold on hold on hold on.' Metz turned round and ticked something on his clipboard. 'If there's room, put them in a truck. If not, shoot them.'

'Yes sir.'

Corporal Kretzmar gunned the jeep up to Metz and screeched to a halt on the gravel.

'I have the extra supplies, Sir', he volunteered.

'What?', said Keller.

'Under the blanket in front of you Sir.'

Keller lifted the blanket to reveal a large canister with a skull and crossbones and the words 'POISON - Zyklon B'. Keller was in the passenger seat and he leaned out to Metz, beckoning him over with a gloved hand. Metz leant over and cocked his head to one side.

'Metz - I'm a man down. It's Schiller. Have you seen him?'

'No. He wasn't there for the screening. Said he was ill. I'll keep an eye out for him, Wilfred'.

They saluted each other and Keller's jeep drove out of the gates. Metz turned back to the house, genuinely worried about my welfare.

***

It was well past two o'clock in the morning when I brought the jeep to a standstill outside Kithausen. We looked up at the wrought-iron sign in black, lit by watchtower lights, above the main gates. *Arbeit Macht Frei.* The words were a sick joke. Sarah shuddered and I put my finger to my lips.

'Let me do the talking', I whispered. Sarah nodded, wide-eyed. I drove up towards the gate and stopped by the wooden sentry-box, beaming. A young sentry stepped out pointing a rifle into my face.

'Identify yourself!', he barked. I leaned over until the light caught my face and I smiled broadly. The sentry peered at me and my Iron Cross.

'Mein Gott!', he exclaimed excitedly. 'Julius Schiller! The movie star!'

The sentry saluted and I raised my palm majestically, Hitleresque once again. Sarah sat frozen next to me, capable of nothing other than a fixed stare.

'At ease, soldier. It's just me and my secretary, Helga Braun', I said lazily. Sarah nodded and forced a smile. The sentry nodded quickly. 'If you'll just let us in.'

The sentry was bursting.

'You are shooting a newsreel, here, yes Herr Schiller?', he gabbled.

'I'm not at liberty to say, soldier', I replied smoothly, winking at him for good measure.

'Of course not sir!'

The sentry winked back at me and unlocked the gate.

'Captain Metz is not here right now, sir, but his office is on the first floor in the block to your right.'

'Thank you, soldier. I'll remember your face. In this business you never know.'

I saluted once more and drove the jeep through the gates and into the concentration camp. The sentry saluted me proudly as we passed. He went back to his wooden sentry box and picked up a field radio. He clicked the transmit button and fiddled with the tuning dial.

'Hey, Jurgen! Come in Jurgen!'

'Jurgen here!'

'Jurgen, listen to this!' The sentry could hardly contain his excitement. 'You'll never guess who just came through here...'

***

Metz and Keller both cursed the bumps in the dark country road. Their convoy of three jeeps, an armoured car and an army truck full of Waffen-SS soldiers ploughed roughly over potholes and rocks towards its destination. It was ten past two in the morning and it was a cloudy night with little sign of the moon. In the first jeep, Keller sat soberly. He had always known there was a chance they might lose the war but the enforced destruction of their programmes confirmed the reality of the larger political situation. In the third and last jeep, bringing up the rear of the convoy, Metz was speaking into a field radio pressed tightly against his ear.

'Thank you Jurgen. Most enlightening. Over and out.'

He removed his finger from the *'speak'* button and smoothed away the bead of sweat from his brow. He thought for a moment and depressed the *'speak'* button again, tuning in to a new frequency this time.

'Doctor Werner? Metz here.'

'Yes Captain Metz?', crackled the young doctor's voice nervously from the radio.

'About the programme. I want you to listen very carefully...plan B...all of them, same dose. Do you copy?'

The radio crackled loudly, the static overwhelming.

Inside the sick bay at Kithausen Concentration Camp the clock stood at twenty-five minutes past two in the morning and Nurse Gortz was shaking uncontrollably. The doctor had been able to give the order but was unable to carry it out. He had left it to her, to the young woman from Hanover with a child in the care of its grandmother and a dead husband. She stood by the large metal medicine tray with a small vial in each hand.

In her left hand was a heavy tranquilizer, as if they needed it she thought, looking across at the seven women as they lay asleep in their beds. That poor woman. The one in the middle. All the other womens' beds had changed owner many times, but not the one in the middle. It had been a special request from a Nazi tank commander with a very low Party number. The woman had nearly died in childbirth, some four years ago, but she wasn't to be so fortunate this time.

Nurse Gortz looked at her right hand and the little vial containing brown liquid marked *Poison*. There was a skull and crossbones plastered on the side. She looked back nervously towards the seven women and remembered all that she had learned at nursing college.

Two years of studying, she mused as she went back to the metal tray to fill the syringes, two years caring for young and old, helping people to survive, to recuperate. Helping people to forget trauma, to deal with pain. They had put on little shows, little playlets for the old people in the Nursing Home on the outskirts of Dusseldorf. She had enjoyed those, enjoyed learning lines and trying to make someone believe something that was not.

Droplets of dark liquid squirted out of the top of the syringe and her hand trembled. She looked up towards where she imagined God was looking down on her. Nurse Gortz had been brought up a Catholic although she had kept quiet about her beliefs since the outbreak of war. No. There was only one belief that could reign in Hitler's Germany and it had nothing to do with God.

Would He forgive her?

14

I couldn't help noticing the similarities between Kithausen Concentration Camp and Bosendorf Studios. The same grey buildings, albeit smaller here, the same barbed wire, even the same guards, just like the two who were now running towards me.

I jumped out quickly from the jeep and Sarah opened her door, watching me. I grabbed the large duffel bag from the back and slipped it over my shoulder. The guards stopped by the jeep and saluted.

'At ease, soldiers'.

One turned to the other and grinned.

'Told you it was him!'

'We'll be on the news, Christian. Can I have your autograph Lieutenant Schiller?'

I smiled stiffly and I signed my name on the back of an SS rations book. The place smelt of death and despair. Now that I'd finally got here, thirty newsreels later, I was terrified of what I might find.

'Come on', I said to Sarah as I watched the guards disappear with my autograph. 'We haven't much time.'

I found the door to the main block open and marched inside towards Metz's office. I needed to find the camp records, the lists of those alive and the list of those already dead. The records would tell me everything I needed to know before I could risk walking around the camp at night searching for one person without raising any suspicion. The camp was very large, it could take us hours to search every block and I was worried about alerting the guards to anything odd.

Sarah was good cover. A man and a woman always looked less threatening than one man alone, even if he was a German movie star.

Metz's office was clearly marked. The man was obviously vain, a sign in brass hanging on the metal door clearly announcing the occupant's position as *Kommandant* and conveniently omitting to mention his SS rank of *Hauptsturmfuhrer*, a lowly captain, which was not nearly as impressive.

I opened the door slowly only to be greeted on the far wall by a stag's head mounted on a dark-wood plaque, a boar's-head similarly-mounted and a number of framed photographs of Hitler and separate photos of Metz. The smell was musty and gave me the impression the taxidermist hadn't used enough embalming fluid. A fox-fur hung on a chair to the right, and next to it were two large metal filing cabinets. A key rested in the top cabinet.

'Eva Wendt or Betty Maude Weinstein', I said. 'Find her here, then we'll find her out there'.

Sarah bit her lip as she looked at the tall filing cabinets.

'I'll do the left, you do the right', I added, pulling opening a shelf.

I looked up at the clock. It was half past two. We needed to be out of here and poolside before sunrise.

I opened the left-hand side of the two filing cabinets, as Sarah had suggested. No, no that wasn't it. The personnel files of the SS guards might make for interesting reading but I hadn't the time. A section on automobiles. Electricity and gas costs. Transport schedules. What about the women? I began tearing through the rest of the drawers. Sickness billets. Travel requests. Metz's daily reports to headquarters. Factory productivity schedules. No mention of inmates' names.

'Germans love their lists. It must be here somewhere!'

Sarah held out a thick sheaf of paper towards me with very fine print.

'I've got something.'

I grabbed it quickly from her. Ten minutes had passed. They'd send someone up soon to ask us if we wanted a coffee, or someone would want an autograph. I pored through the list. It was a list of workers, a list with a number of manuscript amendments and rubbings out. The print was so small and I didn't want to use more than the emergency lighting to read by so as not to attract attention. I turned to the last few pages, to the w, x, y, z section. *Warkowski, Weinstein, Wessel. Weinstein? Weinstein?* No. It was a Rachel Weinstein. What about Wendt? Nothing. I replaced the file in the metal cabinet and gave it a kick for good measure. Sarah looked around nervously.

'Maybe she used another name?', she suggested.

'*Another* one? No. No, I think it would have been Wendt or Weinstein. No, we'll have to go to plan B.'

'Plan B?'

'We better stock up, just in case.'

I looked towards a metal cupboard marked '*Ammunition - Danger!*', opened it slowly and removed a wooden ammunition box marked '*SS*'. I levered off the top, emptied the box onto the floor and a lump of straw fell out. I peered into the straw looking for bullets. I picked another box but there was only straw and firing pins. Sarah watched me nervously. I looked up at the clock. Nearly fifteen minutes had passed. How long would it take to search the camp? I went over to Metz's desk and forced open a drawer with a knife. Inside was a large set of keys.

'We can say we wanted to see what a real camp looked like.'

I grabbed a torch from Metz's desk.

'You ready?'

Sarah nodded grimly, wondering, as she looked at my increasingly desperate face, what I would do when Eva Wendt wasn't there.

The bunch of keys was enormous and there must have been thirty similarly shaped small keys alongside thirty similarly shaped large ones. Silver or brass? I stood by the door to the first grey prison block and turned the key in the lock. Nothing. Nor the second. I looked about, my sub-machine gun hanging low over my shoulder. Sarah stood behind me, keeping watch. Five more keys and then the key turned in the lock. The door opened slowly and I walked inside. Sarah took one more look back and followed me, closing the door behind her.

To the few women still too frightened to sleep, the tall figure of a Waffen-SS officer filling the doorway made them pretend that they were. They lay on racks of beds, ragged poorly-made wooden pallets stacked one on top of the other and side by side, so close that they had to climb over at least ten people to get in or out. I shone the beam from my torch onto their weary lined faces, young faces aged by the work and by the promise of death, desperately trying to find the woman whose name hadn't been on the list but that I prayed was still alive.

'I'm looking for Eva Wendt. Also known as Betty Maude Weinstein', I said as loudly as I dared.

Out of perhaps a hundred women, thirty were now awake. Sarah felt too ashamed to emerge from my shadow. She at least had been allowed to eat and sleep but it didn't look as if these women had been afforded either luxury.   I shone my torch into a sad woman's eyes.

'You? Do you know her?'

She was probably no more than twenty-five, but she looked closer to fifty.   She shook her head, her eyes standing out from her skull and unblinking.

'You?   Have you heard the name?   Eva Wendt? Betty Maude Weinstein?'

Another shriveled sunken-eyed woman shook her head. I wondered if *she* looked like this now, if I would ever recognize her, her hair shorn, like these women, her skin taut and lined, her eyes dulled by the constant threat of death. I had not seen her for a very very long time.

More women shook their heads. No-one spoke a word. No-one questioned me as to why I was looking for this woman in the middle of the night.   The only sounds in the grim dormitory were coughing, wheezing and the rustling of ragged bed-clothes.   I looked again at their faces, moving the torch from left to right and back again, out to the back and to the sides, trying to see every face, hoping, hoping I did not know what. Sarah's hand on my shoulder made me jump.

'We should go.'

I turned and nodded to her and suddenly the whole thing looked futile. There were thirty blocks and I hadn't seen her for five years.

'I worked with her', said a woman from somewhere in the darkness.

I turned to see where the voice was coming from. I shone my torch towards the rear, searching, craning my head out over the barely-breathing bodies.

'I worked with her', came the voice again, this time a little more insistently.

My light fixed on a single face, at the same time young and old, at the same time alive and dead. I clambered swiftly over the beds, desperately trying not to hurt anyone. The women parted to make a way through for me. I reached the voice and squatted down beside a young woman.

'I worked with her', repeated the young woman that had sat next to Eva in the ammunition line at the armament factory, the young woman who had hidden firing pins in her apron to use to pack with straw instead of bullets.

'Do you know where she is?', I asked gently.

The young woman nodded her head slowly and then stared at me, trance-like, just as she'd stared at Eva.

'You're *him*, aren't you?'

'I probably am', I replied, trying to smile.

'She was shot.'

My head slumped.

'You *are* him.'

I didn't look up but nodded my head, sadly. The young woman scratched hers, nervously.

'They took her to the sick-bay. The block at the end.'

'When?'

'A long time ago.'

There were no clocks. *A long time ago* could mean three weeks or five years.

'Thank you', I said quietly as I stood. She'd been shot. That didn't sound like an industrial accident. Neither did it sound like childbirth.

'Come on Sarah. Let's go. And thank you again'.

I clambered back slowly over the beds, retracing my steps and joined Sarah by the door. When this was all over, when someone came to find these women, how many of them would still be alive? What would one name, one woman, one bottle-blonde Jewess matter? I shut the door softly behind me.

The only movement in the courtyard was the sentries, and I saluted them once more as I headed for the block towards the end. We had to be quick now. It was nearly half-past three in the morning and it was a two hour drive back. I could hear the heels of Sarah's shoes clip-clopping on the concrete. We passed four blocks, five, six, seven, each housing countless more women on the verge of starvation. I looked down at the Iron Cross flapping on my tunic. I had never felt so guilty in my life.

I wished I could save everyone in here, all the Jews like me, all helpless, but I was only one man and if I could save *her* then it would be a miracle. The red and white cross above the door gave it away. I inhaled deeply and opened the door, one hand on my sub-machine-gun. Sarah followed me in, hoping.

The room was dark. My eyes adjusted to the light slowly. There were seven beds against a wall and seven figures lay in them. There was no movement from any of the beds. I could hear no breathing. Each of the figures had closely cropped hair. I could still not tell if they were men or women. I walked past each bed and stopped at the bed in the middle. Sarah was next to me.

It was her, Eva Wendt, nee Betty Maude Weinstein, formerly the blondest, most beautiful movie star in all of Germany.

'My God...what have they done to you?' I blurted out.

Her body was now pale and lifeless. Her eyes were sunk deep into their sockets and her skin was stretched taut over her cheekbones. I should have believed Keller. I should have believed Metz. They may have gilded the truth but the truth was clear and plain and right before my eyes. Eva Wendt was dead.

Sarah rested her hand on my shoulder.

'I'm so sorry', she murmured.

I shook my head and dropped to my knees.

'No. No. No. No!'

My hand reached out to touch her face one last time, one last memory. I was too late. The tears welled in my eyes as I struggled deep into my thoughts, deep into the grief I had already felt but had hoped was in vain. And then, obliterating everything else, a high-velocity bullet hit me square between the shoulder blades, burying itself deep into my right side.

I sank to the floor, almost in slow-motion, dying for a forty-sixth time. The side of the metal bed loomed up to my face and my chin took the full force of it. The floor was smooth. I could hear my own breathing and the smell of ammonia wafted around me. Every breath hurt. I reached to my side and pressed my hand there. When I removed it and held it up to my face I saw that it was covered in blood.

I heard another bang, and then another, the explosions of sound echoing around my throbbing skull and then something large and heavy fell on top of me. Instinctively I pushed it off and found myself looking straight into the dead staring eyes of Sarah Bloom, blood seeping quickly from a hole in the middle of her forehead. The pain came now, quickly and brutally, bringing me out of my state of shock and back to the smoothly polished floor of the sick-bay. I turned my head to one side and there in the doorway was Captain Gerhard Metz holding a smoking machine pistol straight at me, straight at the man Metz had duetted with earlier that evening.

He marched swiftly over to me, removed the sub-machine gun from my shoulder and the pistol from my holster. He pulled my duffel bag away and held a *Schmeisser* machine pistol right over my head.

'I am terribly sorry I had to shoot you, Schiller, but I could not take a risk that you would not have shot me.'

The pain was quickening my senses now, bringing me out of the shock. I must fight to control it.

'We would have overlooked it, Schiller. Running off in the middle of the night with a Jewess and a jeep is not a crime. Looking for a Jewess is not a crime, either, despite the fact that you did not believe me when I told you she was dead.'

'You killed her!'

'Do you not want to know why I had to shoot *you*?'

'I'm sure you'll think of a reason.'

'You're not dead. Get up.'

I struggled to my feet. Metz looked dispassionately at Sarah and the seven motionless women.

'Spared the agony of the gas chamber', he said, holding an empty bottle of poison, a skull and cross-bones printed on the side of it. I stared open-mouthed at the bottle, an evil little vial just like those we used to use on stage.

'You fucking bastards! Liars! *Saftsack*! You'll fry in hell you fucking - '

'Outside. I want Keller to hear this.'

Metz shoved his pistol into my back and I walked slowly ahead, limping, to the door, holding my side. I wanted to kill him so much it hurt more than the bullet-wound. I stopped and held onto the frame for support. I turned back one last time to look at Sarah and then at Betty Maude, as they lay together in death.

'Move!' barked Metz as he shoved me hard out of the door and slammed it behind us.

Mayhem greeted me outside in the courtyard. All the powerful searchlights in the towers surrounding the camp were switched on and their massive bulbs flooded the dull grey buildings with their harsh glare. I stumbled forward, pushed by the barrel of the pistol towards a jeep across the courtyard. I could see Keller sitting there imperiously, watching developments and barking orders.

Around us, shepherded by teams of SS foot-soldiers, hundreds of women were screaming and pushing as they were formed into a long line starting from the middle of the courtyard and ending with a window-less single-level building at the back of the compound. Snatches of their screams assaulted me as I was pushed forward, my wound leaving droplets of blood along the earth in my wake.

'I beg you please, sir, please don't!'

'Fur Gott, Gott sei Dank! Bitte, bitte!'

'Hilf mir!'

'Nein nein!'

They were going to the gas chamber. It was four o'clock in the morning at Kithausen Concentration Camp and someone had decided to kill all the Jews tonight, including me. The screams and wails of the women around me were met with rifle butts and boots. They were little more than walking, screaming skeletons. Lights criss-crossed the courtyard, catching faces, confused and scared. I looked up at the nightmare before me. I would be with Eva soon enough.

Keller's face came into view, hard, cold, staring. His black-gloved hand slapped me hard round the face. We were standing near the middle of the courtyard, Keller's jeep in the eye of the storm that whirled around us, the hundreds of women being marched to their deaths.

Metz pressed his pistol deep into my back, forcing me to stand straight.

'This is very disappointing, Schiller', said Keller. 'Very disappointing. I'm afraid you will have no special treatment.'

'Why are you doing this?', I gasped, 'What - what have I...done?'

Keller picked off the Iron Cross from my tunic.

'Captain Metz received a number of radio communications tonight, *Schiller*. One interested him more than the others. He knew you were coming here in order to look for Eva Wendt. I understand you found her?'

I stared coldly at him, feeling weak suddenly from loss of the blood that continued to flow steadily from the wound in my side.

'Remove his uniform. Give me his dog-tags!', ordered Keller. Corporal Kretzmar saluted and began to strip me of every vestige of the Waffen-SS. He ripped off my dog-tags and handed them to Keller.

'You should be shot on the spot!', he shouted. 'You fooled me, you fooled everyone. You and that trickster Bosendorf. You are both going to pay for it, believe me. Hitler wants to meet you both in Berlin.'

They could do with me what they wanted. I just wanted to sleep. I was powerless to stop them and I was conscious enough to know that if I did not receive medical treatment soon I would bleed to death.

'You have committed treason', continued Keller, incensed. 'Treason against the German people!'

He hit me again, a hard slap to the other cheek. I crumpled slowly to the ground. Corporal Kretzmar removed my boots and the last of my uniform, leaving me shivering on the ground dressed in a white vest and underpants, both soaked in blood. All I could see in front of me was the shuffle of women's feet towards the gas chamber.

Metz's pistol did not waver. He knelt over me and spat in my face.

'We captured a British colonel who revealed, just before he died, that your name is *Abraham Goldstein* and that you are a British Jew.'

I think I may have smiled. Nothing they could say to me mattered. Two men pulled me, a dead weight, into the back of Keller's jeep.

'Dress the wound', someone said.

A man tended to me in the back of the jeep, sterilizing the wound and wrapping it tightly with a bandage from a field kit. I'd had a good run, *a good innings* as they used to say in England. I was feeling sleepy now. Harry, the doorman at the *Albany Theatre* in Piccadilly, was waving goodbye to me. But I wasn't Julius Caesar any more. I'd done my forty-five performances. There wasn't an audience of seven hundred waiting expectantly for me to die. There were just screaming women and flames licking up from the grey buildings. The SS were destroying the camp, razing it to the ground. The gas chamber was crammed full and the women who hadn't made it in were being gunned down, their corpses thrown onto the flames of the burning buildings. It was hell. I was in hell, I thought as my eyes started to close, my head heavy. I found a resting place for it on a blanket on the floor of the jeep.

Keller sat in the passenger seat, the battle in Russia lost. The order to destroy the camps, tonight. Schiller, running off to find a dead woman. The British airman, found by a tank commander who revealed his mission was to kill Julius Schiller. Goebbels was already hatching a plan, he was sure, a way of turning things round. Hitler and Himmler were too clever for the Allies. Too clever for Abraham Goldstein. The German people wanted a hero. They would give them a hero. Julius Schiller would die a hero's death and his identity would die with him, just as the British airman – Watkins, Metz had said his name was - had been *shot whilst trying to escape.* Keller smiled. He liked working under pressure. He looked behind him at Abe Goldstein. He had passed out. He grabbed the field radio once more and tuned the dial.

'Keller here. Keller here. Respond. Respond, over.'

The radio crackled.

'Respond. Keller here. Keller – '

'Reading you loud and clear, Keller', blared a harsh voice. 'Is camp sector six mark one liquidation accomplished?'

'Yes, Herr General. The Jews are in the chamber. The buildings are burning. We have captured Goldstein. We're ready- '

A loud wave of static erupted from the radio, so loud that Keller pulled off his headphones. He turned down the volume and replaced them.

'Herr General - can you repeat that please?'

Suddenly a huge explosion rocked the whole camp. The main building seemed to dissolve before Keller's eyes and fly up in pieces towards his jeep.

'Down!', he screamed.

Earth and bits of concrete covered him. Metz ran towards him, finished with supervising the administration of Zyklon B poison gas into the special vents on the roof of the grey windowless chamber.

'Wilfred! Tanks!', he shouted as he jumped in next to Keller. 'It's the Russians - T-thirty-fours. We must leave *now!*'

Behind them, the remaining SS foot-soldiers streamed into a truck, its engine revving loudly.

'Did you hear that?', screamed Keller into the radio. No answer. He turned to the men running from the scene of the blast.

'Retreat! Retreat! *Schnell!*'

As the men clambered into the truck, Keller heard the whistle of a shell, a dull low whistle. He ducked and there was another explosion. He looked up slowly. The truck-full of SS soldiers was no more. The camp was burning and Keller realized that Metz had already put the jeep into first gear and was heading towards the gates.

'Go! Go!', Keller shouted as Metz gunned the jeep and it sped out of the camp gates with me lying unconscious in the back.

The tank-fire seemed to intensify and Metz had his foot flat on the floor, taking the jeep, which could do no more than sixty miles an hour, to its maximum. The two Germans bounced in their seats, tearing over the potholes and heading away from the source of the fire, towards the nearest German tank unit which was only a couple of hours away. As the burning camp dwindled into the distance behind them, Keller and Metz began to breathe more normally.

Keller threw a quick look at the unconscious traitor in the back. Me. I was on my way to Berlin to meet Hitler at last. A third explosion erupted a long way behind us and a ball of flame filled the night-sky. Keller and Metz turned to look behind them, and then back to each other. Slowly, a smile crept over Metz's thin-lipped face.

'I think we made it', he blurted out. With only one hand on the wheel, he patted Keller's knee and smiled. 'We made it, Wilfred.'

A big smile swept across Keller's face. They *had* made it. They would be with Horst Weber's tank unit in less than two hours. Thank God they'd refueled back at camp. They'd be back safe within a day, and then he would deliver this imposter to Goebbels and Hitler. He would no doubt get another medal. Metz too.

Keller looked at him as he drove manically down the bumpy country lane. They could not afford to use their headlights for fear of being spotted, but Metz appeared to be comfortable with driving in the dark. Keller checked the map he held in front of him with a small search-light, crossing off road-junctions in pencil as they passed them. He had jettisoned the field radio. All of its circuits had blown on the second explosion. All they needed, he thought, was a compass and fuel in the tank, and they had both. He wasn't hungry, he wasn't thirsty, he didn't care that visibility was close to zero. A dark night was better for them. And then he held his breath as the unmistakeable rumble of a tank a few hundred yards away broke the silence.

'Metz? Metz? Do you hear that?'

'Of course I do. I just can't see it. Use these.'

Metz scrabbled about under his seat and threw a small pair of binoculars towards Keller. Keller put them up to his face and his expression turned from one of curiosity to abject fear. He could see something large looming ahead of him in the darkness. And now they could both hear the sound of a turret, bearing a massive gun, ratcheting round to face the speeding jeep with the two SS officers and their prisoner.

'Wilfred?', Metz asked nervously. 'What do we do now?'

Keller put down his binoculars and stared straight ahead.

'*Sheisse!*'

Metz took his hands off the wheel and held them up to cover his face as he saw the flash of a tank's gun less than a hundred yards away. It was to be the last thing that either Wilfred Keller or Gerhard Metz would ever see.

We would all be missing our appointment with the Fuhrer.

15

Hans Bosendorf was on the run. He was sixty-four years old, it was July 1944 and he was wanted for treason. Pictures of his face adorned nearly as many walls as that of Adolf Hitler. He had escaped from the Studios a week before. Luckily a friend had warned him that a tank commander somewhere in Russia had uncovered a plot to kidnap Julius Schiller.

'And the funny thing is', Hans's old friend had said on the telephone, 'apparently his real name is Abe Goldstein.'

The second Hans heard those two words his bag was packed. He'd already spent many nights looking at the globe in his office, trying to work out where in the world he could go when the house of cards came tumbling down on Germany. He had not thought that the cards would be tumbling down just on *him*.

It was approaching six o'clock in the morning and Hans's hair had been died black. He was sitting on the only platform at a desolate railway station in the Pyrenees, right on the border between France and Spain. It may have been July but the temperature was hovering around three degrees Celsius. He had had to ditch his camel hair coat, and the leather-soled shoes had been too impractical. He wore hiking boots and a thick black bomber-jacket. He had a woolen cap pulled down over his face and the beginnings of a beard. His passport, the one he had paid dearly for, showed him to be Julio Andres Garcia, a Spaniard, aged sixty-six, from Valencia. If he could get there, to that massive port on the east coat of Spain, there would be a boat that could take him on the long journey across the Atlantic, heading south towards Venezuela. He would work as a grizzled old deck hand, slopping out the latrines and polishing the floors if necessary. He didn't care what he did, because he didn't want to die.

The sun was coming up slowly over the snow-capped mountains, warming the air gradually. Hans was thankful it was July and not January. He would surely have frozen to death up here. The train was due to arrive in forty minutes. He checked his *Lange und Sohne* watch. He knew it was dangerous to keep it but it had been a present from his father and he could not bear to part with it. His money belt contained pesetas for Spain, francs for France and even some US dollars. He also had a small leather pouch which he kept in his underwear that contained fifteen brilliantly-cut diamonds. They would help him survive in Venezuela. Or maybe he would head further south, to Argentina or Uruguay? He wondered if any other Germans would have the same idea. Broadly-sympathetic right-wing regimes thousands of miles away, warm air, clear skies and blue sea were very attractive when the alternative was a battlefield somewhere in Russia.

Hans blew on his fingers and rubbed them together. Ten minutes to go. He tried not to think of what he had done. He was not proud of himself. Until 1939 he had been a film director, but for the following five years he had become a stooge of the Third Reich. He did not feel remotely guilty about Abe Goldstein. He'd given him a chance and the boy blew it by joining the military and getting caught out. If anything, Hans rued, he should hate him, because Abe Goldstein was the reason Hans Bosendorf was on the run. *All for Love*, Hans rued, *All for Love*.

He tried not to think about Eva Wendt. If only she'd told him, he kept repeating to himself over and over, if only she'd trusted him. They'd still be there now instead of....Hans didn't like to think about it. Life was depressing enough. Perhaps the women would be pretty in South America he wondered as he saw a small puff of smoke in the distance and searched for the train somewhere on the Spanish side of the mountain tracks.

***

It was the best fireworks display I'd ever seen. Enormous rockets exploded up into a black sky, filling it with glittering particles of light. Catherine wheels whizzed round, spitting white sparks from their fast-moving circles of fire. Crackers exploded, just like machine gun fire.

And suddenly it was over. There was just sky, never-ending sky, black sky now turning blue, then black again. And it was so hot. Like a furnace. An oven. I was moving, quickly now, moving fast under the night sky, the sounds of traffic approaching, the beep of a taxi horn and the wail of a siren. Shouting, someone was shouting. I thought I'd heard the word but then I could hear so many, selling something. Was it marshmallows? Words ran over each other like fast-flowing river-water, blending into each other, becoming indistinguishable.

I looked up and there in front of me was a dark gaping hole, a hole so black it seemed to suck the light away from everything around it. I was being sucked into the black hole. Faster and faster. My feet were inside it now and the rest of my body would follow. I could swear, as I passed inside its blackness and let it swallow me, that I had seen the sign 'Stage Door' hanging above it, flapping in the breeze.

A hush fell over the audience. I looked up at ten thousand faces in the largest auditorium I had ever played to. They were not well-fed or well-dressed. They were filthy and hollow, their bodies skeletons, barely covered in flesh and bone. Their heads were craned towards me, watching silently, waiting for me to say something. Or perhaps they were simply waiting for me to die. Again. I opened my mouth but no words came out. I tried again. Nothing. This had never happened to me before. Frozen in front of an audience, the largest audience of my life.

I came on stage in my Waffen-SS uniform, Iron Cross pinned to my chest and I knelt over a pale Eva Wendt. She lay motionless, lifeless, her hair shorn and dressed in a blue and white striped concentration camp uniform. I looked down at her face. I looked at my left hand, at the bottle of poison, the evil little vial. Of course! I knew where I was now. The audience had probably not even noticed my momentary hesitancy. I was Romeo, and the lady with the shorn hair lying dead in front of me was my Juliet. Two star-cross'd lovers, about to join each other. I slowly brought my left hand containing the vial towards my mouth and my lines finally came to me.

'*Eyes, look your last! Arms, take your last embrace! And lips, o you the doors of breath, seal with a righteous kiss a dateless bargain to engrossing death!*'

I gulped greedily on the amber fluid inside the vial, draining it completely. My throat burned, my stomach dissolved, my innards imploded. I clutched my chest in agony and collapsed to the stage, my body hitting the sprung floor with a loud wooden thud. There was no breathing now. Nothing. Not a sound. Only the cold wooden stage beneath my body.

Suddenly I was back at Bosendorf Studios, kissing Eva. Now I was on the aeroplane with Hans, watching Berlin vanish and the English channel approach. The meeting in the public house, where Hans had bought everyone a drink. Julius Schiller – a great name. The scuffle with the blackshirts in the alleyway. The last performance of Julius Caesar. The first acting job. My uncle dead under a bus. My mother and father now, pushing me on a swing on Bethnal Green. I was a little boy. And then blackness. I was falling fast through a trap door, heading for the void beneath and then I heard an old man's voice, a slow and deliberate voice, ringing in my ears, saying something that I had heard before, at least forty-five times.

Between the acting of a dreadful thing and the first motion, all the interim is like a phantasma, or a hideous dream.

It was at that point that I opened my eyes.

The first thing I saw was a pretty nurse wearing stockings under her blue and white uniform. She walked past me and smiled. I was lying in a hospital in a row of men, sitting up mostly, chattering and reading. Some were smoking big cigars. I blinked a few times and ran my hands down over myself to check there was nothing missing. Two arms, ten fingers. Two legs, ten toes. The man next to me was puffing on a large cigar. He had a jaunty look to him, his hair flopping over his chiseled face and jutting chin. He was casually turning the pages of a *Superman* comic, spooning up treacle into his mouth from a jar with a big black and green *Tate & Lyle* sticker on the side. I didn't even know if I could sit up. I felt drugged. The man next to me turned and grinned, displaying the whitest teeth I'd ever seen.

'Howdy. Welcome to the world of the livin'', he drawled.

I nodded slowly and smiled. I *was* alive. The man was American.

'Name's Woody. You like treacle?'

Woody held out a spoon of treacle towards me.

'You like treacle?', he repeated, smiling.

I tried to nod but my head was too heavy. Moving made blinding white flashes come out of the corners of my eyes. I rested my head back on the soft pillow.

'Suit yourself', Woody said cheerily.

A crew-cut doctor whispered something to a nurse and walked over to my bed. He smelt of coffee.

'Top of the mornin', mystery guy. You've been out for quite a while.'

'Where am I?'

'US Army Field Hospital.'

'How...how long?'

'Three weeks. They found you in your underpants mumbling Shakespeare or something.'

I remembered the dream.

'Fella, listen OK? I gotta ask ya a few questions.'

'Thus conscience doth make cowards of us all.'

'Y'alright buddy?'

The doctor shone a light into my eyes.

'Pupils dilated, symptoms of head-wound, recovery from major concussion slash coma, subject capable of recognition' he gabbled. 'Can ya sit up?'

I slowly raised myself.

'That's better', he said. 'Now I can talk to you properly.' He held up a clipboard and pen. I looked at him and blinked several times. I was having a problem focusing.

'What's your name?'

'What do you want it to be?', I replied. 'That's what she always said. But she's dead.'

'A lot of people died. But it's over now.'

'The war is over?'

'Certainly is my friend. We won, in case you didn't know.' The words sank in. We won. Germany lost. I was Julius Schiller and I'd lost. I'd been in newsreels wearing a Waffen-SS uniform and sporting an Iron Cross. And now I was in an American Field Hospital with men who would shoot me if they only knew.

'Name?', the doctor asked again.

What's in a name? They don't know my name. They're asking me my name. He said they found me in my underwear. Keller took my uniform. My dog-tags. Oh God. The British! If I tell them I'm Abe Goldstein it'd be just as bad as telling them I'm Julius Schiller.

'My name? Does it matter?'

I looked around me for inspiration. I looked at the GI next to me holding the jar of *Tate and Lyle* treacle.

'Tate', I said decisively. 'T-A-T-E Tate.'

'Christian name?' That was OK. I wasn't Jewish anymore.

'Julian.'

'Julian?'

'Yes. My name is Julian Tate.'

I stated it as definitively as I could, hoping I wouldn't forget it. The doctor wrote down the name quickly.

'Fine, Mister Tate. Any family? Wife, father, mother, son, daughter, brother, sister?'

I stared ahead sadly and shook my head.

'Any place you can go?'

Where could I go? Not England. They'd hang me. Not Germany. They'd recognize me. I looked again at the GI with the cigar and the treacle and the comic. Superman would know what to do. Superman could do anything. He could fly around the world so fast that he made time stand still, or even go backwards. I wanted to make time go backwards, just like Superman. The cover of the comic showed Superman atop a green hill, beneath him a large white sign, the oversized letters marked out in square capitals that spelt *HOLLYWOOD*. Hadn't Keppel, the screenwriter, the man who'd written *All for Love* gone to Hollywood? That night when I'd found out about Betty Maude. And Keppel was a Jew.

I nodded my head slowly at the doctor.

'Yes', I said. 'There's somewhere I can go. There's somewhere I've always wanted to go.'

16

The Atlantic crossing was worse than the aeroplane to Germany with Hans six years before. At least in the plane I hadn't been soaking wet in salty water. At least the ordeal had only lasted a matter of hours. At least I'd had a seat. The sea crossing was lasting for days and there was no respite from the rolling hull and the plunging dips into the gigantic waves. An Atlantic depression seemed to have settled over our liner, following it on its three thousand mile journey. I'd boarded in Hamburg and wangled it so that I never had to set foot on shore at Southampton Dock.

I slept on deck and I'd grown my hair and a moustache as well, dyed them black. The food was disgusting and the water was brown. I had terrible headaches every other day, headaches that made me see stars and grind my teeth together in my sleep. I was Julian Tate, lying prone on the wood, jammed against a bulkhead, my camp bed creaking as each wave pounded against the hull. It was the cheapest crossing to America I could find. *She* would never have traveled like this, I thought, as another spritzer of sea water slapped me in the face.

The other passengers were also refugees, men and women and children who had scrabbled together the fare and were hoping that the promised land would meet them when they arrived in New York. They would see the Statue of Liberty reaching out to them giving them hope, they hoped. I hoped this too. I had no money, no change of clothing and no-one to talk to. I kept away from the Germans because they might have seen my film or my newsreels. I felt and looked older and thinner but it wouldn't have taken a miracle for anyone to recognize me. I kept to myself and the four week journey passed unpleasantly but passed all the same. Columbus had made a similar journey probably under better conditions, four hundred and fifty-three years earlier. Next time, if there was a next time, I swore I'd take the plane.

On the morning of the twenty-ninth day I could see land, the coastline of the United States of America. They needed young men and women to fill their factories, to build their houses and to sweep their streets. I'd've been happy to do any of these jobs but I had a burning ambition, a dream that would have seemed impossible just a few weeks ago but that was now fast becoming a reality. As long as they let me in, I was going to hitchhike all the way to California and I was going to find Peter Keppel the screenwriter.

We landed somewhere called Ellis Island. I stood in a long line of men, women and children waiting to be given entry papers and visas. The sun beat down on us and the line moved slowly. At the head stood an agitated thirty-year-old woman.

'Bekowitz-Marlheimer', she said with a smile.

'Be – what? How d'ya spell that?'

'Ich kann nicht Englisch.'

'You don't speak the lingo?'

'Gott bless America! Gott bless Eisenhower!'

'Alright alright. Who's this?'

'Gott bless America!'

'This your son?'

'Gott bless you.'

'Alright alright. First name?'

'Gott bless you!'

'Jesus Christ alright already!'

He looked at a list of names.

'You can be Jane Benson and your son can be …er…Jake.'

The official wrote out the names quickly. He looked up at the huge line in front of him. He stamped the fresh green cards and handed them to the bright-eyed lady.

'Welcome to America. Next!'

I stepped forward.

'Julian Tate', I enunciated clearly in my new transatlantic accent. The official let out a sigh of relief.

'T-A-T-E?'

I nodded. The official stamped the Green Card and handed it to me.

'Welcome to America. Next!'

The whole process took a few seconds, just as easy as getting into Germany in 1938, six years before. I walked quickly towards a waiting ferry with a big sign for Manhattan. I looked up and the Statue of Liberty's arm stretched out ahead of me, her greenish-turquoise skin making her look like a mermaid. She was pointing the way.

***

The first truck that stopped was bound for Miami.

'Miami? That's south isn't it?'

'You from Europe?'

'Yes.'

'Get in. Name's Bernard Schwartz.'

'Julian Tate.'

We shook hands.

'Where you going?', he asked me.

'Hollywood.'

Bernard started to laugh.

'Hollywood? That's rich. Hollywood!'
I smiled. It did sound rich.
'Why you wanna go there? Full of crazy people.'
'I have a friend.'
'Girl?'

I sat up front with Bernard Schwartz, a handsome dark-haired young man who was on his fifth job for the Wesley Removals Company, a relocation to Miami Beach.

'Forget her', advised Bernie indistinctly, a sandwich in his mouth.

'I can't forget her.'

'Lots of beautiful girls in Hollywood. And Miami.'

'Not like her'.

We quickly headed south along the East Coast Highway, leaving New York State behind us. Within a few hours we hit Maryland.

'Wanna see the White House?', he asked me.

I'd walked up to thirty-second street in Manhattan just to snatch a good look at the Empire State Building. Maybe I should see the White House. Bernard certainly seemed to want to.

'Sure', I replied, wondering what was in the sandwich.

It was dusk and I almost had to pinch myself. The President of the United States of America was in there – maybe - working out how to re-build Europe. Our removals truck circled round and round the perfect wedding cake building and we peered at the lights inside. Someone was standing in a second floor window. That first night we slept in the back of the truck, me on a large sofa, Bernard on a double bed wrapped in plastic, both of us ten feet off the ground on top of tens of wooden packing cases.

'You can go West from here, if you want', Bernard said in the morning as we chewed some donuts together at a filling station.

'We can find you someone who's going to Chicago, maybe a tanker headed back to Texas. That'll get you a lot of the way there. Show you a bit of the country, too. Or I can take you to Miami.'

Mobil Oil had a number of tankers and the drivers were friendly lumberjack types.

'I'll take care a him fer ya', said the blunt-faced, large-bellied driver with chewing tobacco hanging out of his mouth.

'Goodbye Bernie.'

'*Arrivederci* Julian. Maybe I'll see you in Hollywood one day', he said as he shook my hand. 'Might be better than driving trucks.'

'It might', I replied.

The map showed the distance as three thousand miles from coast to coast but I managed to travel nearly four.

Two weeks after I'd said goodbye to Bernard Schwartz I was entering the State of California in the back of a mining truck with a bunch of drunken Mexicans. The route hadn't made any sense. Ellis Island to New York, south to Washington DC, West to Chicago, then to Colorado, south to Houston and finally west all the way. I'd eaten bits of sandwich, beef jerky, bagels, donuts, anything the truck driver or other passengers had on them. For the last two days I'd been eating re-fried beans and sniffing *aguardiente*. I'd had one cup of coffee and a *Coke*, which had given me a real high. It was now the autumn of 1945 and Southern California was warm and sunny. There was no sign anywhere of the biggest war mankind had ever witnessed.

I sat in the back of the powerful Ford pick-up along with Jose, Pedro, Alberto and Gustavo and I let the warm air run over my face. I was in California. I was Julian Tate. I wasn't going to be hung, or shot, or punched or live in fear. Everything seemed so clean, the people laid-back and the cars were so big. There was orange juice with real pieces of orange, somewhere. As the strains of *Estoy tan enamorada, esa Negra tomasa* assaulted my eardrums – the *aguardiente* was strong stuff, I could smell it – I closed my eyes and tried to imagine I was in paradise, but all I could see amongst the palms was her face, watching me.

On a green-brown hill in the distance, glinting in the bright sunshine, lay the enormous white *'Hollywood'* sign. I was wearing a demob suit, a drab grey flannel thing that was too hot and sticky for the ambient eighty degree temperature. My shirt had been white once, and my shoes were a size too big. I had blisters on my feet, weighed only a hundred and forty pounds despite being six feet tall and I had a sty in my left eye. I hadn't shaved for a week and all I had for money were the little green coupons from Ellis Island that entitled me to bread and other basic provisions in the general stores that accepted them. But I'd made it. I'd made it to Hollywood, the dream, the place where all the Jews went and changed their names, just like Hans said. I sat on the brownish grass, wished that Eva Wendt was there with me, and wept.

I walked along the coastline, breathing in the spray from the ocean and watching men and women playing in the surf. I must have walked for miles, clearing the dust from the road from my lungs, replacing it with the breezy warm ocean air. The sign above me read

'*Venice*'. Next to it was a map of the greater Los Angeles area. I was studying it when a middle-aged black man with large sunglasses, a trilby, a moth-eaten suit and sandals started speaking to me.

'Rodeo, Sunset, Mann's, Metro Goldwyn Mayer, Columbia, Mulholland, Beverley Hills, Bel Air, Pacific Palisades, Malibu, Santa Monica, Downtown, Uptown...where you headin'?'

I watched the man take a swig from a whisky bottle in a brown paper bag.

'I'm not sure', I replied slowly. 'I'm looking for someone'.

'We *all* looking for someone, baby.'

'I'm looking for someone called Peter Keppel. He's a writer.'

'You wanna find some Jew writer fella, you gotchersel' a real uphill struggle in *this* town.'

'Why's that?'

'Because', said the black man, looking affronted.

'Because what?'

'Because if you said to me you was lookin' fer a six foot tall studio execootiv that was black, then I'd bees sayin' to ya – hell, I *knows* the guy straight off!'

'And?'

'And that's because there'd only be *one* of him if you catch my drift.'

'His name is Peter Keppel. He's about so high, glasses, medium build. Maybe thirty-five, forty. I think he's been here about five years.'

'D'you say Keppel?'

'Yes.'

He scratched his head and took another swig of whisky.

'Well he ain't no actor. I ain't ever heard o' him'.

'I said he was a writer, not an actor.'

210

'And what're *you* then?'

'I don't know what I am anymore.'

'Thas real funny', he guffawed. 'Man's in the wrong town!' The tanned couples walking by looked at us curiously. We made an odd couple. Two tramps with a bottle of whisky, both wearing far too many clothes for the summer heat, standing by a beach with Pacific rollers thumping down a few yards ahead of us. I watched the faces of the passers-by. They smiled politely and kept their distance. If I was going to find Keppel I'd somehow have to clean up, judging by the stares I was getting.

I walked slowly towards the beach. The black man in shades kept speaking as if I was still next to him. I realized that he was blind. I reached the wet part of the sand and removed my grey-flannel demob suit. I folded my clothes neatly and placed them in a pile on the sand. In only my underwear I ran into the water and dived into the Pacific Ocean.

Still dripping and with no towel, I let the sun dry me as I shaved with a blunt razor. I had no mirror, but I could tell with my hand that I'd done a good job. Clothes. I needed to blend in. Across the street from the coastal highway was a beach store, but it also sold slacks and shirts, not just brightly coloured swim-wear and Bermudas. Luckily it accepted the little green coupons. I bought a pair of slacks, two shirts and a cheap pair of loafers and now I had no more green coupons left. I combed my hair with my fingertips, slicking it back behind my ears.

I could see a sign from the beach and the tell-tale large nondescript buildings that looked like aircraft hangars. Film studios. I gave my old clothes, neatly folded, to the blind man. We were about the same size. I walked down the street a new man, thin and wiry,

211

with nothing other than the clothes on my back, the shoes on my feet and the papers in my pocket. I had a sun-tan from the back of the truck, and no-one paid me the least attention.

Days passed. I found a refuge for young men one block off the Pacific Coastal Highway where I could shower and eat in return for doing household chores and I washed my clothes every day, leaving them to drip-dry in the sun.

Keppel's number wasn't in the telephone book. No-one had heard of him. I visited more than twenty studios, but most of them didn't even let me in the front gate, so I would stand there for hours, hoping to see Keppel drive in or out. And then, one evening, someone was walking into my dormitory telling me there was a man waiting downstairs to see me.

I walked slowly across the cracks in the tiled floor near the ground floor reception area of the hostel, listening to the sound of the cars on the Pacific Coast Highway through the open door. A man stood there facing the street, dressed in a blue sweater and khaki pants. I saw he was wearing an expensive watch. I cleared my throat and watched as Peter Keppel turned round and stared at me.

'Is it you?', he asked incredulously.

I nodded.

'Why are you looking for me Julius?'

I looked at him hollow-eyed, disbelievingly.

'Peter Keppel', was all I could say, 'Peter Keppel', over and over and over.

'You look…thin', Keppel murmured.

'I'm sorry, Peter. I know you came here to Hollywood and I had to make a new start for myself. I thought, he's a Jew. Just like me.'

'I knew it!' Keppel grinned. 'I knew it was something! This'd make some story, Julius - '

'It's Julian now. '

'Anglicised, huh? Nothing wrong with that. I'm a writer. We can have any name we like. The more Jewish the better. But you…'

'I don't want you to write about me. No-one knows who I am. Telling the truth could get me killed. I'll tell you all about it sometime, but maybe not right now. I did some stupid things Peter, but I did them to try and save her.'

'Who?'

'Eva Wendt.'

'The blonde bitch?'

'No! No! You don't understand. Her real name was Betty Maude Weinstein.'

I grabbed him by the shoulders.

'She was Jewish, Peter, she was Jewish. She did it to support her family and they're dead too. Everyone's dead apart from you and me. We're the only ones left.'

'And Hans.'

'What?'

'He sent me a postcard.'

Peter took it out from a pocket in his trousers and handed it to me.

'I thought you might be interested.'

I looked at the picture on the front. It was of a dreamy sandy beach, a turquoise sea and tall swaying palm trees.

'It's from Jerry, you remember, the funny little guy? Hans took him to Argentina.'

I nodded slowly and read the message on the back.

'With HB in Buenos Aires. Back to stunt work. Jerry.'

'So Julian *what*?' asked Keppel. 'The man at the studio told me Tate? Julian Tate?'

'Yes. Julian Tate.'

'Right. Tate. It's a good name. Maybe I can help find you some good roles.'

'No!', I shouted. 'No!'

Keppel looked startled at the reaction and I smiled nervously.

'I mean, no thanks, Peter.'

'You speak English like a native. It's incredible.'

'I *am* English.'

'You're *what*?'

'My real name is Abraham Goldstein and I was born in London.'

Keppel raised his eyebrows quizzically.

'And I don't want to act any more. Ever.'

Keppel stared at me carefully.

'So what can I do to help you?'

'I need', I began slowly, sitting down on a couch in the reception area of the hostel, feeling the soft evening breeze, 'to begin again.'

'I understand.'

'Do you?'

Peter looked at me with a mixture of sympathy and sadness.

'Maybe not.'

'Can you help get me out of this hostel?'

'You can stay with me. Til you find your feet. I've got a spare room. And a communal pool.'

Tears welled up in my eyes.

'Thank you Peter.'

'How long will it take for you get your things?'

'Two minutes. Maybe less. I have nothing.'

'Go.'

I stood up, wiping my eyes.

'There's lots of different jobs I can help you with at the studios. You're a fit guy. We can find you something I'm sure. What do you want to be?'

I smiled.

'I want to be a director', I replied, 'but not like Hans.'

17

It had taken ten years to make my first film, with the screenplay by Peter Keppel, but *'Never Forget'* had made waves and opened to critical acclaim. The audience at the test screening in Santa Monica had given us a thirty minute standing ovation. Tears had run down their cheeks. The substitute ending was the right one. The Hollywood audience loved to cry, but it loved a happy ending. There had been no need to spend so much time worrying about it. As long as it felt natural, which it did.

Ten more years had passed since that first film and it was now 1966, a golden year for Hollywood. Seven films had followed my first, all successful. I now lived alone in a large house in Beverley Hills. I had a swimming pool and more palm trees than there had been in Jerry's postcard from Argentina but it seemed that the titles of my first two films went with me everywhere: *Never Forget* and *All for Love*. It was *her*.

I had become what the newspapers called a recluse, leaving my house only for the studio or a movie premiere. I would not, the newspapers noted, travel outside of the United States.

'An aversion to boats and aeroplanes', was the quote I had given them on the telephone. *'When you invent another method of transport'*, the quote continued, *'then I'll see the world.'*

But for now, I was happy with my house, a butler, a maid and six bedroom suites in Beverley Hills.

I had made enough money to have my own screening room, a cavernous basement with curtains at the front, real cinema seating and even little fluorescent signs above the doors showing the way back to the upper floors. I didn't drink, I never smoked and I had an exercise room which I visited twice daily. I swam a hundred lengths of my pool three hundred and sixty-five days of the year, keeping it heated to a constant thirty degrees.

There was also another pursuit, an obsession that I restricted to night-time. It involved a set of metal film canisters, twelve in all, containing the full presentation of the feature film *The Duke and the Chambermaid, All for Love,* starring Eva Wendt and Julius Schiller. All the canisters were damaged and some of the film inside was burned. Peter Keppel had saved them when he made his way from Germany to America twenty-five years ago.

Every night, when it was late and the butler and the maid were asleep, I walked down the softly-carpeted steps to my basement screening room. It was sound-proofed and I was able to operate all of the equipment myself. I kept the battered canisters locked in the projection booth in the centre above the back row. Fifty seats, but only one was ever taken after midnight.

I always started with the last reel. It was getting stretched as it was old and I had played it numerous times, too many times to count. I could not risk getting it copied. I could not risk anyone recognizing me.

It was a Friday night and I sat in the darkness, watching the flickering screen in front of me. The black and white film played silently, the images reflecting on my face in the stalls. My hair was graying at the temples, but I looked strong and fit. The years had been kind to me at least in that way.

It came to the moment where we would kiss. I could remember it like it was only yesterday. I looked so young, and she looked so beautiful. I got up out of my red leather seat in the centre of the back row and walked into the projection booth. I pressed the pause button on the projector. The film froze on the screen at the exact moment I had wanted it to. The duke was holding the chambermaid in his arms and kissing her passionately.

I moved out of the booth and walked slowly up to the screen. I stood against it, my shadow falling over my own much younger face on screen. My hand reached out and I touched her face. I held my hand against the screen, the tears flowing quickly down my cheeks. And then a voice came from out of the darkness.

'She was one in a million.'

It was Peter Keppel. My hand did not move from the screen.

'How many times have you watched that reel?', he asked. I looked up at the screen wistfully. I must have watched it thousands of times, every night for nearly fifteen years.

'Cary Grant was looking for you', continued Keppel. 'Something about a comeback. He liked our last offering. Bacall's interested, too.'

'She's not right', I replied, after a long pause. 'Not right at all.'

'What about Doris Day? It'd be a new thing for her.'

I didn't answer. I just kept staring up at the screen, up at the woman I loved, the woman I would always love. Keppel stood up from his seat at the side of the back row near the exit and walked towards me. He rested his hand on my shoulder.

'My friend - '

'How did you get in?'

'Roberta was up'.

I nodded. Roberta was my maid and housekeeper and she liked Peter Keppel. The two of them spoke Spanish together sometimes, talking about the lights in the harbour in Valencia, sitting on the porch with mugs of coffee. Keppel shook his head sadly.

'To pursue the dream is commendable, but this is obsession.'

'I'm not obsessed.'

'The studio says you're holding up the casting. Again.'

'They can afford to be patient. God knows we've made them enough money.'

'It's not about the money...it's about you. You're a recluse here.'

'You know why I live the way I do.'

'Twenty years, my friend. Twenty years. No-one's going to arrest you now. There's no barbed wire here. Come on. You need to eat. I know a place. Let's get some fresh air. It's open all night. Just off Sunset.'

Neither my face, nor my hand moved from the screen.

I did feel hungry though.

***

Peter Keppel had a new Mustang convertible and he enjoyed driving it at night with the hood down. Sunset Boulevard was not quite deserted, the air was fresh and Peter had very little hair left to be blown by the wind. We reached the restaurant after only fifteen minutes. The neon sign announced '*Maxines*'. It was nearly two in the morning but the place was almost full, bustling with waitresses, party-people and others that were simply hungry. Maxine, a fifty-something with a taste for kaftans, greeted everyone as they entered. She knew Peter Keppel and she gave him a good table.

Ten minutes later, a Spanish omelette sat in front of me, untouched. Opposite, Peter was tucking into a steak and fries. It was bloody, just the way he liked it. I studied the omelette. It looked good, but I couldn't eat. A Spanish omelette at two in the morning on Sunset with a screenwriter. Had Hans been this lonely?

I stared ahead of me. Peter spoke to me in short snatches between mouthfuls of fries. I didn't hear a word. I *was* obsessed, I realized, obsessed with a woman that had been dead for twenty-two years. Peter Keppel was right, again. My thoughts were disturbed by a man's hand reaching out to shake hands with me over my omelette.

'Mister Tate?'

I didn't look up. The voice sounded familiar.

'Mister Tate? That you?'

I nodded into my omelette.

'I admire your work. Here, lemme give ya my card.'

The man's suntanned hand placed a white business card onto the table next to the untouched omelette.

'Looks good. Maxine does a mean Spanish omelette.'

'Yes. Yes she does.'

I picked up my fork, took a mouthful and looked at the small white card in front of me.

'Yeah, I like your films a lot, Mister Tate. Bear me in mind, OK? Especially anything with cars.'

'I liked *The Great Escape*', Keppel chimed in, his mouth full of fries.

The man nodded and head back to the door. We heard the roar of a sports car outside a second after the door shut behind him.

'You know who that was?', Keppel asked.

The name on the card was *Steve McQueen*, a telephone number below it. An idea was forming slowly, *the great escape*. I stood up.

'Peter?'

'Yeah?'

'I'm going to go for a little walk. Order me a coffee?'

'Sure. Everything OK?'

'I don't know. I just need to be alone for a minute.'

'OK. You look kind of agitated, my friend. You'll be OK?'

I nodded.

'You were right. I needed to get out. Ten minutes. Clear my head.'

I pulled on my camel-haired coat. Just like Hans, I thought as I headed round the corner off Sunset. The little street was a cut-through, away from the traffic and *Maxines* and towards a set of blocks set up on the hill. I could see the lights in the valley below twinkling behind me. I could see the lights in the apartment block in front of me. It looked like a number of people were still up. I walked deliberately, slowly, my footsteps resonating on the tarmac. There was no traffic so I just kept to the middle of the street, away from the dark doorways and trash cans. I had my head down, deep in thought and so I did not see the two Hispanic thugs sitting smoking. I just walked past them, oblivious.

I had tried to find out where she was buried, had thought about visiting the grave, if there *was* one. But I'd had nobody to write to, and there was no agency or government or family I could contact without drawing suspicion to myself. I didn't know if Abraham Goldstein was wanted by the British. I didn't know if Julius Schiller was wanted for war crimes. I didn't want to know, so I'd remained here, in my own little bubble, nearly six thousand miles away. Was it safe now? Was

221

it safe to travel abroad? People would forget, wouldn't they?

I knew I hadn't changed that much physically, but no one would be expecting to see Julius Schiller. No-one would remember me. I hadn't been much of a star, had I, really? One film, one film with the dazzling Eva Wendt. And as far as I knew, I had the only copy at my house in Beverley Hills. I was Julian Tate now. *Mister* Tate. Even to big-shot stars, A-listers like Steve McQueen, I was Julian Tate the director.

'Hey? Mister? Got a light?', asked a voice from the darkness of a doorway.

I kept walking, sticking to the middle of the street. The two thugs nodded to each other, got up and followed me. I could hear their footsteps behind me. Ten feet, five feet. I stopped and turned round. Two thugs, not with black-shirts, no Fascist insignia this time. An alleyway. A streetlight. I remembered. I was even wearing the same coat Hans had worn.

'I used to smoke, but I quit', I said calmly.

'Thas' an espensive coat, amigo', said the taller of the two Hispanic men, leering at me.

'You gotta wallet?', asked the squatter of the two.

They stood on either side of me, blocking my path in both directions, the hills and blocks above, the valley, the lights and Sunset down below.

'Giv'i' to me', he hissed, pulling out a switchblade from his jacket.

The taller thug grabbed me round the neck and I felt his arms tighten. The squat guy punched me in the stomach and I dropped to my knees. I continued to struggle but I couldn't stop them ripping my pockets with the knife and taking out the wallet and some loose notes, maybe five hundred dollars. One of them punched me in the face. *Where was the knife?*

I struggled to stand up, my nose bleeding and my stomach in agony. I fell over again onto the street, near a doorway, away from the light. I could hear myself breathing heavily and I heard two sets of sneakers running swiftly away. Someone else was now running towards me. I lay in the doorway, waiting for the face to come into the light. Five seconds later, Keppel was kneeling over me.

'You OK? How bad is it?'

'I'm OK.'

'Can you get up?'

I looked up at him.

'Yes. I think I can.'

'You want me to help you? Anything broken?'

'History repeats itself, Peter.'

'What? What are you talking about, Julius?'

'It's *Julian* and I'm talking about Hans Bosendorf. He couldn't find what he was looking for until he came to England and I found him in a gutter. He was wearing a coat just like this one.'

Keppel looked down at me, puzzled.

'You saying this only happens to movie directors in smart coats? Cos I gotta tell you Julian, this is the world we live in.'

Keppel started helping me up. He put his arm under mine and hitched me to a standing position against a wall.

'I must get out more', I said as a smile crept across my face.

'I thought -' Keppel began.

'Thanks for coming to get me.'

'Yeah, well it's my fault you're here.'

I took a step and wobbled, reaching to the wall for support.

'A very wise man once said to me', I said, 'that the answer to most of our troubles is staring us right in the face.'

'Anyone I know? 'Cos you're starin' at the wall.'

I took another step away from the wall, more firmly this time. I stretched my arms up and winced.

'You were right, Peter. I don't get out enough. And, you know what? You know all my troubles? The studio's problem with me? *Your* problem with me?'

'I don't have a problem with you. Come on, let's get a doctor to look at those ribs -'

I winced and clutched my chest in pain.

'I've been running scared, Peter.'

'Come on Julian.'

Peter helped me hobble down the alleyway, back towards the lights stretched out beneath us on the other side of Sunset Boulevard. The stars in the sky were hazy, but they were still there. I looked up at them.

'Peter - remember that saying? If the mountain won't come to Mohammed?'

'...then Mohammed must go to the mountain. So?'

My step became firmer and the haze seemed to lift from the stars in the night sky.

18

My hands were shaking as I looked out of the window. Twenty-thousand feet below me the Atlantic rollers looked like tiny white crests, appearing and then vanishing again into the grey-blue ocean. I was on the last leg of my journey.

Air travel might have improved greatly in the twenty-seven years since my last flight, but the sharp bumps and dips of propeller planes had simply been replaced by the whine of jet engines and steep turns at much higher speeds. Take-off was murderous. The sound had been deafening. Those lights flashing, everyone smoking, everyone chatting while my hands gripped the sides of my seat and my feet buried themselves into First Class's thick carpet. Only a few hours and it would be over, thank God.

It felt like I'd been up here for nearly a day. Los Angeles to New York and then Lufthansa direct to Frankfurt where I would get a train to West Berlin, the only little bit of America behind the Iron Curtain. Keppel had volunteered to fly with me, but I'd turned him down. This was to be *my* pilgrimage and such pilgrimages were best made alone.

The German aeroplane – especially in first class - was very comfortable, but I couldn't help but feel uncomfortable. There were sofas and friendly air-hostesses in tight uniforms to serve champagne and oysters. There were businessmen and government officials. I sipped water with some bicarbonate of soda mixed in for my stomach. I'd been to the bathroom twice in the last hour.

The man sitting next to me was British, an old university professor who'd just finished a lecture tour of the United States and was now on his way to do some research in Germany. He introduced himself as Arthur Pilkington.

'Julian Tate.'

'You look familiar.'

'I'm a film director.'

'Ah. That explains it. Anything I would know?'

'Probably.'

'You're an *American*, Mister Tate?'

'You guessed.'

'Your accent is very...*transatlantic* I believe is the correct terminology these days, that's right, *transatlantic*. Have we not met before, perhaps in England? Your face *is* very familiar.'

I buried myself in my copy of the *Hollywood Reporter*.

'Mister Tate? When were you last in England?'

'I forget', I replied, Abe Goldstein flooding back to me. 'I travel a lot.'

'Ah', Pilkington replied expansively. 'Care for some claret?'

'I don't, thank you.'

'Chip?' Pilkington held out a steaming French fry from his plate. 'They're really rather good.'

As if to demonstrate, he popped it into his mouth.

'No thanks. I have to watch my weight.'

'Ah yes yes yes. You *Americans*' – Pilkington used the word rather disparagingly – 'are silly like that. You probably have an exercise bicycle and a swimming pool.'

'Yes.'

'There we are then.'

'Yes. There we are.'

I turned another page of the *Reporter* and pretended to look interested in an article comparing Mary Tyler Moore to Lucille Ball.

'Did you fight in the war?', Pilkington asked, popping a chip into his mouth. 'I was too old you see, so they kept me hidden away in a fourteenth-century garret. Ha Ha! You'd be about the right age I expect to have been called up by Uncle Sam. Were you there at D-Day? Juno Beach perhaps?'

'I prefer not to talk about the war, if it's all the same to you.'

'Of course my dear fellow, perfectly understand. We've all got our demons, Christ I should know!'

Pilkington laughed as he popped another chip into his mouth. I looked at Pilkington out of the corner of my eye and found Pilkington doing the same thing.

'Gotcha!', roared Pilkington heartily.

'I'm tired', I said. 'I'm going to try and sleep now.'

'Of course of course. I'm sorry. Excuse me for being tiresome.'

'It's quite alright.'

I closed my eyes and turned away to face the window.

'*Sweet dreams, Julius*', I thought I heard the old man say as I drifted off to sleep.

***

The sign read *Willkommen an Deutschland!* - Welcome to Germany! Pilkington was far behind me, moving slowly. I had one small carry-on bag, an attaché case.

'Welcome to Germany, Mister Tate' said the tired middle-aged blonde sitting at the glass-fronted counter in front of me. She looked like she'd been there for years and she looked up wearily as she stamped my passport.

'It's been a while', I replied.

She looked like a battle-hardened, older version of Helga Braun. I looked down at her name badge. It *was* Helga Braun. I turned away quickly. She frowned.

'Haven't we...?'

I walked past her quickly towards the baggage reclaim, looking straight ahead of me. I wondered if she'd made any movies. Probably not, judging by the expression on her face.

I took the train from Frankfurt and crossed into East Germany only with the benefit of the special pass I'd managed to obtain from the cultural attaché at the United Nations. I was making a cultural visit.

By 1966 Germany's guilt had begun to fade, but Berlin was a city cleaved into two. To the West, Berlin was thriving with real businesses making real money, real people enjoying cinemas, theatres and sport and a slow but steady process of regeneration. On the other side of the Wall, to the East, Berlin was in decline.

Reachable only via *Friedrichstrasse* train station or *Checkpoint Charlie*, the East was a grey, drab, grim reminder of the ability of the Soviet Union to suck all life out of pretty much everything, including its people. West Berlin was an oasis in the heart of the Eastern Bloc. The exchange rate was officially one West German Mark for one East German Mark, but on the black market the rate was more like seventy to one. I had stacked up with a large number of black-market notes and I folded them and hid them in my shoes before passing through *Friedrichstrasse*, carrying only my attaché case which they hadn't even bothered to search.

'Bosendorf Studios', I said to the cab-driver on Alexanderplatz. I had to see it one last time. The cab was a Lada, made somewhere like the Urals and the engine sounded like it was made out of wood rather than metal as it rattled and spluttered. The cab driver scratched his head. My German was nearly as rusty as the Lada, but I thought I'd said it clearly enough.

'Bosendorf Studios', I repeated. 'Do you know it?'

'Used to know it', the cabbie replied. 'Long gone, though. Old man Bosendorf did a runner at the end of the War. Government took it over.'

'What's it now?'

'Get in.'

The streets were much as I remembered them. Little had changed. Instead of military uniforms the people were in grayish clothes. A few new grayish buildings appeared on the horizon and then twenty enormous blocks of apartments that looked like battleships against the grayish sky. They were the ugliest buildings I'd ever seen. The cinema was still there, the one Hans used to go to, the one I'd seen on my way into Berlin all those years before, but now the movie was in Russian, not German. I couldn't see any other sign outside. If there were any Jews left, I thought sadly, they could go and see it.

The road was recognizable. I'd tried to visit the street where Eva's parents had lived, but the cabbie told me it didn't exist anymore. Allied bombing had taken care of it. As we headed out of the city the memories flooded back to me. The night we met her parents, the drive in the Volkswagen prototype that the Germans had turned into a best-seller.

The road bent round to the right and there ahead of us should have been the gates to Bosendorf Studios, rising proudly out of the green belt around the city. But there was no green belt. It was a conurbation, and a large grocery store now marked where the gates had been. A long line of people, mainly women, stretched out from the front doors.

'See how they stand in line', the cabbie said. 'We all have to stand in line under *Kruschev*. I waited four years for this taxi.'

The cabbie looked into his rear-view mirror. We had an escort a hundred yards behind us, one large black car in a sea of small Trabants.

'Are you staying long in the East?', the cabbie asked.

'A few hours.'

'Good. It is for the best.'

'I'd like to get out now.'

The cab came to a halt. I stepped out, leaving my attaché case inside. I crossed the road and walked up to the grocery store. Behind it was a warehouse and trucks driving in and out, unloading fruit and vegetables from large pallets. There was no sign of the studios, no sign at all. They'd been razed to the ground. I had come here just to see it again before I started work tomorrow but now all I wanted to do was go.

'*Friedrichstrasse*', I said abruptly as I got quickly back in the cab.

'Already?'

I could feel my hands sweating and I wondered why the cabbie kept checking his rear view mirror. I looked behind us and saw the large black car a hundred yards or so away. Someone was always following me.

'I've had enough of the East', I said. 'Just get me out of here.'

Hirschbaum Studios was back in the relative civilization of West Berlin. Privately owned by Joel Hirschbaum, a wealthy young producer, it prided itself on being able to cast for international films from the widest pool imaginable. Most importantly, Hirschbaum was able to gain access to girls from all over Germany, including those from the East via a *'special cultural arrangement'* which boiled down to a special cultural payment to a certain special cultural official. This access had been crucial in my decision to make the trip.

Betty Maude Weinstein had been born in Leipzig, now in East Germany and behind the Iron Curtain. There must, I reasoned, be other girls like her. And if I found one, then she'd have to be willing to make the seven and a half thousand mile journey back to Hollywood to star in my film. She didn't even need to speak English; we could always dub her. The story behind the film had already been translated into hundreds of languages.

Joel Hirschbaum was a young man with wire-framed glasses and a firm hand-shake. He was tall and dark-haired and he looked very pleased to welcome a famous Hollywood director to his studios. He spoke English fluently with an American accent.

'You had a good trip, Mister Tate?'

'Yes thank you. How many have you got for me?'

'We have over three hundred girls for you to meet, Mister Tate.'

'Three hundred?' I'd expected fifty.

'Three hundred who conform to your *exact* requirements. I had nearly five thousand letters. I've had my team sifting through them all.'

'I see.'

'It is prestigious for them, Mister Tate. And for me also.'

'So when do we start? Three hundred...'

'This afternoon if you feel up to it.'

'Why not?' I replied.

The film studio was brightly lit and very much like the old Bosendorf main studio, partly because nearly everything inside appeared to be about twenty years old. I sat in a director's chair on the edge of the stage to one side, in darkness. Hirschbaum stood out front, watching the girls as they came on, coordinating by whispering into the walkie-talkie that fed through to the dressing rooms where the girls were waiting. At the back of the studio on two folding metal seats sat two somber men in grey suits holding clipboards, monitoring the proceedings.

'Thirty's enough for day one', Hirschbaum said to me.

Maybe we'd find the one I was looking for and everyone could all go home, including me.

Each girl was blonde, most were blue-eyed, and they were aged between eighteen and twenty-five, although from my cursory glance at the girls earlier backstage, I was sure it was more like fourteen to forty. Some of their photographs were obviously taken in a favourable light, or at least ten years before. I'd said *recent*, but Hirschbaum obviously preferred the scatter-gun approach.

The girls had clear instructions. Move into the spotlight when called. If not asked to leave instantly, recite a speech in English and answer a few questions. If at any time they were asked to stop, or Julian Tate said *thank you* or *vielen dank* then they should curtsey and leave with their twenty Marks traveling expenses.

'Miller!', called out Hirschbaum.

The first girl walked into the spotlight and stood stock still, the light blinding her. Greta Miller was a pretty blonde with voluptuous breasts and a button nose. The nose was too small, too perfect and the breasts were too in my face, *too* voluptuous. I wasn't making that kind of movie. Ten seconds went by.

'Vood you like I say sometin'?', she blurted out in a high-pitched German accent.

'No, thank you', I replied.

'That will be all thank you, Fraulein Miller' said Hirschbaum.

Greta Miller cast down her eyes, curtseyed and walked out of the light.

'Marta Regelsburg!'

A statuesque figure walked forward, like Marlene Dietrich, smoking a cigarette. She strode confidently into the light and posed, hand on hip, seductively. Better. This was better. Hirschbaum had done his homework.

'What have you prepared today?', I asked from the darkness.

A low growl, panther-like, came back at me.

'Something by Shakespeare.'

Better and better.

'Which play? Which part?'

'Is a mixture', she replied, 'I think you like it.'

'Okay. Off you go.'

She stubbed out her cigarette and knelt on the floor. She looked up into the Gods with a wild look in her eyes and her voice boomed out slowly.

'Out vile damn'd spot!'

She raised her arms up to the roof, screamed and tore at her face with her hands. I put my fingers in my ears.

'*Vielen dank!*', I shouted. 'I said *thank you!*'

'Svetlana Podarova', cried Hirschbaum as girl three walked into the spotlight. She was very pretty, but she was barely five foot tall and looked no more than fourteen. I leaned back in my director's chair, keeping well away from the light.

'Herr Hirschbaum? I have a better idea. Can you get everyone in here, together, for tomorrow?'

'*Everyone*?'

'Everyone. I just need to see their faces.'

'All two hundred and ninety-seven?'

'Yes.'

'I had not budgeted for this.'

'Tell me what the extra is, double it and I'll pay it.'

Hirschbaum shrugged and looked to the rear of the studio. The two men in grey suits shifted uneasily on their metal chairs, whispered to each other and nodded. Hirschbaum turned to me and smiled.

'You are a good businessman, Mister Tate.'

'I had a good teacher, Herr Hirschbaum. Those your investors at the back?'

He didn't reply.

When the telephone rang that night I knew it would be Keppel. All the executives at the studio were worrying about their director going AWOL on a mission to cast the female lead in Germany.

'People don't want to see German actresses anymore, Julian', Keppel said. 'Maybe as the bad girl, but not the star.'

'I just need the face, Peter, the face. We can do what we like with the rest. Dub her, change her name, but we need the right girl for this. It'll make the movie.'

'You're happy with the lead man, though?'

'Yes. He's English, he's perfect.'

'You've got four days, Julian, four days then they're gonna use central casting. Two little starlets lined up, prettier than God.'

'God's an old man with a white beard.'

234

'God's whoever you want him to be, my friend.'
'I'm tired Peter. I'll call you tomorrow. I'll know by the evening.'
'Goodnight Julian.'
'Goodnight Peter'.

***

The next day I woke at six. I had my own trailer on the studio lot for the few days of my visit and it was very comfortable. Hirschbaum reserved it for stars. I got dressed and walked out onto the lot. No barbed wire, no sentries and there was already some activity in one of the studios, a war-film Hirschbaum had said.

I made Hirschbaum's job difficult by *not* sending him a picture of Eva, only a sketch, but I couldn't risk that he'd make the connection between Eva Wendt, Julius Schiller and me. I described to him what I was looking for. A blonde with depth, a girl of five-eight or so with confidence, intelligence and beauty, maybe eighteen to twenty-five years old. I had the sketch done at my house in Beverley Hills from a publicity shot of Eva holding a cigarette in a long holder and staring smoulderingly at the photographer.

As I opened the door of the canteen a number of men stood around with grimy faces, dressed in Second World War uniforms. Germans could only make films about the war if they showed the Nazis in a despicable light. Redemption and guilt made them rewrite their country's war history and destroy the propaganda films that Goebbels had pumped out from Bosendorf Studios. A general in the Waffen-SS sipped a cup of coffee and ate a croissant whilst a make-up lady applied the finishing touches to a gash on his forehead. The general was chatting to a British airman and I walked

235

tentatively to the counter and picked up an orange juice and some oatcakes. I walked over to an empty table and sat down, trying to avoid the Nazis.

The oatcakes weren't bad at all and the juice was fresh. The canteen was filling up and the girls were arriving early, ready for their screentests with Julian Tate. They didn't know what I looked like and so they couldn't know that I was sitting there amongst them, the tens of blonde girls streaming in, some with their agents and mothers. I could tell which were from the East and which were from the West. The difference in clothes and make-up was easy to spot. Three hundred clones ordering black coffee, bottled water and smoking cigarettes, some from long holders just like the sketch I'd sent Hirschbaum. I sat and watched them.

My eyes caught the flick of the girl's hair, the only brunette in a sea of blondes. Her face was hidden by three other girls. They turned together and walked over to the far side of the canteen. I watched her walk, the swing of her hips, the confidence of her steps. I caught myself staring and looked quickly back down into my orange juice as Joel Hirschbaum sat next to me.

'Did you sleep well, Mister Tate?'

'Yes, yes thank you.'

'They're all here.'

'I can see.'

'Pretty', Hirschbaum smiled, 'aren't they?'

'Yes.'

'Two hundred and ninety-seven blondes.'

'And one brunette.'

'She can dye it if you like her.'

'I'll see her first.'

'Ten minutes?'

'Fine.'

I had butterflies in my stomach as I sat in my director's chair facing the blacked out main stage with Hirschbaum sat next to me.

'Ready?', he asked. I nodded.

'Just like I said, please.'

Hirschbaum shrugged and whispered something into his walkie-talkie. From the silent void came the sound of stiletto heels clip-clopping slowly towards us. I closed my eyes. That sound. The shoes came to a halt and I opened my eyes again. A silhouette of a woman was barely visible against the unlit black backdrop. A lighter clicked, a young woman's face lit for a split-second by the flame and then a plume of smoke rose from the darkness.

'Somebody has a sense of humour', she said in English slightly tinged with a German accent.

I could hear myself breathing now and I peered into the darkness.

'Herr Hirschbaum', I murmured, 'the spotlight if you please.'

Hirschbaum whispered into the walkie-talkie and with a dull boom a dazzling spotlight flooded the stage with light, making the young woman in the centre blink.

I blinked too as I stared at her, wondering if I was dreaming. Standing calmly, confidently in the light, smoking from a long cigarette holder was a twenty-one-year-old Eva Wendt with brown hair. She could not see me and I held the silence for as long as I could, watching her with my mouth open.

'What is your name?', I asked slowly.

'Good morning Mister Tate', she replied. Her voice was clear and strong. 'I'm Clara Weber.'

I had my mouth open but no words were coming out.

'I'm sorry about my hair Mister Tate. I can always dye it.'

'No. No it's OK. It's…fine.'

I stood from my director's chair and walked slowly towards her, into the light. I got closer and closer and only stopped when I was no more than a foot away from her. I stared into her eyes. She looked at me enquiringly, innocently, waiting for me to say something.

'Your name is Clara', I said finally.

'Yes, that's right.'

'Clara Weber?'

'Yes. But it can be anything you want it to be'. The likeness was *too* perfect. It was a miracle.

'Is something wrong, Mister Tate?', asked Hirschbaum.

'The likeness is incredible', I whispered. 'Incredible'.

We stood in the spotlight looking at each other and then I turned to Hirschbaum.

'You've done a great job, Hirschbaum. Thank you.'

'Would I be right in saying I don't need to call in the next one, Mister Tate?', he asked hesitantly.

'You would be right.'

Hirschbaum mouthed *Gott sei Dank!* to the roof and whispered something into his walkie-talkie.

'What sort of girl are you looking for, Mister Tate?', Clara asked. 'I can be whoever you want me to be.'

'I don't want you to change a thing. You're perfect.'

'I am?'

'Yes. How old are you?'

'Twenty-two.

'Good. Can I see your passport?'

'Alright, alright I'm twenty-six.'

'I leave tonight for Los Angeles. I want to take you with me.'

'What?'

'You're hired.'

'But...but I haven't read anything yet Mister Tate.'

'Doesn't matter. You're hired all the same. Where did you learn to speak English?'

'At school.'

'You said you were twenty-six?'

She nodded.

'Perfect.'

'I'm hired?', she asked Hirschbaum. He nodded vigorously at her. She ran over to him and hugged him.

'Oh thank you, Herr Hirschbaum, thank you!'

'Don't thank me young lady, thank Mr Tate.'

Clara skipped up to me and took my hand. She even had the same name as Eva's character in *All for Love*. It was a sign. This must have been how Hans Bosendorf felt when he discovered Eva. The same excitement, of knowing that I could not fail. I couldn't wait to tell Keppel and watch those studio executives' faces.

'Mr Tate, I can't begin to tell you –'

'Don't say a thing. You need to get packed. I'd like to leave as soon as possible. We can sort out your visa *en route*.'

'If you say so. Everything's at my parents. We're only ten minutes' away on *Dennerstrasse*.' Clara looked away nervously. 'Oh dear. There is one...*small* problem.'

'What small problem?'

'My parents. I didn't even tell them about the audition. I don't know how they'd feel about me leaving the country.'

'Your parents?'

'Yes, perhaps I was wrong not to?'

'No no, I would like to meet them. Very much. We can tell them the good news together. They'll understand.'

***

Arthur Pilkington had delivered his lecture in Frankfurt and made his way back to London two days later. He loved to travel but he liked nothing better than to return to Cambridge in the summer time. The flowers were in bloom and the students, having finished their Tripos examinations, had nothing better to do than take their girl-friends on punts down the River Cam wearing straw boaters and striped jackets and popping open bottles of chilled white wine. He could hear their laughter as he sat at his desk beneath the open window set in mullioned fourteenth century stone. That morning he'd completed *The Times* crossword in forty minutes. He took pride from the fact that he had kept his mind sharp and that even in his late seventies he could always remember a face and put a name to it.

His mind did not fail him now. The man on the plane, he was sure, was Julius Schiller, also known in England as Abraham Goldstein, a Shakespearian actor, last performance *Julius Caesar* at the Albany Theatre if Pilkington remembered rightly. Also a Lieutenant in the Waffen-SS, awarded the Iron Cross for bravery in the field. Star of a film by Bosendorf Studios and appearances as himself in many propaganda newsreels on behalf of the Third Reich. Twenty odd years had passed and they'd never found out what happened to Watkins and the rest of the parachute team but maybe Julian Tate could be of some assistance.

Poor Marjory, he rued, tapping out his pipe gently. She'd been inconsolable, and quite rightly hadn't believed a word of it.

'*You killed him you shits!*' she cried to the Brigadier she found in the small basement Whitehall office. '*You buggering killed my Harvey!*'

He felt sorry for Marjory, but it was all over such a long time ago now, what good would it do her or anyone to dredge it all up, to uncover more incompetence and death. Military Intelligence had drawn a line sharply under *Operation Goldstein*. *It never happened*, ran the rubric. *Killed in action over Germany*, ran the epitaphs and the telegrams, including the one to Marjory. Everyone had assumed that Schiller or Goldstein was dead too. The Russians had found his dog-tags and Iron Cross outside Kithausen Concentration Camp along with a number of charred and unidentifiable bodies.

But what if the bugger was alive and well and directing films in Hollywood? With his swimming pool and his sun-tan? He was rich, whereas Marjory only had her meagre war widow's pension. Pilkington gazed over to the telephone. It would only take one call.

He remembered the German scientists, the makers of the V2 rocket and the atom-splitting experimenteers. Some were in the United States, some here, the rest in Russia and they were all well-off and well looked-after. They were Nazis but everybody loved them now. Most of the others had been released from prison, even in Russia where they'd lost nearly twelve million people in the war. The top brass were either executed at Nuremburg or committed suicide or were hunted down by Simon Wiesenthal and others like him. Everyone knew South America was a veritable breeding ground for them but Pilkington hadn't reckoned on Hollywood.

He looked again at the telephone and filled his pipe with some fresh tobacco.

19

The telephone rang and a hand reached over from under a linen duvet to pick it up.

'Yes?', said a sleepy voice into the receiver.

'Keppel?'

Peter Keppel blinked and looked over to his alarm clock. It was three o'clock in the morning.

'Julian? D'you know what time it is?'

'I know. I'm sorry. I had to call.'

'No, believe me, you didn't.'

'I've found her.'

'Who?'

'I've found a girl for the film. She's perfect.'

'That's great Julian. Now can I go back to sleep? I'll tell the studio tomorrow *when I wake up.*'

'Fine. You tell them. I'll be back with her as soon as I can. Get someone to do me a contract.'

'Good night Julian', said Keppel, replacing the receiver. He rolled over and tried to get back to sleep.

I put down the telephone and turned to Clara.

'You all set?'

She nodded.

'Can I smoke in the car?'

'You can smoke wherever you want to, Clara.'

Hirschbaum lent us a limousine, a black one, together with a peak-capped chauffeur. A few minutes later the car glided smoothly out of the gates and out onto the streets of West Berlin.

'I'm glad you're not from the East side', I said. 'Makes the whole visa protocol thing much easier.'

Clara took another puff from her cigarette.

'Do you conduct all your auditions like this, Mister Tate?'

'This is the first time I've done one like this.'

'I thought so. I'm very flattered.'

'So tell me about your parents.'

'They're just…normal. What do you want to know?'

'What does your father do?'

'He was a policeman, but he took early retirement.'

'And your mother?'

'A *Hausfrau*. She worked a little I think during the War, in a factory, before I was born.'

'And your father?'

'What about him?'

'What did he do during the war?'

'I don't know, Mister Tate. I know he was away for a while when I was little. You can ask him, but please, remember it is a sensitive subject for most Germans.'

'I won't mention it, don't worry. It's just so I know how I can pitch things to them.'

'*Pitch things*?'

'Giving you a studio contract. Maybe three or more years away from home.'

'I see.'

'What about you, Clara? Would you mind working in Hollywood? Being away for three years? Maybe longer?'

'You are joking Mister Tate! It's my dream.'

'That's what Laszlo Lowenstein said.'

'You mean Peter Lorre?', she replied quickly.

She took another puff from her cigarette and stubbed it out into the ashtray in the armrest. I watched the way she did it. It was just like Eva.

'Do you have any brothers or sisters?', I asked.

'No', she replied, sadly, 'no I do not.'

Our limousine crossed a wide junction and turned left at a sign for *Dennerstrasse*.

'This is it', said Clara. 'Number ten'.

The limousine stopped outside a small terraced house with Dutch gables. The chauffeur got out and opened the door for Clara, then for me. We stepped out onto the pavement and gazed up at the house.

'Very nice', I said.

My voice, I realized as I spoke, sounded nervous. Clara held out a key and looked at me, sensing my trepidation. She grasped my hand and smiled.

'Don't be nervous. They *are* very nice.'

I'd decided on the way there to offer them two – no - three trips a year to see their daughter, paid for by the studio, or if they wouldn't pay then I'd foot the bill.

I found it difficult to take my eyes off her. Thank God I came to Berlin. The key turned in the lock, Clara opened the door and we walked inside.

I followed Clara down a hall and into a drawing room full of family photos. In pride of place on the mantelpiece sat a photo of Clara, aged about ten or eleven, standing in between what must have been her parents, who were seated. It was a very formal picture, but there was a hint of a smile on Clara's face.

'I was eleven, she said. 'I remember them taking that picture.'

I looked carefully at the photograph. The mother was a chubby woman with eyes a little too close together. She had a rubbery nose and low cheekbones. She looked about forty-five or fifty. She was clearly a plain woman. My eyes moved over to study her husband's face. He was flaxen-haired, short and thick-set. He had a large bulbous nose and thick lips. His forehead was high. Clara looked nothing like either of them. I heard footsteps approach from down the hall.

'Mama? Papa?', Clara called out nervously. 'There's someone who wants to meet you.'

I moved away from the photograph on the mantelpiece, straightened my jacket and combed my hair nervously away from my forehead. *Smile and wave*, I could hear Hans saying, *smile and wave*. I did just that as Mr Weber walked in stiffly through the living room door. It looked like he had a bad back.

'*Guten tag*', he said, holding out his hand formally. '*Ich bin Horst Weber*'.

'Julian Tate'.

We shook hands.

'American?'

I nodded. Horst Weber frowned momentarily and then turned to introduce his wife in perfect English.

'May I present my wife, Greta Weber.'

I craned my head to look past him at Mrs Weber. She stepped forward, forced a smile and bowed. She held her husband's hand nervously. In the flesh she was dumpy and plain, just like the photo. I looked at both parents, then at Clara, who was smiling nervously at me.

'Mr Tate is a movie director, papa, from Hollywood.'

Mr Weber looked worriedly at Mrs Weber.

'Hollywood? Really? Is that so?', he said guardedly. 'Please sit down Mister Tate. May we offer you some tea?'

'Yes. Yes that would be lovely.'

I sat down on one of two leather armchairs. It creaked as I settled into it. Horst Weber put his hand gently on his wife's shoulder.

'*Schatze*?' Mrs Weber smiled and did a little curtsey. '*Konnen Sie vier Tassen Tee machen*?'

Mr Weber rested his hand on his daughter's shoulder.

'Help her, dear, would you?'

'Yes, papa.'

Mrs Weber led the way out of the living room followed by Clara. Mr Weber walked stiffly over to the door and shut it. He walked back to the empty leather armchair and sat down slowly.

'*Es ist besser*', he said flatly.

'I'm so sorry to barge in on you like this, Herr Weber...'

'I know', he said slowly, 'why you are here.'

'You do? Did somebody call?'

'No-one has called.'

'Then...?'

'One moment please.'

He stood stiffly again and moved over to the large dark-wood desk by the window. He sat down and opened a drawer, his eyes fixed on me. I saw him flick a quick glance inside. I cleared my throat.

'Your daughter, Clara said she didn't tell you about the audition. I came over with her to break the good news - '

'The *good* news, you say?'

Mr Weber rested his hand in the drawer.

'Yes', I said enthusiastically. 'She's exactly what we're looking for, Mr Weber. She's perfect for my film. I can help make your daughter a star and she'll make a lot of money.'

Mr Weber peered closely at me as his hand reached inside the desk drawer.

'Really?', he said, absent-mindedly. He pulled out a photograph. 'Money, you say?'

He shut and locked the drawer and walked over to me.

'Would you like to see this?', he asked, oddly.

'Yes of course', I replied, wondering if Mr Weber was always this detached.

He handed me a photograph and I held it in both hands. It was of a man in Waffen-SS uniform standing next to a tank and the man was clearly a younger Mr Weber.

'I spent five years in a filthy Russian prison', he said in a low, bitter voice. 'Just for fighting for my country like all the others. For doing my duty…'

'I'm so sorry, Mr Weber, but it was all such a long time ago.'

'Please let me finish Mr Tate. I did my duty. No more, no less. Imagine, if you will, that one day I capture a British airman and that he tells me of a fantastical plot to capture a British Jew by the name of Abraham Goldstein, and that Abraham Goldstein is masquerading as a Waffen-SS officer named Julius Schiller. Do I believe the British airman? Is he lying?'

I looked up at him in amazement.

'My wife could never have children. What were we supposed to do? When the man called and told her about the adoption program...'

'*Adoption program*?'

My eyes widened. I looked again at the photographs around the room, of the parents who looked nothing like their daughter.

'We could not turn it down. We even named her after the maid in your film. Clara is the correct name, is it not?'

'Yes.'

'It was...fitting. We always knew who the mother was. And as for the father…' Mr Weber peered at me closely. 'I knew it was the same man that the British airman had come for.'

The door creaked open and Clara entered beaming, holding a tray with a teapot and four cups and saucers. I stared at her disbelievingly. Mr Weber stood stiffly.

'Sorry about the delay. I told mama and she dropped a tea-cup.'

Clara looked at both of us.

'Oh dear? Was I wrong not to tell you about the audition, papa? Are you upset?'

Mr Weber stared at her sadly.

'No my dear', he said softly, 'I've been wrong not to tell *you*.'

'About what?'

In the kitchen, Mrs Weber was sobbing into her apron, her head resting on the kitchen table. Tears were streaming down her face. She remembered it like it was only last night. The tiny baby had been taken from the maternity unit at Kithausen Concentration Camp twenty six years ago in the middle of the night - the seventeenth of July 1940 to be precise. A nurse had delivered it to her a few hours later wrapped in warm clothing.

She had rocked the baby in her arms and walked upstairs with it to the nursery. She had gently soothed it in its cot and then rested it on its back to sleep. Mrs Weber remembered it so well, that first night, so well. It was the night she had been waiting for all of her life. Horst had come back in fifty-one and they had brought the baby up together, but she always wondered if one day someone would come to take her away from them.

An hour passed and back in the living room, Clara, Horst Weber and I had stopped drinking tea.

'Would you have ever told me, papa?', she asked Weber. 'I mean, if Mr Tate hadn't found me?'

'I don't know Clara. Please try and understand. What would you have done in my shoes?'

'I don't know, papa, I don't know.'

Clara cried and Horst Weber looked away guiltily.

'I'm so sorry. Perhaps I was wrong. I've been wrong about many things in my life. It is fate that has brought Mr Schiller – I mean Tate – here today. Fate that led him to you, my beautiful Clara. But I can see why he chose you, why he was drawn to you. You do look exactly like the woman who gave birth to you.'

Clara looked up slowly.

'Do you have a picture of her?', she asked. 'I should like very much to see it.'

I nodded and pulled out a publicity photograph of Eva, cigarette holder in hand.

'My God!', she whispered. 'This is me. This is me with blonde hair.'

She turned to Horst.

'You saw her movies?'

'Yes. All of them', he replied. 'Several times.'

'*All* of them?', I asked. 'Several times?'

'*Ja*. You could say…you could say I was a fan.'

'I have one of her films back in Los Angeles', I said. 'It's damaged, but it's the one we made together. It was called *All for Love*. The one where the heroine, your…mother…Eva….played the character with your name.'

'I would very much like to see it', she whispered. 'I would like that very much indeed.'

I walked over to Horst Weber's desk and unlocked the drawer. He watched me carefully.

'How did she die?', she asked me. 'I would like to know.'

I shook my head and opened the drawer. I looked inside and Horst Weber looked away guiltily.

'There's a gun in this drawer, Mr Weber.'

'I know there is.'

'You weren't planning to shoot me, were you?'

'Please understand, Mister Tate. Please understand, Clara. There were some things I did not tell your mother. There were some things I could not tell anyone.'

'What things?'

'Things that would have meant Clara was taken away from us.'

'What are you talking about, papa?'

'What do you mean Mr Weber? What things?'

He moved over to a small drinks cabinet and pulled out a bottle of schnapps and three glasses.

'I think, Mr Tate', he said slowly, 'that perhaps we should all sit down and drink something a little stronger than tea.'

20

Horst Weber took a sip of schnapps from his glass and wiped the sweat from his forehead.

'It was the seventeenth of June 1944. The German army was falling back behind a Russian onslaught. My own tank unit had been ordered to stand and fight, but the generals had persuaded Hitler to retreat and save our men. There were embarrassments, embarrassments that needed to be eradicated from history'.

'Go on', I urged him.

'The adoption programme and the women under it were scheduled for liquidation. This meant that they would be disposed of by lethal injection and their bodies burnt.'

He paused, waiting for the inevitable reaction.

'Units were sent to all camps to remove all traces of these subjects and all the others. Eva Wendt, also known as Betty Maude Weinstein, was at Kithausen camp when the unit commanded by *Obersturmbannfuhrer* Wilfred Keller arrived. I do not know exactly how it happened, but I do know that the doctors and nurses were instructed to give two injections to each of the adoption programme subjects. One was to be a heavy tranquiliser, the next lethal poison. I tried to stop it. What must have happened, what I believe did happen, was as follows.'

'The nurse tasked with the injections could not bring herself to kill the women she had tended to and seen give birth. She must have substituted a different drug, perhaps one used to temporarily paralyze and give the apparence of death.'

'But I saw her! I saw her!', I blurted out.

'You have read *Romeo and Juliet*, Mr Tate?'

'Of course.'

'Then as you will recall, Juliet did not die from the apothecary's potion.'

My mind flicked back to the scene I could never forget. Eva, lifeless on her bed, Sarah Bloom lying dead next to her. Mr Weber re-filled the glasses of schnapps as he spoke.

'The Russians arrived and the Germans fled. When the Germans were gone, Eva Wendt woke up and I believe...I believe she tried to find you both.'

'She woke up?'

'That is what I said. She must have been very tired and malnourished. They found a set of dog-tags for Julius Schiller and also an Iron Cross. I believe she must have thought that you were dead.'

'Oh my God!'

'Yes.' He paused. 'And I am afraid there is more.'

He took another sip of schnapps and gazed at Clara.

'She tried to find you, my darling. But she did not know if you were a boy or a girl, nor what your name might be, and there was no way of tracking you.'

'I can only imagine what she must have felt like', whispered Clara. 'It is horrible, too horrible.'

'Yes. I'm afraid that it was. It became too much for her to handle. She tried to kill herself, so they put her in a place where she would be safe.'

Horst Weber stood.

'And then?' I asked.

Silence. He looked away guiltily.

'And then? Which place? Where did they put her? Mr Weber! Please! How do you know all this? What happened to her?'

'Nothing happened to her', he replied. 'I believe she is still there. It is in East Germany.'

***

I got a pass through Joel Hirschbaum's contacts. Joel had lent us the limo with his driver and we'd gone through *Checkpoint Charlie* under special license.

After a three hour drive our car approached familiar wrought iron gates, behind them the large country house I'd stayed in with Keller and Metz, the one with the pool. The sign outside now read *Zanatorium* and every surface seemed to be painted white. This was the place I'd duetted with Captain Gerhard Metz and slapped Sarah Bloom in the face to save her life, much good it had done.

Clara sat next to me still in shock, which was how I felt as well. Finding an actress, finding a daughter, and maybe, maybe, finding *her*. I dared not think it. I dared not. I reached over for Clara's hand. She gave it willingly.

The driver stopped at the gates, leaned out and pressed the button of an intercom. An indistinguishable voice came out of the plastic box and the driver announced who we were and who we had come to see. I noted that the reply was not *she is not here*. No-one was denying that she was there.

The gates swung open and the car swept inside towards the large villa, the swimming-pool now filled in and the beautiful lawn now a ragged brown expanse.

'I've been here before', I said, 'before you were born.'

She looked at me with a puzzled expression as the car came to a smooth stop on the gravelled drive. She stepped out without waiting for the chauffeur to open the door. I was already ahead of her.

'I know this place', I kept repeating. 'I know it.'

She followed me in through the large oak front door, which was unlocked, and into a large high-ceilinged entrance hall. I approached a receptionist in a nurse's uniform at the front desk.

'You must be Miss Weber?', she said instantly to Clara. Clara frowned.

'And Mister...Tate?'

We nodded in tandem.

'The doctor will escort you. Please take a seat.'

She motioned to a line of unoccupied metal chairs along the side of the room.

'Is Eva Wendt here?', I blurted out.

'The doctor will explain everything. He will be along shortly.'

'Thank you, nurse, thank you.'

I paced the entrance hall, looking for the doctor.

'May I smoke?', Clara asked the nurse.

'No smoking', she replied.

I looked up at the large white face of the clock. Ten minutes to three. I watched the second hand tick by. *Tick tick tick.* I drummed my fingers against my leg along to its beat. I looked next to me and reached for Clara's hand.

Tick tick tick. The face of the clock dissolved before my eyes, leaving in its place the face of a white-coated doctor in his fifties with large black-framed spectacles and a gentle smile.

'I believe you're looking for me,' he said quietly. 'I'm Doctor Semmel.'

I stood quickly.

'Julian Tate. Clara Weber' I replied.

Semmel shook my hand and bowed to Clara. As he looked up at her face his mouth dropped open and his eyes widened.

'Mein Gott', he exclaimed. 'Mein Gott!'

I looked at the man's expression, the same look on my face I had had when I first saw Clara at Hirschbaum Studios.

'She's here, isn't she?' I asked. Semmel looked at me oddly.

'You better come with me.'

The corridor was very long. I couldn't remember this part of the building. It looked newer than the front of the house and the floor was hard, concrete, overlain with solid grey and blue rubber tiles. Doctor Semmel led us towards the end and we turned a corner. Ahead of us was a continuation of the corridor, not quite as long, with a stained glass window at the end. Semmel walked towards the window as the sunlight shafted through the glass.

He stopped at the last door on the left, just under the window and removed a large set of keys from the side-pocket of his white coat. He picked one, fitted it in the lock and turned. Clara and I stood side by side, holding hands nervously. The lock clicked and Doctor Semmel rested his hand on the door knob.

'I think it is best', he said, quietly, almost whispering, 'if the gentleman goes first. There has only been one other visitor in twenty years.'

He looked up sadly at Clara.

'Your father Horst. He came here several times.'

'Several times?', I found myself repeating.

'Yes. You knew her, didn't you, Mr...Tate?'

'Yes I did. I...worked with her.'

255

'I see. Be prepared, then. She may not be exactly as you remember her.'

'I'm prepared. Give me your cigarettes, Clara.'

Clara handed them to me, taking one out for herself which she lit.

'Sorry, doctor', she smiled, exhaling nervously. He shrugged.

'You go', said Clara. The doctor's right. I'll be just out here.'

I swallowed and walked inside.

It was dark. I stood very still, letting my eyes adjust. I could hear myself breathing heavily. I felt for a light switch on the wall and prayed. The room was suddenly flooded with light and I blinked, trying to focus. I could not believe what I saw.

Covering every square inch of wall were photos of Clara as a baby, a child, and a teenager, publicity photos of me, tens of them, different poses, some with Eva and a poster of *All for Love*, the one film we made together. And then I saw her.

Sitting on the window sill, in front of closed shutters, bars visible behind them, sat a woman in her early forties, staring at me curiously. It was Eva Wendt. It was Betty Maude Weinstein, sitting on a window sill, alive, breathing and staring at me as if I were a laboratory specimen. Did she recognize me? I knew I was older, but surely...?

She looked pale and thin, but she was alive. There was too much to say, so we stood, staring at each other silently, each taking in the other, searching for the right words.

'I need a cigarette', she said finally.

I fumbled in my jacket and pulled out the packet of Marlboros I had taken from Clara at the door. I handed her a cigarette and, with my hand trembling, lit it for

256

her with a match. She took a deep breath of the smoke and exhaled slowly, looking up at me curiously and blowing the smoke into my eyes.

'Thank you', she said.

She moved closer to me and stopped just inches from my face. I looked into her eyes. She hadn't changed. She wore no make-up, her hair was brown, her face was paler, but she hadn't changed. I had found her at last. I would nurse her back to health, if she needed nursing. I would take her away from this place if it took all the money in the world.

It came from nowhere, like a lightning bolt. Her hand swept up from her side and slapped my face hard, on my right cheek. I blinked, my face stinging from the pain. *Don't move*, I told myself, *don't react* but she slapped me again, with the back of her hand on my other cheek and raised her hand a third time. I grasped it firmly. Tears welled in her eyes. She clasped my shoulder with her free hand and drew herself to me, holding me tight and crying bitterly into my shoulder.

'I thought you were dead', she said, 'I thought you were dead. They showed me your…your *medal*…your Nazi medal…'

'Shhh. Not now. Not now.'

'But I *saw*…'

'I know my darling, I know.'

'But you're dead! You're dead! Why didn't you come for me? Why? Why?'

'Because I thought *you* were dead', I replied.

I squeezed her tightly and kissed her. A flicker of fear swept across her face and she held me suddenly by my shoulders.

'There's something, something…', she said as she burst out crying. 'I can't tell you, I can't…it breaks my heart, Abe.'

'What is it? Tell me. Whatever it is, trust me and tell me.'

'It's about you and me. The two of us. We...we produced a third.'

'No, Eva! Please stop! I know what you're going to say. Listen to me. Listen to me very very carefully. I have to prepare you for something.'

'What? What else is there?'

'Sit down with me, here'. I motioned towards the bed. 'Please. Humour me. Trust me.'

She moved over to the bed and sat down slowly, smoothing out her plain dress.

'Can I have another cigarette?', she asked. I handed her one and lit it for her. She took a long drag and directed a plume of smoke towards the window.

'Well?', she asked, tears in her eyes.

'I know', I began slowly, 'that you were pregnant with our child.'

'You knew? How could you?'

'I didn't know until yesterday.'

'What?'

'I found out yesterday.'

'Yesterday? Abe, what happened yesterday?'

'How do you think I found you?'

She shook her head, dazed and I pointed to the pictures of Clara on the wall.

'I found *her* first.'

'I was never a fit mother. Never!'

'Nonsense. You will always be her mother. You are Clara's real mother.'

'I said she should never know, that she should stay with them. He brought me the photos, the poster. He said he loved me.'

'Horst Weber said he loved you?'

'Yes', she replied meekly. 'He did. And I knew he loved my daughter and that he'd take care of her.'

'She's here, darling. She's here with me now.'

'Here?', she said in a panic. 'Here at the sanatorium?'

She stood quickly and swept the hair away from her face.

'I cannot see her like this.'

She wiped her face with the hem of her dress.

'I'm a movie director now. I live in Beverley Hills, in California. I came to cast for a film, looking for someone like you. I could never forget you – my first film was called *Never Forget* – and when I came here I found Clara Weber. She's agreed to come to Hollywood.'

'Hollywood?', she murmured, disbelievingly. 'Hollywood? Are you crazy'

'No. Neither of us is. Will you come with me, Betty? I have a large house but it's empty without you. I sit every night and watch *All for Love* and stop the film when we kiss. Do you remember? Do you remember the kisses, Betty?'

'I remember slapping you.'

'She's outside the door, Betty. Would you like me to go and get her?'

21

Hans Bosendorf was nearly eighty years old but he still felt strong enough to make the trip. Jerry had become his butler, protector and driver. The fifteen sparkling gems that Hans had smuggled out through Spain to South America had converted into close to a hundred thousand American dollars, which in the mid-nineteen forties had been a small fortune. They'd landed at the port at *Barranquilla* on the north coast of Colombia twenty one years ago in the middle of a tropical storm, and slowly they'd made their way south.

The number of Nazis they met on their travels was astonishing. It seemed as though the whole of the Third Reich was here, minus the big-shots who'd paid the price for their madness. Everyone had with them funds in one form of currency or asset. There were dollars, forged English pounds, Swiss francs, gold bars, stamps, rare coins, precious stones and works of art. All of them were convertible into hard cash one way or another. Hans had heard of the Nazi who had bought a twelve-bedroomed farmhouse in Uruguay with three thousand acres of land in exchange for a *Canaletto*. It wasn't exactly the *Lebensraum* that Hitler and Himmler had envisaged, but it was *Lebensraum* all the same.

Hans had been an expert at the make-believe world of the cinema, and now his expertise was called on by the new German émigré class. He was much in demand. They needed someone who could help the past lose itself, who could construct a new public persona for them, help them pursue business interests without the fear of being hauled off to jail. Even the big-wig Adolf Eichmann, architect of the death of countless tens of thousands in Eastern Europe in concentration camps had come to him for help, and, detestable little shit that he was, Hans had taken his money just like he had taken it from the others. Constructing a believable back-story was an art that Hans had practiced all his life. But, when Eichmann was caught by the Israelis, Hans figured that things were getting a little too close for comfort.

The nineteen-forties and fifties had been tense enough, paying off countless government officials, contributing to a variety of special *charitable trusts* that were no more than government-approved protection rackets. But the Israelis, and *Mossad* in particular, scared Hans Bosendorf. He personally had done nothing wrong, he figured, but if they found some of his friends and they fingered him then he would be guilty by association. He didn't want to die in disgrace. He wanted a final fling, a grand spectacle. He had a nice house, but a house was not portable, a house was reachable and instantly traceable, even though the deeds were held in the name of a Panamanian company. Hans had a plan and it involved hiring a crew to help him. He'd never been there, but he'd always talked about it. He felt he knew it better than anyone else who'd never been there. It was time, he thought, to put his money where his mouth was. He was going to sell his house, buy a yacht and sail it to California.

'If I can – *ba ba!* - make it there', he sang softly to himself on the veranda of his palatial home, sipping a glass of dark rum, 'I can make it – *ba! ba!* - anywhere.'

He knew the song was about New York, but in his mind's eye he could see the sign, the big white letters on the hillside, the stars on the streets and in the sky.

***

I decided that I loved aeroplanes after all. I watched the blue of the Atlantic out of the small round window as the four-engined jet passed over Ireland. I had donated more than ten thousand dollars to the sanatorium's central fund and Doctor Semmel had been happy to process Betty's release. We sat now in first class, the three of us, refreshed, newly-coiffed and suited-up, me in a *Hermes* wool-twist, Betty and Clara in matching *Chanel*, sipping champagne.

A week had passed and I'd had to field a number of angry calls from the studio and from Peter Keppel, asking me where the hell I was and what the hell I thought I was doing. I'd waive my fee, I told Keppel, and my leading lady would also waive hers. Funnily enough, the studio agreed quickly to the delay.

'Isn't flying wonderful', said Betty, lighting up two cigarettes and passing one to Clara.

'Terrible habit', I said.

'Don't tell me. It's going to kill me and my daughter.'

'Everyone smokes in Germany', said Clara. 'They smoke to forget where they are.'

'You'll see Beverley Hills', I said, 'and believe me, you'll want to give up right away.'

'So', said Betty, slipping her arm through mine, 'you are a rich man now, Mister Tate?'

I smiled back at her.

'The richest guy on the planet. And we're gonna make you a star, Clara. No-one's gonna burn your films like they did with your mother's.'

'You still promised I can see *All for Love.*'

262

'Of course. We can all watch it together. We have our own private cinema.'

We laughed and clinked our champagne glasses as Europe slipped away twenty-five thousand feet beneath us.

Six rows back, in the business section in row eight, sat two nondescript men in their thirties in dark suits, white shirts and ties. They both had mid-brown hair, mid-brown eyes, were of middling height and had lean, taut faces. They were sipping Coca-Cola and had joined the flight at Heathrow Airport.

***

Sailing under an American flag was easy if you had the money, and Hans had the money. He'd bought a sixty-foot motor yacht, or rather the Cayman Island company that owned a sixty-foot motor yacht. It was two years old, twin-engined and capable of twenty-five knots. It had six berths and he only needed three crew including the captain, plus Jerry, so he took two berths for himself. While he was at it, he bought himself an American passport. There were some excellent fixers in South America, and he'd somehow got a passport and even a social security number in the name of Hal Boden, a retiree from Miami who'd decided to sail round the United States. Hal Boden had died in an unfortunate accident off the coast of Jamaica, the fixer had told Hans, giving Hans the passport and the boat in a great two-for-one package, with a dead crew-member's passport for Jerry in the name of Mark Quinn from South Carolina. Changing the photographs had been simple, and it was nice that *Hal* sounded like *Hans*.

It was time for Hal to come out of retirement, thought Hans, as he stood on deck, feeling the warm breeze of the West Indies wind against his face. They'd decided to make good their cover by sailing around the Caribbean and then passing through the Panama Canal to test all their papers. If everything worked there, they would head on up the coast until they got to San Diego, where they would berth and Hans would take Jerry to LA. Anyhow, that was the plan.

It wasn't only the Jews, he rued, that went to Hollywood and changed their names.

**

A year passed. It was now 1967 and Hollywood was an exciting place to be, especially for the Tate family.

Clara Weber had changed her name to Tate and although she could never bring herself to hate her adoptive parents Horst and Greta, she felt more comfortable being away from them. She still wrote, but she avoided telling them about her real parents, Beverley Hills, the money, the weather and all the other things that made her feel happy to have left Germany a long way behind her. Her past had begun in the war under extraordinary circumstances, and she didn't want to think about it more than she had to. The chance to act in a film, let alone star in one, was frightening, but it was something she had known she would always want to do. It was, she now knew, in her blood.

Horst Weber continued to write letters to the woman he used to visit in the sanatorium, the woman he was secretly in love with but she burned them, unopened, when she saw the postmark. Eva Wendt, nee Betty Maude Weinstein, became Eve Tate, my wife and Clara's mother. Hollywood loved all three of us.

Tatler and *Vanity Fair* gave the whole family an interview with a full colour spread. They were almost the first pictures I had seen of myself in print. From recluse to *bon viveur*, the transformation had been remarkable and Peter Keppel watched it all from the sidelines. Keppel had penned a screen adaptation of the play that I had always wanted to direct and luckily the studio had wanted to produce. The male British lead was an unknown, but Keppel couldn't help but smile at the resemblance he had to a young Julius Schiller. The female lead, performing for no fee, was Clara. It was to be the studio's biggest release that year and the publicity surrounding me, my new wife and film-star daughter was helping the studio enormously with the marketing.

Bright lights showed up blemishes and scars and needed constant covering up, and the lights were shining very brightly indeed for Julius Schiller, serial number 1103444921032, Lieutenant Waffen-SS, holder of the Iron Cross for Bravery, propaganda actor, killed in action, July 1944.

I could see the lights of the movie theatre in Santa Monica in front of me. It was my favourite theatre and the studio had agreed to premiere the film there that night before it went on general release in the United States the following week. It was Friday night, it was *shabbas*. We should not have been taking a ride in a car, even if it was a limousine. Eva and Clara should not have been smoking cigarettes and I should not have been on my way to work.

In the crowd near the front stood an old man warmly dressed in a camel-haired coat, despite the warm evening air. He had come to see for himself. Jerry had shown him the copy of Vanity Fair but he knew he had to see the real thing before he could possibly know for sure. He found his eyes met by another's. His gaze rested, entranced, on the pretty

265

young blonde standing next to him in front of the cinema. His eyes gleamed as he handed her a business card in the name of Hal Boden.

'*Mein Liebchen*', he purred, 'you have lovely eyes.'

Our limousine pulled up outside. A crowd had gathered and there were huge banks of photographers, blazing away with their Nikons and their Leicas, the flashes like an earthbound firework extravaganza, a glitterball of lights. A red carpet stretched from the sidewalk to the theatre and the fans and the press lined each side of it, the flashbulbs from their cameras dazzling. The noise was audible even behind the double-glazed windows of the limousine. I looked up at the sign for the movie, the bright neon sign that burned red against a white fluorescent sheen. *Romeo and Juliet*. I looked over to Eva, my very own star-cross'd lover, and took her hand.

'We did it, Mrs Tate'.

'Yes we did, Mr Tate.'

'We pulled it off.'

I turned to Clara and squeezed her hand.

'You go first, Clara. It's you they want to see, not us. You ready?'

'I'm ready.'

It was like a Hollywood ending. It was like the way the studio had made us change the final scene of the film, had made us skew the screen adaptation of one of the most famous plays in the world in order to suit the test audiences. I had agreed to it because I could see the irony in it. After all, Eva Wendt had not died, and neither had I, despite all evidence to the contrary.

I tapped the glass in front of me and the chauffeur stepped out. He walked round slowly to the door and opened it. Clara deposited her cigarette into the ashtray in the back of the seat in front of her and, resplendent in evening gown, stepped out of the limousine to a burst of light and a roar from the crowd.

'Clara! Clara! Clara!', they cried.

She held the center of the red carpet like she'd been taught, even though, inside, she was more nervous than she'd ever been before in her life. She stood there in scarlet and she smiled and waved.

In the limousine, Eva and I leaned forward and watched her.

'They love her', I said.

'I love her too', Eva replied, 'and I love *you*'.

She kissed me softly on the lips.

'Ditto', I said, smiling.

Keppel looked away, a smile also on his face as Eva brushed some imaginary dust from my collar.

'I had it dry-cleaned, you know', she chided.

'Shall we?', I said, motioning to the open door.

'You first', she replied.

I stepped out onto the red carpet to another flurry of flashbulbs. I could hear a television reporter speaking to camera next to me and suddenly the camera with its bright light focused on my face, beaming me into millions of homes. I must remember to smile and wave, I thought. Eva joined me and put her arm around me. I kissed her on the cheek. Peter Keppel stepped out slowly, but the cameras were all directed at the Tate family, standing in a row, holding hands and grinning. Keppel gave a big thumb's-up sign to me and I grabbed his arm and pulled him onto the carpet. The crowd applauded and cheered as the four of us raised our arms in unison.

I held my two leading ladies tightly. This was possibly the happiest moment of my life and it was playing itself out in front of the world's television cameras. The horrible memories of the past were gone. A hideous dream. We were together *now* I thought as I kissed my wife passionately and the flashbulbs dazzled again.

'Julian! Julian! Julian!', they chanted. I smiled, thinking about the last time they'd chanted my name, about seven thousand miles and twenty-eight years ago.

We linked arms, the four of us, turned and walked up the red carpet towards the beckoning doors of the cinema. Posters were splashed everywhere announcing *'Romeo and Juliet, a Julian Tate film, a love story re-made for the modern age!'*

I took no notice of the two men of middling height in identical grey suits who followed me swiftly up the red carpet, in their hands an extradition order.

22

Frame after frame clicks through the projector, the old thirty-five millimeter film keeping pace with the sturdy reel, stretching a little with age, lengthening each shot, blurring the focus and blending the bright into the dark. Infinitesimal shades of gray intersperse with light and shadow, granular dots come together and dissolve. When they re-assemble, they form new outlines, their images shift in a never-ending flux like the gleam of the moon on a cloudy night above an ebony ocean.

The flickering images flit before me from a different time, a different era, lighting my face and filling the screen. There's no sound. There was sound once, but it must have faded from the print many years before, the only print remaining I am assured. I think they're wrong. I think the sound was overlaid on most screenings, synchronised on a separate recording and spooled up to start at the right moment. It doesn't really matter though, because an image can be copied and copied again, trapped for an eternity.

The camera, they say, doesn't lie, and a picture, like the proverbial song, speaks a thousand words. I watch the pictures in front of me again and again and I know the story they *don't* tell. I know why I keep watching the images, the flickering grey-toned screen. I'm willing the images to change and show me the flipside. I know they won't, though. They won't show the truth. All I want now is the truth, but if no-one wants to *believe* the truth then the fiction wins out. That's what I'm a little worried about, I must admit, that the images override what really happened. Images need no introduction, no justification. They are prima facie evidence, incontrovertible and damning. They survive and will haunt me forever. They may fade, they may decay, but they are still possessed of a greater longevity than I.

The truth will be buried with me when I die. We'll decompose together, different elements of the same being, the man and the man-made. No-one will be able to reconstruct us, to make us whole again. No-one will be able to draw unpleasant conclusions by matching one to the other. Nothing, I realize now, despite the celluloid in front of me, is black and white.

So they play me the newsreels, one after another, over and over. I sit for days in windowless rooms while they interview me. I am patient. I answer all their questions. After all, as I keep telling them, I have nothing to hide, nothing to be ashamed of. I've done nothing wrong, you see. Anyone in my position, and I mean anyone, would have done exactly the same. *All for Love*, I repeat to them, *All for Love*. I don't know why, but they don't get it. They don't believe me.

Luckily they've stopped hanging people in England, even for treason. Here in this cell they let me write, awaiting my own trial. They give me paper, pen and ink and they even encourage me. The warden here is very good, quite likeable really in his own way, a literary man. He says it's best to put it all down, that people might want to know that I did nothing wrong.

My daughter Clara is my most precious legacy. She visits me, with Eva, when they allow. And Peter Keppel has been to see me a couple of times. Not as often as I'd like. I need to discuss this with him, you see, get his professional opinion as a writer. Hans died, he told me, leaving all his money to Jerry. I think everyone else must be dead now.

I ask myself time and time again: who did I hurt? I didn't kill anyone. I wasn't a traitor, like they said. I'm not embarrassed about what I did.

If they let me out I'll make a film about what really happened.

And I promise it will have a happy ending.

Printed in the United Kingdom
by Lightning Source UK Ltd.
119914UK00002BA/127